RAINBOW WARRIOR

The 10th Bernie Fazakerley Mystery

by

JUDY FORD

RAINBOW WARRIOR

Published by Bernie Fazakerley Publications

Copyright © 2018 Judy Ford

Drawing of Police Dog Q © 2018 Sally Marshall

All rights reserved.

ISBN: 1-91-108349-X
ISBN-13: 978-1-911083-49-8

DEDICATION

Dedicated to the police dogs and handlers of Thames
Valley, Hampshire & Isle of Wight Dog Section

CONTENTS

Dedication iii

Contents..iv

Acknowledgements..vii

Disclaimer..ix

Glossary of UK police ranks xi

Sketch Map of Blackbird Leys and Surrounding Area xiii

Detailed map of Blackbird Leys..xiv

Chapter 1: Friday Night..1

Chapter 2: Saturday Morning 20

Chapter 3: Saturday Afternoon 37

Chapter 4: Saturday Evening..52

Chapter 5: Sunday Morning..66

Chapter 6: Sunday Afternoon...77

Chapter 7: Sunday Evening 86

Chapter 8: Monday Morning...97

Chapter 9: Monday Afternoon...107

Chapter 10: Tuesday 125

Chapter 11: Wednesday Morning...136

Chapter 12: Wednesday Afternoon 145

Chapter 13: Wednesday Night 156

Chapter 14: Thursday Morning 159

Chapter 15: Thursday Afternoon 177

Chapter 16: Friday morning 199

Chapter 17: Friday Afternoon 211

Chapter 18: Saturday Morning 229

Chapter 19: Friday 236

Chapter 20: Six weeks later 247

Thank You 258

List of Police Personnel 259

More about Bernie and her friends 262

About the Author 264

ACKNOWLEDGEMENTS

The drawing of Police Dog Q on the back cover and the dedication page was done by Sally Marshall. The police dog silhouette on the front cover was derived from this picture. More of her work may be found on her Facebook page:
www.facebook.com/Sally-Marshall-Art-558425041178487

Members of the *PeskyMethodists* Facebook group and many other friends on Facebook and Twitter suggested police dog names and helped me to choose "PD Q" (suggested by Alison Wallbank) and "Wesley" (suggested by Matthew Reed and by the Wesley Church Centre in Chester) for the two dogs who take part in the action in this book.

PD Q was inspired by this book: *Fabulous Finn* by Dave Wardell with Lynne Barrett-Lee, Quercus Editions Ltd, London, 2018, ISBN 978-1-78648-906-7, which also provided useful information about the work of police dogs.

Sarah Rickard, an ex-colleague from my NIHR Research Network days, gave valuable insight into the world of the gay community and helped me to avoid some serious faux pas. Any ignorance or insensitivity that remains is my fault not hers!

I would like to thank Gillian Gilbert for reading the manuscript, giving helpful comments and pointing out typographical errors.

Many Facebook friends contributed ideas to this book.

Special thanks go to Maryalice Hogg-O'Rourke, who has been a continuing source of encouragement.

I am indebted to the authors of a wide range of internet resources, which have been invaluable for researching the background to this book. These include (among others):

- Spinal Injuries Association (www.spinal.co.uk)
- Wikipedia (https://en.wikipedia.org/)
- Google Maps (www.google.co.uk/maps)
- The Disabled Police Association (www.disabledpolice.info)
- Tweets from the many police officers (human and canine) with Twitter accounts

Every effort has been made to trace copyright holders. The publishers will be glad to rectify in future editions any errors or omissions brought to their attention.

DISCLAIMER

This book is a work of fiction. Any references to real people, events, establishments, organisations or locales are intended only to provide a sense of authenticity and are used fictitiously. All of the characters and events are entirely invented by the author. Any resemblances to persons living or dead are purely coincidental.

Most of the locations and institutions that feature in this book are real. Their inhabitants and employees, however, are purely fictional. In particular,

- While Cowley Road Methodist Church is real, Sally Pearson, who is depicted here as its minister, is not; nor is she based on any minister of religion from any denomination.

- Antonio's hairdressing salon is purely fictional, as is its owner, Marcus Antonio (AKA Mark Brown).

- Design Ability has no connection with any company of that, or any similar, name.

- Although the two public houses (the Blackbird and the Bullnose Morris) are real, none of their employees portrayed here are based on anyone associated with those businesses in any way.

- The Oxford Mail is a real newspaper, but its reporting of the Oxford Pride event, as described here, it entirely fictional. Actual reports may be found here: http://www.oxfordmail.co.uk/news/16266530.PIC_GALLERY__Kaleidoscope_of_colour_for_Oxford_Pride_parade/

- Descriptions of incidents at the Oxford Pride event 2018 are entirely made up.
- None of the police personnel portrayed here is based on any police officer from Thames Valley Police or any other police service.
- The Oxford Science Park hosts many innovative small businesses, but Design Ability is not one of them; nor is the company specialising in software for driverless cars based on any company there or anywhere else.

GLOSSARY OF UK POLICE RANKS

Uniformed police

Chief Constable (CC) – Has overall charge of a regional police force, such as Thames Valley Police, which covers Oxford and a large surrounding area.

Deputy Chief Constable (DCC) – The senior discipline authority for each force. 2nd in command to the CC.

Assistant Chief Constable (ACC) – 4 in the Thames Valley Police Service, each responsible for a policy area.

Chief Superintendent ('Chief Super') – Head of a policing area or department.

Police Superintendent – Responsible for a local area within a police force.

Chief Inspector (CI) – Responsible for overseeing a team in a local area.

Police Inspector – Senior operational officer overseeing officers on duty 24/7.

Police Sergeant – Supervises a team of officers.

Police Constable (PC) – 'Bobby on the beat'. Likely to be the first to arrive in response to an emergency call.

Crime Investigation Unit (CID) – Plain clothes officers

Detective Superintendent (DS) – Responsible for crime investigation in a local area.

Detective Chief Inspector (DCI) – Responsible for overseeing a crime investigation team in a local area. May be the Senior Investigating Officer heading up a criminal investigation.

Detective Inspector (DI) – Oversees crime investigation 24/7. May be the Senior Investigating Officer heading up a criminal investigation.

Detective Sergeant (DS) – Supervises a team of CID officers.

Detective Constable (DC) – One of a team of officers investigating crimes.

These descriptions are based on information from the following sources:

[1] Mental Health Cop blog, by Inspector Michael Brown, Mental Health co-ordinator, College of Policing. https://mentalhealthcop.wordpress.com/, accessed 31st March 2017.

[2] Thames Valley Police website, https://www.thamesvalley.police.uk , accessed 31st March 2017.

SKETCH MAP OF BLACKBIRD LEYS
AND SURROUNDING AREA

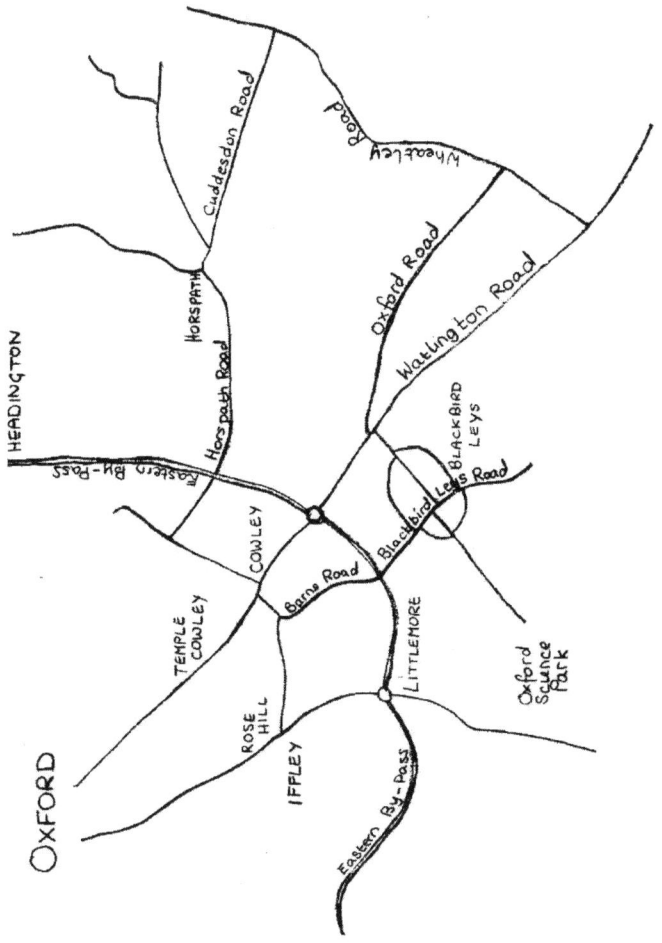

DETAILED MAP OF BLACKBIRD LEYS

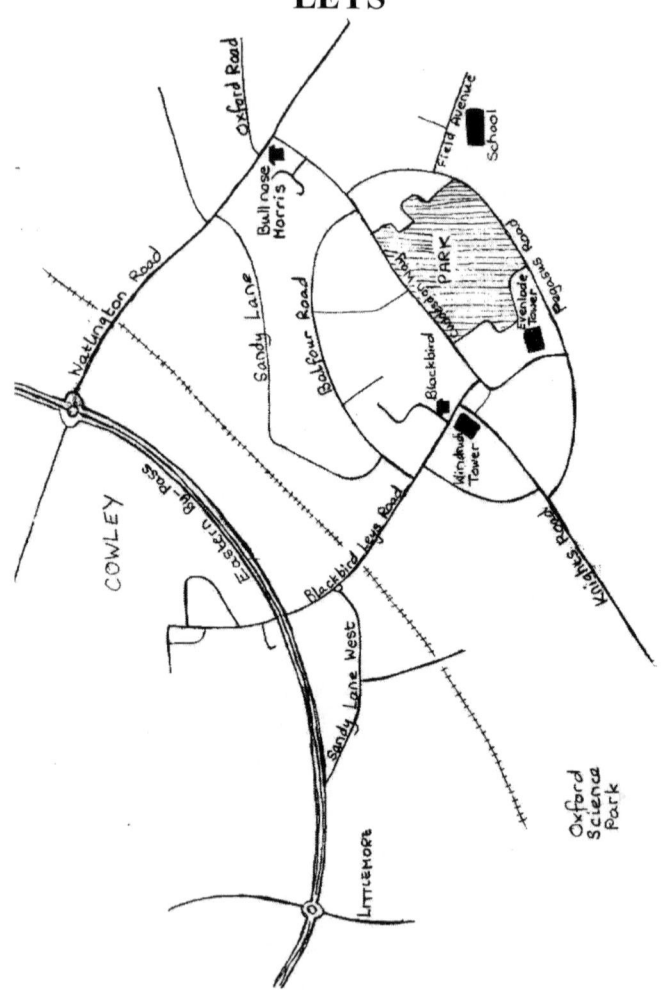

CHAPTER 1: FRIDAY NIGHT

'Last orders!' called out the bar-tender across the crowded room.

Simon drained his glass and set it down on the table in front of him. He had been chairing an informal planning meeting for a project to provide rugby training for youngsters from the Blackbird Leys estate during the school summer holidays, which would be starting in a few weeks' time.

'One for the road?' he asked, looking round at his friends sitting around a small table at the side of the room. 'I'm getting them.'

'Not for me,' Wayne answered, shaking his head. 'I'd better be heading back.'

He got to his feet, picking up his jacket from off the back of his chair and shrugging it on over his broad shoulders.

'We'll give you a lift.' Simon's wife, June, pushed away her empty orange juice glass to make room on the table for her handbag, and started searching for her car key.

'Thanks, but I'll be fine on the bus.' Wayne raised his hand in a gesture of farewell and turned to go.

'I'd better be making tracks too,' said Gary, the fourth

member of their little committee. 'Janice won't let me out to play with you again if I'm not back on time!'

'Oh yes!' Simon joked. 'I forgot. You turn into a pumpkin at midnight, if you don't get back to the little woman on time!'

All three got up and started making their way towards the exit, weaving between the many small tables and dodging other customers who were either intent on getting in one final drink before closing time or else preparing to leave themselves. Ahead of them, Wayne's muscular figure in its distinctive green jacket disappeared through the door.

'Wayne seems like a nice boy,' June murmured to her husband. 'And I'd never have known if you hadn't told me. He seems completely normal ...'

'Well, what did you expect?' Gary asked tersely. 'Did you think he was going to be some sort of alien from outer space?'

'No of course not! I've just never met one before and I didn't know what to expect.' June blushed and chattered on in an attempt to hide her embarrassment. 'What's that caption on the back of his jacket? I couldn't get the words.'

'*Design Ability*,' her husband told her. 'It's his company name.'

'You remember I told you he's got an engineering degree?' Gary added. 'He started this business with one of the other students on his course.'

'You mean his rich daddy set them up in it,' Simon derided. 'That's how these Oxbridge types get on.'

'They seem to be making a go of it,' Gary defended his friend. 'Wayne tells me they're looking to hire more staff for this new Oxford office.'

Once outside the building, they stepped to one side of the path while June continued to ferret in her handbag for her keys. Looking towards the street, Gary saw the light from a streetlamp picking out the words on the back of his friend's jacket as Wayne prepared to cross the road to the bus stop.

He continued to watch as the young man strode purposefully across. Then, just as he reached the opposite kerb, everything started happening very quickly. An engine roared and a silver car sped up the road and hurtled towards them. Gary stared in dismayed disbelief as it mounted the kerb and ploughed into Wayne, hurling him across the pavement. As if in slow motion, his body described an arc in the air before colliding with the corner of the bus shelter. The car swerved to regain the road, its rear wing grating against a cast-iron litterbin. Then it accelerated away.

'Stop!' Gary shouted helplessly, running out into the centre of the road to get a better view of the car's registration plate. 'Stop you bastards!'

The car disappeared round a bend in the road. Gary turned and hurried over to the crumpled heap that was Wayne's body. Someone else was already there, kneeling over him and peering down intensely. Gary crouched down too and the other man looked up. He was dark-skinned with hair in dreadlocks and a cigarette in his mouth. When their eyes met, he removed it and stubbed it out on the pavement.

'He's out cold,' he told Gary. 'Better call an ambulance.'

Gary put out his hand and touched Wayne's shoulder, but the other man pushed it away.

'Better not move him. Wait for the paramedics.'

'They're on their way.' Gary turned at the sound of Simon's voice from behind him. 'June's called 999.'

As if on cue, a police patrol car appeared, its blue light flashing. It pulled up and a large uniformed officer got out.

PC Gavin Hughes looked around, quickly sizing up the situation. Then he took off his jacket, folded it to form a makeshift pillow and crouched down to place it gently under Wayne's head. His radio crackled and he spoke into it with calm urgency, asking for more police officers and checking that an ambulance was on its way. He gently checked Wayne's pulse and breathing, and then looked round at the small crowd of onlookers.

'I got a message this was a hit-and-run,' he said. 'Did any of you see what happened?'

'It was a silver BMW,' Gary answered eagerly. 'New: 18-reg. I couldn't get the whole number, but it was definitely 18 and I think it ended with a K. It headed off towards the ring road.'

'Thanks.' Gavin imparted this information to his colleagues via the radio. 'Now, can you tell me who this is?' He looked down at Wayne, who was still lying motionless and unresponsive. 'Any of you his mates?'

'His name's Wayne Major,' Simon volunteered. 'We'd all been – that's me and my wife and Gary here – in the *Blackbird* having a few drinks. Wayne was going to get the bus back. He'd just got across the road when this maniac slammed into him.'

'Thank you. Can you give me the name of his next-of-kin? Is there someone who'll be expecting him home?'

'That'd be his parents, I suppose,' June began, 'but he doesn't live with-'

'No,' Gary cut in. 'The person you need to contact is his partner. I can give you the name and address. They live in Cowley.'

Gavin took out his notebook and carefully noted down the details. Then, seeing Wayne stirring, he gently placed his hand on his shoulder to restrain him.

'Just lie still there,' he said gently. 'The ambulance will be here any moment.'

Wayne's eyes flickered and an expression of puzzlement passed over his face briefly before he lost consciousness again.

A siren and more blue lights announced the arrival of the ambulance, closely followed by a second police car. After exchanging a few words with the paramedics, Gavin went over to brief his colleagues.

Malcolm Appleton, still nervously sporting his recently-acquired sergeant's stripes, had been showing the ropes to a new recruit when they got the call to assist at this crime scene. He was relieved to see that the first officer on the scene was a reliable PC with plenty of experience but no desire for promotion. Gavin would know what to do without being told, and would not attempt to score points over a rookie sergeant.

***

On a routine patrol on the Eastern By-Pass, PCs John Gamble and Louise Otterbourne received a call to intercept a car, which was reported to have gone through a red light at the junction with Horspath Road. The powerful silver car had left the northbound side of the ring road, travelling at speed and narrowly avoiding a collision with an oil tanker coming in the opposite direction. A member of the public had rung the police, saying that it had continued at a dangerous pace through the small industrial estate near the junction and on out into the open country beyond.

Louise and John gave chase, past the sports ground and cricket club and on into the village of Horspath itself. They slowed to take a sharp bend near the pub and general stores; then the road straightened out and they could see the distant tail-lights of a vehicle ahead. Louise put her foot down in an attempt to catch up, but the car seemed, if anything, to be gaining ground. Then suddenly the lights jerked to the right and disappeared. What had happened? Had the car left the road?

They hurried on and then slowed down as they approached the point where they thought the lights had disappeared. They continued at a snail's pace, peering to left and right in the hope of seeing some trace of the missing vehicle. When they reached the T-junction with Wheatley Road, they realised that they must have missed it. Louise turned the car round and they retraced their route, still looking out intently for any signs that a car had left the road.

'There it is!' John shouted at last, pointing to the left. 'Look! There!'

Louise slowed to a stop and they both got out. John shone a torch on the number plate of the silver car that he had spotted with three wheels on the rutted track that led through an open field gate and the fourth dangling over the ditch, which, together with a thorn hedge, separated the field from the road. In their haste, the driver of the car had taken the corner too close.

'It's that hit-and-run car we're supposed to be looking out for,' Louise said, noting the registration year and the final character. 'They said 18 and ending in K.'

While she radioed in this information, John prowled round looking for some indication of which way the occupants of the vehicle had gone. Unfortunately, the ground next to the driver's door was grassy and there were no discernible footmarks. The muddy track was more promising, but in the dark, he could only make out tyre marks and what might be hoof-prints left by horses or cattle.

'I've asked for backup,' Louise reported a minute or two later. 'We're in luck. Mel's not far away with Q.'

***

'I'll go in the ambulance to provide continuity of evidence,' Malcolm told Gavin, as the paramedics prepared to set off for the hospital. 'Can I leave you to inform the next-of-kin?'

'Right you are.'

'And Ben,' Malcolm turned to his more junior colleague, 'I want you to stay here to protect the scene of crime.'

PC Ben Timpson nodded and took up a position next to the litterbin, proud to be given such a responsible role, but a little nervous of being left on his own. Gavin looked round at the group of onlookers.

'Thank you all for your help,' he said. 'We've got your names and addresses and you'll probably get a visit from CID in the next few days to talk to you about what you saw. But now, it would be best if you all went off home.'

He stood, watching them. After a few moments, they started to drift away until the two police officers were alone.

'I'd better be off to break the bad news to the victim's family,' Gavin told Ben. 'You're doing a great job,' he added kindly, seeing the young man's anxious expression. 'And if there's any trouble, don't be behindhand with calling for backup.'

***

The end-terraced house where Wayne and his partner lived had cream-painted walls and white UPVC window-frames. Most of the small front garden had been paved to make a hard-standing for a green van, which was decorated with a logo based around a stylised wheelchair and bore the words *Design Ability* in large white letters.

Gavin parked outside and walked up to the front door. There were no lights visible and the curtains were drawn both upstairs and down. He pressed the bell, holding it down for several seconds, anticipating that Wayne's partner might be asleep. Then he stepped back and waited patiently.

He was just beginning to wonder whether he ought to ring again when a light went on upstairs. A short while later another came on in the hall. A dark figure appeared behind the frosted glass in the door and there was the sound of a key being inserted into the lock. The door opened and a face looked out.

It was a young man. His dark brown hair was cut across at the front in a long fringe, which covered his eyebrows and threatened to obscure his deep brown eyes.

Gavin could not decide whether this face reminded him most of an Old English Sheep Dog or a frightened deer. On seeing a police officer in uniform, his expression changed in an instant from exasperation to consternation.

'I – I thought it must be Wayne forgotten his key,' he stammered. 'What's happened? Is something wrong?'

'Mr Dean O'Brien?' Gavin asked calmly.

'Yes.' The young man's eyes opened wider, definitely more startled deer than sheepdog now. 'What is it? Is it Wayne? Has something happened to him?'

'There's been a road traffic accident,' Gavin told him. 'Can I come in?'

'Yes, of course.' Dean flung open the door and stepped back to allow Gavin to enter the small hall. 'Come through here.'

He led the way into a long room, with windows at the back and front of the house.

'I think we'd better both sit down,' Gavin said, looking towards a sofa and easy chairs grouped around a large television screen. 'If that's OK?'

'Yes, yes.' Dean perched on the edge of a chair, while Gavin settled himself on the sofa. 'But tell me about Wayne? Is he badly hurt?' He paused and looked at Gavin with his large liquid eyes wider than ever. 'He's not …?'

'He was hit by a car, which mounted the pavement on Blackbird Leys Road.' Gavin told him gently. 'He struck his head and that rendered him unconscious.'

'But how is he? I mean – will he get better?' Dean pushed his hair back from his eyes with his left hand and Gavin noticed a wide gold band on his ring finger. There had been a similar one on the victim's hand, he remembered.

'It's too early to be sure, but the paramedics told me that, apart from being knocked out, his injuries seem fairly minor. He's in good hands. He'll be at the John Radcliffe[1]

---

[1] The John Radcliffe Hospital is a large teaching hospital situated

by now. I'm here to take you there to see him – if that's what you'd like.'

'Yes!' Dean leapt up. Then he stood gazing down uncertainly at his pyjamas and bare feet.

'You take your time,' Gavin said reassuringly, getting to his feet and laying his hand gently on Dean's shoulder. 'I'm not in any rush. You go and get yourself ready, and I'll be waiting for you down here.'

Dean disappeared upstairs, leaving Gavin standing thoughtfully in the sitting room. He looked around him. There was a piano against one wall with a row of photographs on top of it. Gavin wandered over to look more closely.

In the centre stood a large picture of two young men in grey suits with carnations in the buttonholes, standing next to each other, holding hands and smiling broadly. Gavin recognised the steps and distinctive yellow bricks of Oxford Register Office in the background. The smaller of the men was easily identified as Dean, by his conspicuous dark fringe. The other must be Wayne. The build was right, but the cheerful face looked very different from the bruised and grazed one that Gavin had looked down upon shortly before.

***

'I hear you've got a hit-and-run driver you want us to find for you,' PC Melanie Stanton called out to Louise as she climbed out of her van.

'That's right,' Louise answered, looking up from where she had been examining the scratched paintwork on the nearside rear of the abandoned car. 'Whoever it was looks to have made off across country. They can't be far. It can't have been more than five or ten minutes after they crashed that we called you.'

---

in the Headington district of Oxford.

'OK.' Melanie went round to the back of the van where her two dogs were waiting in their cages, alert and eager to get to work. 'Sorry Wesley,' she said to the liver-and-white Springer Spaniel, which was pawing excitedly at the bars and whining to be allowed out. 'This one isn't for you, I'm afraid.'

She unfastened the other cage and quickly attached a long leash to the large German Shepherd bitch, who lay inside. *Police Dog Q* was an experienced general-purpose dog, who could be relied upon in a variety of policing situations. When it came to tracking down miscreants using her powerful sense of smell, she was second to none.

Louise came round and greeted Q warmly, fondling her head and patting her on the shoulder. She was an animal-lover herself and enjoyed any opportunity for fraternising with members of the Dog Section.

'Hello there, Q! Do you remember me?'

Q wagged her tail and looked up at Louise with her tongue hanging out, ears pricked and eyes alert.

Holding tightly to Q's collar, Melanie led her round to the open driver's door of the abandoned car. Soon they were off, following an invisible trail diagonally across the field.

Louise watched, knowing that Melanie and Q would get on better without her and conscious of the need to remain with the car to ensure that any forensic evidence at the scene was preserved. Where had John got to? He had been trying to follow a set of indistinct footprints, which he had found a few feet from the field gate. He had disappeared into the darkness several minutes ago and was now nowhere to be seen.

Her question was answered almost immediately by a series of short barks from Q and an exasperated cry from Mel.

'Why can't you lot ever just stay put and wait for us to get here? How can you expect a dog to track down villains when you go wandering round the crime scene leaving scent trails all over the shop?'

Louise hurried after them.

'John,' she said, slightly breathless after her sprint across the field, 'may I introduce PD Q and her chauffeur, Mel Stanton. Mel, this is PC John Gamble. He thought he'd found footprints leading from the car.'

'They're clearer here,' John added in an attempt to justify his actions. He pointed downwards with his torch. 'See! It looks like two sets of prints overlapping one another.'

'OK. Let's see what Q has to say about them,' Mel responded.

She led the dog a little further along the trail of prints, beyond where she judged John's own scent trail must end. Then she gave orders for Q to resume tracking. Q sniffed around obligingly, but without any sign of enthusiasm. She seemed confused and perhaps a little bored. She returned to her handler's side and looked up with an expression that told Mel that they were on the wrong track.

'Nothing doing here,' Mel reported to the others. 'Looks like these prints are old. Let's get back to the car and start again. And this time,' she added, giving John a hard look, 'will you both keep still and leave it to Q to do the tracking?'

It did not take Q long to find a new scent trail to follow. She set off confidently over the grass with Mel following behind, sometimes having to break into a run to keep up as the big dog plunged ahead through the darkness. She let out the lead to its maximum length.

A splash ahead of her warned her that Q had found water. She called out to her to stop and hurried to catch up, reeling in the lead as she did so. She found Q standing in a small stream, which formed the boundary between this field and the next. Mel shone her torch around, looking for a place where she could cross dry-shod. Soon they were both on the other side with Q looking eagerly up at Mel awaiting instructions.

'Good girl! Track on!'

At once Q was away again, running across the wet grass. Mel could tell that the scent trail that she was following was recent and clear. Surely, this must be the way that the driver of the car – or at least one of the occupants – had come?

Q's pace slowed as she approached a field boundary. Mel again reeled in the lead and used her torch to examine the obstruction. It was a hedge. There were plenty of places where Q would be able to push her way through – and where Mel, with more difficulty would be able to follow – but the danger was that there might be barbed wire concealed within the bushes, which could penetrate even Q's thick fur, not to mention the damage it might do to Mel's regulation uniform trousers.

Fortunately, the suspect that they were following appeared also to have been wary of pushing their way through the hedge. A little way to their right, Mel found a gate and Q confirmed that the trail continued on the other side. Immediately they were off again, racing across the uneven turf into the unknown.

***

I'm ready. Can we go now?'

Gavin turned to see Dean standing in the doorway, dressed in jeans and a polo shirt.

'Yes.' Gavin followed Dean out into the hall. 'You'd better put a coat or something on,' he added, looking down at Dean's bare arms. It's getting chilly out.'

Dean reached out to a row of hooks on the wall of the hall and selected a green jacket its breast pocket decorated with another copy of the logo that Gavin had seen on the van outside. He put it on and then turned away from Gavin to open the door for them to leave the house, giving the burly police officer an opportunity to observe the words *Design Ability,* in a distinctive script, standing out white against the dark green.

Dean's hands were shaking as he fumbled with his keys to lock the front door after they had gone through. Gavin placed his hand on his shoulder in a gesture of reassurance.

'Try not to worry. Like I said, he's in good hands.'

'But you said he hit his head,' Dean argued dismally as they made their way down the short path to the waiting police car. 'And you said he was unconscious. I've seen people with brain injuries. One of them was paralysed all down one side, and another had to start learning to talk all over again.'

'And I've seen men knocked out cold one evening and back on their feet and in work the morning after,' Gavin insisted.

'And Wayne's always been so active,' Dean persisted, as if he had not heard. 'He'll hate it if he can't do his sport anymore.'

***

Melanie cautiously held up a strand of barbed wire, which spanned a narrow gap in the hedge, to allow Q to pass underneath and then carefully climbed over it herself. The ground gave way beneath her and she found herself sliding into a ditch. She scrambled out and looked around. The surface on that side felt much firmer under her feet. Shining her torch downwards, she saw that she was back on tarmac.

Suddenly everything became much brighter as a vehicle approached with its headlights on full-beam. Mel took hold of Q's collar and instructed her to sit while they both waited for the car to pass.

It did not. Instead, it pulled up a few feet in front of them. The lights dimmed and became less dazzling. A uniformed figure got out from the driver's side.

'Hi Tracy!' Mel called out, recognising Police Sergeant Tracy Burton. 'What are you doing here?'

'I was about to ask you the same thing. I'm looking for a place called *Hoo Down Farmhouse*. They've reported a car stolen and it looks as if it's the same as one that knocked down a pedestrian outside the *Blackbird* three quarters of an hour ago.'

'And the same as the one that Louise found abandoned half an hour ago. That's where we've come from. Q's been tracking the driver.'

Q looked up at the sound of her name. Then she stood up and strained to move off. Clearly, she still had a scent to follow and was keen to get back to work.

'OK Q, track on!' Mel commanded, releasing her collar but keeping her on a short leash.

The dog led them confidently along the road a short distance and then turned in at a driveway on their right. Mel ordered her to wait while the two police officers shone their torches around looking for a name or house-number to indicate where they were. The drive was flanked by two tall brick pillars from which hung a pair of wrought iron gates standing open.

'There we are!' Tracy said triumphantly, pointing up at a sign attached to one of the gateposts. 'Hoo Down Farmhouse! Looks like we've found it.'

'But if the car was stolen, how come the driver came back here after crashing it?'

'Mmm. It makes you wonder, doesn't it,' Tracy agreed thoughtfully.

***

Gavin had visited the Accident and Emergency department at the hospital more times than he cared to remember in the course of his twenty-nine years as a police officer, and he knew his way round very well. Not even he, however, could arrange for Dean to see his partner immediately upon their arrival, because Wayne was on his way to the radiology department for a brain scan. The harassed-looking nurse, who briefly abandoned his heavy workload to speak to them, assured them that everything possible was being done and that a doctor would come to speak to them in due course.

Gavin gently steered a white-faced Dean, whose anxiety-levels had clearly increased at the mention of the CT scanner and the possibility of bleeding in the brain, into a quiet waiting area away from the chaos and noise of the Friday-night A&E Reception. Malcolm was sitting there waiting for news of the victim's condition. He got up and came across to greet them.

Or rather, he greeted Gavin while giving nervous sidelong glances towards Dean. Like every officer in the force, he had been on an LGBT[2]-Awareness course, supposedly to prepare him for dealing sensitively with members of the Gay Community. However, with no personal experience to draw on, this had only made him apprehensive lest he do or say the wrong thing and inadvertently cause offence.

'He's still unconscious,' Malcolm told Gavin. 'They've taken him down to radiology for a scan. I told them I'd wait for him to come back, but now you're here …,' he looked at his watch. 'I could do with getting back and filing a report of the incident. Do you think you could …?'

'No problem. I promised Dean I'd stay with him in any case.'

'Dean? Oh yes, of course! You mean …?' He forced himself to turn to address the young man, who had been listening wide-eyed to the police officers' conversation. 'I'm sorry. I should have introduced myself. I'm Sergeant Malcolm Appleton. I came in the ambulance with your friend. The doctors say he's not badly injured, except that they're not sure what damage the bang on his head may have done.'

Dean nodded in silence and gave a small involuntary

---

[2] Lesbian, Gay, Bisexual and Transgender

gulp. Gavin placed his arm around his shoulders and propelled him gently towards two empty chairs in a corner of the room.

'You sit down here, son, and I'll go and get us both a nice cup of tea. I know hospitals: the wait is always longer than you expect.' He turned to Malcolm. 'OK Malc; you get off and write your report. We'll be fine.'

'Thanks.' Malcolm turned to go. Then he hesitated and turned back. He approached Dean and looked down at him. He could feel his cheeks reddening as he spoke, rather hurriedly, conscious that his embarrassment must be palpable to the young man. 'I'm really sorry about what happened. We'll do everything we can to find whoever did it, I promise.'

Then he was off. By the time Dean raised his head to look bemusedly after him, he was striding purposefully through the door on his way back to the more familiar territory of crime reports and police files.

***

Dean looked just a little better when Gavin returned a few minutes later with two plastic cups of tea from a vending machine in the corridor outside. He looked up and managed a weak smile, taking the cup and cradling it in both hands.

'I've rung Wayne's mum and dad. They're coming over right away.'

'That's good.' Gavin sat down beside him, placing his own cup on the empty seat on the other side of him. 'Do they have far to come?'

'Bromsgrove. It usually takes a bit over an hour if you get a good run.'

'They're driving then?' Gavin silently hoped that Gavin's parents had not celebrated the end of the working week with the traditional "few pints". Having his father-in-law arrested for drink-driving would not improve Dean's state of mind.

'Yes. I hope they'll be OK. They only got back from visiting Wayne's sister in Swansea a couple of hours ago, but Barbara says they went straight to bed and now they're feeling fine.'

'I expect she's right.' Gavin tried to be reassuring, despite his own misgivings. 'It's amazing how adrenalin can keep you going in this sort of situation. The exhaustion only kicks in later, when it's all over.'

They sat in silence. Gavin vainly tried to think of something to say to keep the conversation going and to distract Dean from dwelling on his partner's injuries, which, even if not life-threatening, had the potential to be life-changing.

'I wish we'd never moved to Oxford,' Dean said suddenly. 'I'm sure Barbara and Graham didn't want us to, but we got the opportunity to take a unit on the Science Park and Wayne said that an Oxford address would be good for the business. I'm sure he's right about that,' he added loyally, 'but it must have looked a bit ungrateful after all they've done for us.'

'You've got a business?' Gavin tried to pick up on something positive to talk about. 'What line of work is it?'

'We design equipment to enable people with disabilities to be more independent.'

'That sounds interesting,' Gavin began, still working on his distraction routine. Then an idea struck him and several things started to drop into place in his mind. 'You're – you're not the two lads who made DCI Porter's wheelchair, are you?'

'Yes. Do you know him?'

'I could hardly not know him! He's a legend in the force – and not just in Thames Valley either. But as it happens, I do know him personally too. I expect he's forgotten all about it, but he was on the panel that interviewed me when I first applied to be a copper. He gave me a real grilling and I was surprised they didn't turn me down.'

'That's how it all started – with Jonah Porter. Bernie – you must know Bernie too, I suppose – asked my tutor to find some students to make some gadgets to help him with things. That was when he was still on the rehab ward at Stoke Mandeville[3]. He chose Wayne and me, and everything just snowballed from there. Wayne's dad has his own engineering firm. Well, I suppose I ought to say had, because he's sold most of it now. Anyway, he set us up as a subsidiary and bankrolled us for the first few years after we graduated. That's why it seemed a bit ungrateful to move away from them just when he was retiring and we'd got things on an even keel. And now …!' Dean's voice cracked and he wiped his hand across his eyes.

***

'Excuse me!' A young woman in hospital uniform approached them some half an hour later. Gavin looked at her identity badge: *Zena Gamble, Healthcare Assistant*. 'Are you waiting to see Wayne Major?'

'Yes!' Dean jumped to his feet. 'Is he OK? Can I see him?'

'He's been transferred to the neurosciences ICU,' Zena told him. 'If you come with me, I'll take you there.'

'ICU?' Dean queried anxiously. 'That's intensive care, isn't it? Does that mean …? Is he …?'

'I'm afraid I can't answer your questions, but when we get to the unit there'll be someone who can.'

'But, he is going to be alright, isn't he?'

Gavin put his hand on Dean's shoulder again and gave it a reassuring squeeze. 'Let's just go and see, shall we?

[3] The National Spinal Injuries Centre at Stoke Mandeville Hospital in Aylesbury is one of the largest spinal injury units in the world. It was made famous by the pioneering work of Sir Ludwig Guttmann who founded the Paralympic Games.

***

A nurse came to meet them at the entrance to the ICU. 'I'm Megan Gould,' she told them. 'I'm the named nurse responsible for Wayne Major during this shift. I'll take you to see him in a minute, but first I need to explain a few things. Don't worry,' she added, seeing Dean's expression of alarm at these words, 'it's nothing dreadful. You just need to understand what's going on.'

Dean nodded eagerly. 'Yes. Go on!' he urged.

'Wayne is currently in a medically-induced coma. The doctors have done that to help his brain to recover from the trauma that it experienced when he hit his head. That means that he won't respond when you talk to him, but he probably can hear you, so you ought to be careful what you say. Don't discuss his condition, for example; just let him know you're there and you could maybe hold his hand or something like that.'

'How long?' Dean asked, his voice grating as his mouth suddenly became very dry. He swallowed twice and cleared his throat. 'I mean, how long will he be kept like that?'

'That depends on how he's doing. The doctors will be monitoring the swelling in his brain and as soon as that responds to treatment, they'll probably start bringing him out of the coma. It varies a lot, so I'm afraid I can't give you a straight answer. It could be just a few hours or it could be quite a bit longer than that.'

Megan led the way inside the unit. Dean followed, looking round in a daze at all the complicated medical equipment.

'You'll find he's connected up to lots of tubes and monitors,' Megan warned him, noticing his wide-eyed anxiety. 'I know it looks scary, but try not to let it worry you. It's all just so that we can do our best for him.'

CHAPTER 2: SATURDAY MORNING

Gavin looked at his watch. Seven o'clock. It had been a long shift, but he had one final call to make before going home to breakfast and then to bed. He drove through the leafy suburb of Headington in the pale morning sunshine and turned in at a wide drive between stone gateposts, with copper beech hedges on either side. This house was larger and older than its neighbours, and set further back from the road.

Gavin parked neatly alongside a large car with a disabled badge on the window. He got out and started up the sloping path to the front door. He looked at his watch again and then up at the bedroom windows. The curtains were open and there appeared to be a light on. Light also shone through the small window to the left of the door. He had been right in thinking that the family would be early-risers, even at the weekend. He pressed the bell-push and stepped back a pace to wait for a response.

The door was answered by a tall man with greying red hair.

'Gavin! What brings you here?' Peter Johns knew Gavin well through having worked with him during his own forty years as a police officer.

'It's bad news, I'm afraid. I thought you'd want to know that Wayne Major's in hospital. He was involved in a hit-and-run on Blackbird Leys Road last night.'

'You'd better come in.'

Gavin stepped over the threshold and wiped his boots meticulously on the mat, before following Peter through a door on the right. He looked round at a pleasant sitting room with windows on two sides, a pair of comfy chairs at the far end and a desk with a computer and other electronic devices on it. The room also contained a number of strange pieces of equipment upon whose uses Gavin could only speculate. This was the study and sitting room belonging to DCI Jonah Porter, who had been a permanent guest in Peter's home since the death of his wife four years earlier.

'Jonah's getting dressed,' Peter explained, crossing the room to a door beyond. 'But I know he'll want to hear about it right away.'

He opened a door at the side of the room and led Gavin into Jonah's bedroom. It was cluttered with more of the mysterious gadgets and seemed crowded with people, now that Peter and Gavin were there. In the centre of the room, there stood a high, metal-framed bed, similar to those found in hospitals. There was another, narrower bed against the wall under the window. Pushed up against another wall, Gavin recognised Jonah's electric wheelchair, in its reclined position so that it looked more like a hospital trolley than a chair.

On either side of the bed, two women were standing, bent over and clearly busy with some task. Gavin realised that they were engaged in putting a pair of trousers on to the occupant, who was lying motionless on his back. DCI Porter looked very different, in this helpless position, from the dynamic and demanding senior officer with whom Gavin was familiar. In his hi-tech wheelchair, the paralysis caused by a bullet in the neck nine years earlier seemed almost irrelevant. Without it, he appeared smaller somehow and painfully vulnerable.

The women looked up at the sound of the door opening. 'Gavin!' Peter's wife, Bernie, recognised the big policeman at once, and at once realised that he would not be here at this hour without good reason. 'Is something wrong?'

'It's Wayne,' Peter explained. 'He's in hospital.'

'He was knocked down by a car at the bus stop opposite the *Blackbird*,' Gavin expanded. 'He's in the neuro-ICU.'

'How? What happened? Have you got whoever did it?' Jonah, unable to move, exploded into angry and anxious speech.

'It looks like joy-riders to me, Sir,' Gavin replied, addressing the senior officer in the formal manner that he was accustomed to using at work. 'The car was reported stolen shortly after the incident took place. I don't think they've traced the driver yet.'

'What about Dean?' Bernie's eighteen-year-old daughter, Lucy, asked in a troubled voice. 'You *have* told him?' she added anxiously.

'Yes. I went and got him from home and took him to the hospital,' Gavin assured her.

'And how's he taking it?' asked Bernie. The whole family were extremely fond of the two young men.

'Shell-shocked is how I'd describe it. Doesn't know what's hit him. I stayed there with him until Wayne's parents arrived. Mrs Major seems to have taken him under her wing now.'

'That's good.' Bernie looked just a little less anxious. 'I know Barbara has a soft spot for Dean. She'll take care of him. But it must be dreadful for them too, of course,' she added quickly.

'Who's in charge of the investigation?' Jonah demanded. 'What are they doing to track down the driver?'

'I don't think that's been decided yet,' Gavin told him. 'It's been a busy night.'

'I suppose so.' Jonah sounded distinctly dissatisfied, but he did not express out loud his frustration at the apparent lack of urgency, which he recognised was not Gavin's fault. He turned his head to address Bernie. 'Now hurry up and finish getting me up and into my chair. We've got a busy morning ahead of us.'

'Doing what, exactly?' Peter asked, although he already had a good idea what Jonah was planning.

Bernie and Lucy, meanwhile, hurried to fasten Jonah's trousers and then began the process of transferring him from bed to chair, where it would be easier to put on his shirt.

'First off, I'm going to the hospital to see for myself how Wayne's doing,' Jonah said briskly.

'I want to go too,' Lucy interjected.

'We can't all roll up at the ICU together,' Peter argued.

'Well *I'm* going,' Jonah insisted. 'I want to talk to the doctors and find out what their prognosis is. And I want to check that Dean's OK.'

'We all do,' Bernie agreed, 'but Peter's right – if we all go, we'll only be in the way.'

'And then, after that, I want to call at the station to check that they're taking this thing seriously,' Jonah continued. 'If it's been put down to joy-riders there's a danger that it will simply drown in a sea of cases that we don't have the manpower to investigate properly.'

'You're not on duty over the weekend,' Bernie pointed out, trying to sound firm but knowing in her heart that she was wasting her breath. Since his disabling injury, Jonah was supposed to stick to a strict office-hours-only working pattern, to preserve his strength and to allow him time for the physiotherapy and other time-consuming routines necessary for his well-being. This did not suit his energetic personality and, despite Bernie's best efforts in her role as his Personal Assistant, he frequently broke the rules.

'That's got nothing to do with it!' Jonah declared forcefully, twisting his neck in order to address Bernie, while Lucy leaned him forward to tuck in his shirt at the back. 'I won't be working – just checking that this isn't going to be swept under the carpet.'

'Don't you think that for once in your life it would be a good idea to trust someone else to be able to do things right?' Peter asked with a sigh. 'You aren't the only decent officer on the force you know.' He turned to Gavin. 'Thanks for coming. We appreciate it. Now we'd better let you get off home. At least – you're welcome to stay to breakfast, but I imagine Chrissie will be expecting you?'

'Yes.' Gavin glanced down at his watch again. 'She always does a fry-up for me when I'm on duty over Friday night.' He looked round at the others. 'I'll be going then.'

'Hang on!' Jonah called him back. 'Just one more thing: are you sure it was just a driver losing control? Or could it have been deliberate?'

'How d'you mean, Sir?'

'It just occurred to me: could this be another of these attacks that I'm looking into?'

'Which attacks?'

'On people who took part in the Gay Pride march last month. It started low-key, but they've been escalating. Could this just be the latest development?'

'I suppose it could, Sir,' Gavin answered dubiously, 'but I don't really see how they could've identified him. It's not as if he was coming out of a gay bar or something. And it was dark. How would they know who he was?'

'Nice try, Jonah,' Bernie smiled. 'But it won't work. You're not going to get yourself put in charge of this enquiry, so why not give in gracefully?'

***

In another home in another part of Oxford, another family was in the process of preparing for the day ahead. DI Anna Davenport had recently returned from maternity leave on a part-time basis, while she adjusted to life with her youngest child, Donna, whose unplanned arrival a few months earlier had precipitated the departure of her husband of sixteen years.

'It's OK, Mum, I'll take her.' Anna's other daughter, seventeen-year-old Jessica, reached out for the infant who was coughing and crying in turns in Anna's arms. 'You get on and eat your breakfast or you'll be late.'

'I don't know.' Anna, sounding doubtful, nevertheless handed the baby over. 'I think she may be sickening for something.'

'I'm sure you're wrong, but I've got the number of the children's ward *and* our GP *and* the community paediatric team, so I can get help if I need it. Now eat up while I take her upstairs and change her. I can smell that she needs it! And I bet that's all that's wrong – she's just uncomfortable.'

Jessica left the room. Anna watched her go, listening to the retreating footsteps mounting the stairs. It was strange. When Jessica and her brother were born, she had happily handed over their care to their father after only a few weeks, in order to return full-time to her career. This time, nearly nine months after Donna's birth, she still found it hard to be separated from her, even briefly. Was it Donna's disability – she had been born with spina bifida – that made the difference? Or was it her enforced career break, during which the child had hardly been out of her sight, that had made the bond with her youngest child so painful to break?

She sat down at the table and poured muesli into a bowl. Jess was right: she must get on. She could not afford to be seen as unreliable. Her boss, DCI Porter, had pulled a lot of strings to obtain her current working arrangements and there were plenty of people who would be on the lookout for an excuse to dispense with her services.

If only she could find a nursery or childminder that would take Donna on! It was strange the way they all suddenly had full books as soon as they heard about

Donna's disability. It was good of Jess to offer to look after her sister, but she had her schoolwork to think of as well and Anna was anxious that her A' level results would be affected. In any case, working just two long shifts each weekend was unsustainable financially in the long run, as well as being a sure and certain barrier to any further promotion.

She finished her breakfast and put the empty bowl and coffee mug in the sink for Jessica to wash later. Then she went upstairs to collect her jacket and briefcase and to say goodbye to her daughters. Her son, Marcus, stumbling bleary-eyed back from a visit to the bathroom, almost collided with her as she reached the landing. He mumbled a greeting as he returned to his room intent on a few more minutes – or hours – in bed.

'I'm going now,' she told him. 'There's what's left of yesterday's chicken in the fridge for your lunch and you can go to the chippy for dinner if you like.'

'OK. See you later,' he mumbled, taking the five-pound note that she held out to him and disappearing with it into his room.

*****

'The restaurant will be serving breakfast now,' Megan said quietly, looking round at Graham and Barbara Major and then finally allowing her eyes to rest on Dean, who had spent the night sitting at Wayne's bedside with Wayne's left hand clasped between his own two. 'Why don't you go and get yourselves something to eat?'

'I don't want to leave him,' Dean protested almost inaudibly, his throat dry and his voice cracking.

'Dr Weber will be here at eight,' Megan continued. 'She's Dr Mutambara's registrar. If you go and have breakfast now, by the time you get back she'll be able to tell you how things are going.'

'Come along!' Graham got up. He liked to be active

and in control of every situation. Watching and waiting over his son, who seemed to him to be more dead than alive, had been a difficult experience. He patted Dean on the shoulder. 'We can't do anything for him at the moment. Let's go and get something to eat and then come back and see what the doctor has to say.

***

Chief Superintendent Alison Brown called Anna over to her the moment she walked into the open-plan office that housed the Crime Investigation Department.

'I'm putting you in charge of investigating a near-fatal hit-and-run that took place last night,' she told her. 'Sergeant Appleton will fill you in on the details. I've told him to wait in your office. You'd better see him first thing, before he goes off duty.'

Anna hurried to obey. This sounded a little more promising than the other cases that had come her way since returning from her maternity leave. Was it significant that this was the first occasion when a female officer had been in charge of allocating the jobs? No. She had no evidence for that. More likely it was that there had been a reluctance to trust her with important cases too soon after her return to work – or perhaps the chronic shortage of officers had left Alison with no option on this occasion.

When she got to her office, she found not only Malcolm Appleton but also Louise Otterbourne waiting for her. Malcolm summarised what had occurred and then handed over a folder of reports.

'The car has been recovered for forensic examination,' he finished. 'Tracy Burton, who responded to the call reporting the theft, tells me that the owner was far from pleased at not being able to have it back, so you can expect some flak from him. He's some sort of businessman who's used to getting his own way. The other thing about him is … well, Louise had better tell you. She was there.'

'It's the dog,' Louise explained. 'You remember I told you Mel Stanton had PD Q tracking the driver of the car? Well, it seemed odd to her – and I agree – that the trail led to the house where the car's owner lived. We were wondering if it wasn't really stolen at all.'

***

The combination of Jonah's warrant card and his wheelchair convinced the charge nurse who opened the door when he and Bernie rang the bell at the entrance to the ICU that he should be allowed in. He led the way to a small office where Dr Luisa Weber, a tall fair-haired woman who spoke with an almost imperceptible German accent, was giving Wayne's family an update on his condition.

'We'll give him an MRI scan this morning,' she said, as they entered. 'The CT scan that we did last night suggested that there's been a small bleed in the brain. We want to check on that and also to look for any signs of increased intracranial pressure.'

'What does that mean?' Dean asked anxiously.

'When the brain is subject to trauma, there is often an inflammatory response, which increases the pressure inside the skull and can cause damage to the brain. We've been administering drugs to reduce the pressure, but we need to check that they've been working. If the pressure is getting too high, we may have to reduce it by using surgery. Usually that just involves drilling a small hole through the skull to drain off some of the cerebrospinal fluid.'

'Is that dangerous?' Dean's eyes were wide open and scared.

'No – it's a routine procedure,' the doctor assured him. 'It's often used for monitoring the pressure as well as for treating it, so we may decide to do it even if the pressure isn't reaching dangerous levels yet. It's OK. It won't cause any permanent damage.'

'And when will you bring him out of this coma that you've put him in?' Graham asked. 'How long is he going to be like this?'

'That will depend how he progresses. I'll be able to tell you more after we've done the second scan, and when we get the lab results back from his bloods. There are biomarkers that we can look for that indicate the degree of inflammation that has occurred.'

'And afterwards – once he's awake again?' Graham's voice was unintentionally aggressive in his desire to learn more about the longer-term future for his son. 'How long before he's back on his feet again?'

'Again, it's too soon to say,' the doctor sighed, looking round apologetically, knowing how inadequate her answers were. 'He may make a complete recovery. But you do need to be prepared for it to take a long time, and … and it may be that he will be left with some permanent disability. We just don't know at this stage.'

'What sort of disability?' asked Jonah. 'Are we talking the sort of thing you get after a stroke?'

'Yes. That's right,' Dr Weber confirmed. 'Traumatic brain injury is essentially the same as a stroke – and if you have any experience of stroke, you'll know that the long-term effects are very variable. The sorts of things that we could be talking about are speech impairment, partial paralysis, difficulty with swallowing … a whole range of things, like I said.'

'And he might never get better?' Dean asked in a small voice.

'I'm really sorry,' the doctor looked round at them all again. 'At this stage, we really don't know.'

There was a knock at the door. The charge nurse put his head round it.

'There's another police officer here wanting to talk to the family,' he told them. 'Shall I bring her in here, or …?'

'If she doesn't need to speak to me, I could do with getting on,' Dr Weber replied. 'I've got other patients to see. And we'll need this room for the interdisciplinary team meeting soon. Can you find them somewhere to talk in the waiting area?

***

Jonah was pleased to see Anna waiting for them when they all trooped out after Nurse Mark Aston, who led the way to a seating area in the corridor outside the ICU.

'Are you the SIO[4]?' he asked. 'I was hoping they'd find someone reliable.' He turned to address the others. 'This is DI Anna Davenport,' he told them. 'She's one of our best. Anna – Wayne's parents, Barbara and Graham Major, and his husband, Dean O'Brien.'

Anna shook hands with all three and then indicated to them that they should all sit down.

'As DCI Porter says,' she began, 'I'm leading the investigation into this incident. Would you like me to tell you what we've managed to find out so far?'

'Yes,' Graham replied quickly, 'and what you intend to do to bring whoever did it to book.'

'We've found the car,' Anna told them patiently, hoping that the victim's father was not going to make trouble. 'It's being examined by our forensics team for evidence of who was driving it. According to the owner, it was driven away sometime yesterday evening. I've got officers checking out known offenders with a history of taking without consent. We're also looking at footage from traffic cameras along the route that we think the car followed after the collision with your son.'

'Is that all?' Graham sounded disappointed that there was no talk of an imminent arrest. 'What about putting out a call for witnesses? Someone must know who it was.'

'Please!' Dean appealed to him, 'Don't make a fuss.

---

[4] Senior Investigating Officer: the officer leading the investigation into a crime.

Catching them won't help Wayne.'

'I know it's frustrating,' Jonah intervened, 'but really this is all standard police procedure in a case like this. We can't work miracles, but don't worry, we'll get there in the end.'

'We've got several witnesses who saw the incident,' Anna added. 'I'm going to be interviewing them later today. As DCI Porter says, we'll be working as fast as we can, but these things take time.'

'And if we take shortcuts, we may not be able to make a charge stick,' Jonah continued. 'Just knowing who did it isn't enough. We need to collect sufficient evidence to get a conviction.'

Reluctantly, Graham accepted this argument and sat back in silence while Anna went through some questions with Dean about Wayne's movements the previous evening and checked the contact details of the friends that he had been with in the pub. After obtaining the Majors' address and mobile phone numbers, she got up to go.

'Thank you all for your help.' She shook hands all round again. 'And can I say again how sorry I am that this has happened and assure you that we will be doing everything we can to find out who was responsible.'

Jonah followed her out, without stopping to take his leave. Bernie said brief goodbyes to Dean and the Majors and then hurried after him. She caught up with them in time to hear him telling Anna that he intended to accompany her back to the police station.

Ignoring Bernie's protestations that this was not his case and anyway he was not on duty that day, Jonah insisted that he had some important additional information and must be allowed to share it with Anna's team.

***

'I'm convinced that you ought to be considering the possibility that this wasn't just a random incident,' Jonah told Anna a short while later, in the privacy of her office at the police headquarters. 'It could be a targeted attack.'

'What sort of attack? And why would you think that?'

'I'm wondering if it could be linked to this spate of homophobic attacks that we've seen since the Oxford Pride parade last month. All the victims have been people who were featured in the Oxford Mail item on *Gay-led Businesses* that it published as part of reporting on Oxford Pride this year. Have a look here.'

A slight movement of the fingers of his left hand made the computer screen attached to his wheelchair rotate allowing Anna to see a sequence of photographs and accompanying text. The first picture was a wide-angle shot showing a large group of people, several of them carrying rainbow banners, many in colourful clothes, one drag queen towering above the rest of the crowd on impossibly high heels.

'This is just a general view,' Jonah said, manipulating a small joystick to move a pointer across the screen. 'But even in this, some people are easy to spot.'

Bernie's eye was immediately drawn to two figures at the front of the picture, holding hands with their backs to the camera. Even if Wayne's muscular physique and Dean's wiry build had not been sufficiently familiar to enable her to identify them, the green jackets with their prominent white lettering would have made them instantly recognisable.

Anna, on the other hand, was struck by another couple.

'Isn't this Monica Philipson?' she asked in a puzzled tone, pointing at another face from the crowd in the picture on Jonah's computer screen, 'with her arm around Alice Ray?'

Jonah turned the screen around again to look more closely. 'Yes. That's right,' he confirmed.

'But -,' Anna began. 'I mean ... are you telling me they're ...?'

'Didn't you know?' Bernie asked. 'They've been

together for … six months, would it be?'

'About that,' Jonah agreed. 'I suppose it all happened while you were on maternity leave.'

'But Monica isn't … She can't be,' Anna protested weakly. 'A few years back she had a serious crush on *you*, Jonah.'

'But get on and show Anna the article,' Bernie urged to fill the uncomfortable silence that ensued. Jonah obligingly scrolled down to show more pictures and text.

'The newspaper thought it was running a story about the contribution that gay entrepreneurs make to the local economy and showing the range of activities that they are involved in,' he told Anna. 'They particularly homed in on businesses, like Wayne and Dean's, which have a positive social aspect to them.'

'Wayne Major and Dean O'Brien head up *Design Ability* a small design and engineering firm dedicated to promoting independence for disabled people,' Anna read out, studying the photograph of two young men standing next to a green van with white lettering on the side.

'The first incident was at this company,' Jonah said, scrolling down to show a picture of a row of three cars parked outside an ordinary-looking shop-front. 'It's just an ordinary private hire firm, whose owner just happens to be gay. They have a special scheme, working with a local charity, to provide transport at cost for people who can't afford things like visiting relatives in hospital or getting to the old folks club. After the article in the Mail, the shop was vandalised and then a few days later a note was pushed through the door telling them to get out or else. Based on the content of the note, the issue seems to be the fact that cabs from this firm are used to supply transport for the school run. All the drivers have had their criminal records checked and all the paperwork is in order, but it seems that some people still don't like the idea that their child could be in a car with a gay man.'

'So these people are equating *gay* with *paedophile*?' Anna asked.

'That certainly looks like one aspect of it,' Jonah agreed, 'but I'm not sure that it covers all the cases. This one, for instance, doesn't really seem to bear quite that same interpretation.'

The next picture was of a hairdressing salon, which Anna recognised as a well-known business in the centre of Oxford. She had been there herself once or twice, but found the prices too high for anything except very special occasions.

'Marcus Antonio – or to give him his real name, Mark Brown – has had this shop for thirty years. He claims he's never had any trouble until now. His customers are almost all women and he reckons they actually enjoy being attended to by a camp gay man. I rather get the impression that he revels in it and goes rather over the top to promote this image. His shop has been vandalised too. He reported it right away, but didn't link it to the Gay Pride article until later, when he received a death threat through the post.'

'At his shop?' asked Anna, 'or at home?'

'At the shop. It came the same day as the taxi firm reported getting their note. That's what made us think they might be linked.' Jonah scrolled down further. 'Finally, we have this social enterprise, which takes unemployed youngsters and trains them in bicycle maintenance. They get given old worn out bikes, and they fit them out and sell them on - mainly to students, who use them while they're at the university and then sell them back at the end of their course. Again, there's no particular reason to associate this with anxiety about paedophilia. As before, there's nothing very remarkable about the organisation or its manager, except that he just happens to be gay and to have featured in the article in the Mail. Again, his business premises were vandalised, but this time, they went further and attacked him personally.'

'How?'

'Just verbal abuse and threatening behaviour,' Jonah

admitted, a little regretfully Anna thought. 'A man approached him as he was leaving work and shouted out a load of expletives. He got on his bike and headed for home and he thinks he lost him, but he's worried in case he followed him and now knows where he lives.'

'Did he recognise the guy?' Anna asked.

'No. He said he'd never seen him before. We tried to get a description from him, but he was too shaken up by the incident to remember anything much.'

'Do you think it really was a targeted attack?' Anna asked. 'Couldn't it have just been chance encounter with a drunk looking for a fight?'

'Perhaps,' Jonah conceded, 'but the incidents do seem to be escalating, and isn't it too much of a coincidence that it happened at the same time that the other businesses were targeted.'

'And is *Design Ability* the *only* business featured in the article that *hasn't* been attacked?' Anna asked.

'No. There's also a wedding planning service run by a lesbian couple and a lingerie shop belonging to a trans woman. They haven't reported any incidents. I've got it on my *to do* list to check that it isn't just that they don't trust the police enough to tell us about it.'

'Very much aimed at gay men then,' Anna murmured. 'I wonder if that tells us anything.'

'That's the one thing that doesn't seem particularly strange about the incidents,' Jonah answered. 'There are always far more attacks on gay men than gay women. But everything else about them seems all wrong. They're not at all like normal homophobic attacks – if it's acceptable to talk of any attacks as "normal" – which are usually drink-induced and done on impulse. This looks more organised and pre-meditated, as if someone has a grudge.'

'And you think Wayne's "accident" could actually be a further ratcheting up of the attacks?' Bernie asked.

'That's right.'

'But, as Gavin so astutely remarked,' Bernie objected,

'it seems incredible that the driver of a speeding car could recognise Wayne from behind in the dark.'

'*You* recognised him in that picture,' Jonah countered. 'They didn't recognise *Wayne*; they just recognised the lettering on his jacket.'

'Well, I suppose it makes sense for you to include this as potentially part of the pattern of attacks, but I'd better get on with investigating it as a hit-and-run,' Anna said decisively. 'Here's my list of witnesses who were there and saw the car.'

Jonah and Bernie scanned down the list that she held out to them.

'Leroy Gilbert?' Bernie asked. 'Living in a flat in the Windrush tower?'

'That's right. How did you know?' asked Anna.

'He's a friend of ours – well, sort of. His family were Peter's neighbours when he lived down Cowley Road.'

'He was in the bus shelter when it happened,' Anna told them. 'The other witnesses were all on the other side of the road – outside the pub. I'm going to interview them all later today. I've also got a list of kids from the Blackbird Leys estate with histories of joy-riding. So there's plenty to keep me busy,' she concluded, with a wry smile.

CHAPTER 3: SATURDAY AFTERNOON

It took some doing, but Barbara eventually managed to persuade Dean to leave the ward and come with them to eat lunch in the hospital canteen. Dean looked round in a daze at the choice of meals on offer, unable to think of anything while his mind was filled with the picture of Wayne lying lifelessly in the hospital bed attached to so many tubes and wires. He allowed his mother-in-law to select a baked potato with cheese and salad, which was a combination that she knew he liked. She hesitated over a dessert, aware that he was health-conscious, but thinking that he needed something substantial to keep his energy levels up. In the end, she plumped for a banana, which was undeniably a fruit but was also calculated to provide additional calories. She picked the same options for herself, while Graham took advantage of his wife's preoccupation with their son-in-law to choose steak-and-kidney-pie and chips, followed by chocolate pudding, a combination which she would normally have frowned upon.

They carried their trays of food over to a table in a secluded corner of the room and sat down to begin their meal. Dean was surprised to discover that he was hungry and soon demolished the potato. He was in the process of unzipping his banana when he heard someone speaking to him from behind. He looked round to see a middle-aged woman wearing a green shirt with a clerical collar inserted at the neck. It was Sally Pearson, the minister from his church.

'I was so sorry to hear about Wayne. How's he doing? Is there any news?'

Dean looked at her, struggling to think of anything to say. Sally, detecting his discomfiture, filled the awkward silence by continuing.

'I don't want to intrude. I just thought I'd let you know that I'm here for you. If there's anything I can do, you will let me know won't you?'

'Yes,' Dean nodded. Then, with an effort, he collected his thoughts and looked round at Graham and Barbara. 'This is Sally,' he told them. 'She's the minister at my church. Sally – this is Wayne's mum and dad, Barbara and Graham.'

Sally shook hands and they exchanged inconsequential pleasantries. Then she drew up a chair and sat down next to Dean. She spoke earnestly to him.

'I know that you don't want to leave him,' she said, having been briefed on this point by Bernie, 'but it's important that you look after yourself too – for Wayne's sake. If you need to take time out, there are plenty of people who would be happy to sit with him for you.'

'Thanks, but I'd rather be there myself.'

'I know, but if this goes on for some time,' Sally persisted carefully, 'there will be other things you have to do – other responsibilities that you have. Keeping the business going, for example, ready for when he's ready to come back to it.'

'I can take care of that,' Graham intervened. 'I know the business inside out.'

'That's good,' Sally agreed, smiling with relief. At least

she could allay Bernie's anxieties on that count. However, a moment later she realised that she had relaxed too soon. Dean cried out in dismay as he remembered the plans that he and Wayne had had for that afternoon.

'I've just thought! What about Carl and Harry? We were supposed to be taking them out this afternoon.'

Sally looked round enquiringly. Barbara's mouth fell open, her look of distress mirroring Dean's despairing expression.

'I'll go over there and explain everything,' Graham said, after a short pause. He was secretly pleased to have something concrete to do to help the situation. This passive watching and waiting did not suit his energetic personality at all. He got to his feet. 'I can be there by two-thirty if I go now.'

'You will be careful, won't you?' Dean pleaded anxiously. 'You won't frighten them? Don't tell them about Wayne being run over.'

'No, of course not. I'll just tell them that he isn't well, so you can't come after all.'

'We'll have to let the Home know the full story,' Barbara added. 'Then the Care Workers can prepare them for … well, for whatever happens. It looks as if it may be a while before Wayne's ready to see them again.'

'You don't think they'll say we aren't suitable anymore?' Dean asked apprehensively, his voice rising in alarm. 'After we've got so far?'

'No, no, of course not,' Graham said, a bit too quickly and heartily to be convincing. 'It'll just all take a bit longer, that's all.'

'Carl and Harry are two boys that Wayne and Dean are hoping to adopt,' Barbara explained to Sally, seeing her bewildered expression. 'They're brothers, who have been classed as "difficult to place" by Social Services, because of their behaviour, but they seem to have really hit it off with Wayne and Dean.'

'We've got the house all ready for them,' Dean added.

'They're coming to stay ... or – or they *were* coming to stay once they break up for the summer. Do you think ...? I mean, what if ...?'

'Just try to take one thing at a time,' Sally urged gently. 'I'm sure nobody will take any decisions about the adoption until we know how things are going to turn out with Wayne. Have the doctors said how long it's likely to be before they know that?'

'The registrar said that she'd give us an update after lunch,' Barbara told her. She looked round at their empty plates. 'Shall we all go up to the ICU and see if she's ready for us?'

***

Anna took DC Alice Ray with her to interview the teenagers from the Blackbird Leys estate who had been identified as having a history of "twocking"[5] and consequently might have been the driver of the car when it hit Wayne.

Sitting alongside Alice, who was in the driving seat, Anna could not help giving sidelong glances at her, looking for any external signs that should have alerted her to her colleague's sexuality. Didn't lesbians usually have their hair cut very short? Alice's was tied back in a neat pony-tail. What about makeup? Alice's was very discreet, verging on invisible, but then so was Anna's own, since they were both dressed for their job.

She forced herself to concentrate on her work. She looked down at the list of names and addresses that one of the civilian staff had compiled for her. Some of them were dismally familiar.

'Let's start with Jason and Ryan Paul,' she said, naming two persistent offenders. 'Jason has taken cars before and

---

[5] Taking a conveyance without consent (abbreviated to TWOC) is an offence under the Theft Act 1968.

Ryan seems to be following in his big brother's footsteps with anti-social behaviour and petty theft.'

'Is that the same family as Dave Paul?' Alice asked. 'The guy we got sent down a couple of years ago for GBH?'[6]

'That's right, and it looks as if young Jason may be on the way to following in his father's footsteps. He's been cautioned for threatening behaviour and carrying a knife in public.' Anna sighed. 'This is another of those families that seem doomed to carry on making the same stupid mistakes from generation to generation.'

They pulled up outside the small modern terraced house where the Paul family lived. There was an overflowing rubbish bin in the front garden and a dilapidated blue Vauxhall Astra, with a flat tyre on its nearside front wheel, filling the short drive. They squeezed past it to reach the front door. There was no bell or knocker so Alice rapped hard on it with her fist.

They waited. Getting no reply, Alice banged again while Anna took a few paces back and looked up at the windows for signs of life. They were about to give up and move on to the next entry on their list, when the door opened and a woman looked out. She was dressed in a pale blue onesie. Her hair, which was blond, with a darker shade showing at the roots, was tousled as if she had just got out of bed. Her eyes were anxious and hostile.

'Mrs Paul?' Alice asked in a friendly manner. 'I'm Detective Constable Alice Ray, and this is DI Davenport. We need to have a word with your sons Jason and Ryan. Are they at home?'

'Why? What's wrong?' Lyn Paul looked at them nervously, fumbling in her pocket for a packet of cigarettes and a lighter.

'There was an incident last night,' Anna told her, 'and

---

[6] Grievous Bodily Harm. Inflicting grievous bodily harm is an offence under the *Offences Against the Person Act* of 1861.

we just want to ask them if they saw anything or know anything about it.'

'What sort of incident?' mumbled Lyn, bending down slightly and cupping her hand around the cigarette that she was intent on lighting.

'A car was stolen and driven at speed around the estate,' Alice answered. 'A pedestrian was injured. We're talking to anyone who may have seen something.'

'Jason's not here.' Lyn's eyes widened and she looked scared. Anna wondered how much she knew about what had gone on the night before.

'And Ryan?' Alice asked.

'He's in his room – but he won't be able to tell you anything. He wasn't out last night. He-'

'We'd still like to speak to him,' Anna cut in, speaking calmly but firmly. 'May we come in?'

Mrs Paul grudgingly stepped aside to allow them through the door.

'Go on up,' she said, waving her arm in the direction of the stairs. 'It's on the right.'

They climbed the stairs and then stood looking round the small landing. The door immediately to their right was slightly open. Anna knocked on it and waited for a reply. There being no response from inside, she knocked again, hard enough this time to make the door swing open to reveal an untidy bedroom, which Anna had to admit reminded her very much of the one that her own teenage son occupied. There was a wardrobe, with one door swinging open and a jumble of clothes hanging out. More clothes lay strewn higgledy-piggledy across the floor, sharing the space with magazines, some of which looked to be pornographic, and several empty coke cans and pot noodle containers. The walls were covered with lurid posters, which Anna would certainly not have liked to have around her when she was trying to sleep.

Ryan Paul was sitting on the bed with his head bent over a mobile phone ignoring the intruders.

'Ryan?' Anna opened the conversation in a casual voice aimed at reassuring the suspect. 'I wonder if we could have a word? I'm Inspector Davenport and this is Constable Ray. We're hoping that you might be able to help us.'

Ryan continued to tap away on his phone without any sign that he had heard her speak or was aware that they had entered – just like Marcus when he knew that he had done something to provoke his mother. Anna stepped further into the room and spoke a little louder.

'Ryan! Put that phone down for a minute. We need to talk to you.'

The boy continued to ignore her, but the rhythm of his fingers on the phone faltered almost imperceptibly. He knew they were there and did not want to answer their questions.

'There was an accident last night,' Anna told him, coming up close and looking down on his bent head and still active hands. 'Outside the *Blackbird*. Did you hear about it?'

There was no reply. Ryan bent his head a little lower as if trying to hide his face or else to shield the phone from Anna's prying eyes. With a swift movement, Anna reached out her arm and took it from his hands. She put it down on a shelf inside the open wardrobe, out of Ryan's reach. He leapt up and stretched out his hand to retrieve it, but Alice stepped forward and stood in front of the cupboard, facing the bed.

'What d'you do that for?' Ryan demanded, finally acknowledging their presence. 'Give it me back!'

'You can have your phone back just as soon as you answer a few questions,' Anna told him. 'So first: what do you know about the accident last night.'

'Nothing,' Ryan answered sulkily, and then, defiantly, 'Why should I know anything about it?'

'We thought you might've heard people talking.'

Ryan shrugged and shook his head. Anna decided to try another approach.

'Where were you last night?' she asked.

'Here.'

'All evening?' Alice enquired sceptically. 'It was Friday night. Didn't you go out with your mates?'

'No. I was here.'

'What about Jason?' Anna could see that Ryan was not going to budge from his story. 'Was he here too?'

'Yeah,' Ryan answered promptly. Then he hesitated, looking round at Anna and Alice as if trying to work out how much they already knew about his brother's movements. 'Well,' he added at last, 'he was here when I got back from school. I dunno about later.' Then, defiantly, 'I was in here, wasn't I? Not snooping on Jason. What d'you think I am? His probation officer?'

'OK, Ryan. We'll leave it at that – for the moment,' Anna said, confident that they were not going to learn any more by continuing their questioning. 'Just bear in mind that it won't do you any good, if it turns out you did know something about who it was who took a car and nearly killed someone with it and you didn't tell us. Do you understand?'

'Can I have my phone back now?'

'Here you are.' Alice picked up the phone and handed it to him. 'And don't forget: we're watching you.'

Lyn Paul was sitting in front of a large television screen with another cigarette when they went back downstairs. Like her son, she did not look round as they entered her small front room.

'Can you tell us where each of your sons was last night between ten and midnight?' Anna asked her.

Lyn turned slowly in her chair and looked round at the two police officers.

'Last night?' she queried vaguely. 'I wouldn't know. They're not kids anymore; they don't tell me where they're going.'

'But they were both out last night?' Alice asked quickly.

'I can't remember. Like I said ...'

'What time do you eat at night?' Anna asked.

'Eat?' Lyn looked puzzled. Anna realised that family mealtimes were a foreign concept in this household.

'Yes,' she replied. 'You must all eat. Did Jason and Ryan eat at home last night, or did they go out?'

'Ryan stayed in his room,' Lyn shrugged, picking up the TV remote and starting to flick through the channels. 'I think Jason went down the *Bullnose*[7] with his mates.'

'He's still under-age, isn't he?' Alice asked sharply. 'Does he often spend time in the pub?'

'Like I said, they don't tell me where they're going.'

'You're their mother,' Alice persisted. 'You're responsible for them.'

To their surprise, at this, Lyn roused herself and stood up to face the two police officers. 'Don't come here telling me how to raise my own kids! And anyway,' she added, the fire going out of her eyes as quickly as it had come and her face taking on a rather hopeless expression, 'What d'you expect me to do? The last time I tried to tell Jason what to do, he gave me this!'

She pushed her hair back from the side of her face to reveal a large bruise.

'That's assault,' Alice gasped, taken aback at this unexpected development. 'We could charge him.'

'Like you charged his dad? No thanks.'

'You ought to let us do something,' Alice insisted. 'You're not safe, living here with someone who-'

'Just forget it!' Lyn interrupted in a hopeless voice. 'There's nothing you can do that won't make things worse.' She slumped back on to the couch and resumed flicking through the television channels.

'Come on,' Anna said to Alice in a low voice. 'There's

[7] The Bullnose Morris is a pub situated on Watlington Road at the edge of the Blackbird Leys estate. It is named after the classic car, which was manufactured at the Morris motor works in Cowley, Oxford in the first quarter of the 20th century.

nothing more we can do here. Let's go.'

She put down a business card on the sofa next to Lyn.

'OK Mrs Paul. We're going now. If you think of anything that might help us to find out who was responsible for the hit-and-run last night – or if you change your mind about needing help with Jason – just ring this number.'

***

'We've reviewed the MRI scan and the blood results,' Dr Weber told Dean and Barbara, when they returned to the ICU. 'The consultant is satisfied that the bleeding has stopped and the swelling is improving. So we're discontinuing the medication that was keeping him in a coma. It should be just a matter of time before he comes round.'

'And after that?' Dean asked nervously.

'We'll just have to take things as they come. As I said before, we won't really know the extent of any brain damage until he's been conscious for a while. And don't worry if he seems disorientated at first. That's only natural. You can help to bring him round by talking to him. Just speak normally and don't worry if he doesn't respond. Like I said, it all takes time.'

***

'According to these notes, Ethan Roberts is a mate of Jason Paul's.' Anna said, as they got out of the car at the next stop on their quest. 'They were at school together – when either of them was in school at all, that is. Now they're both unemployed. It was Ethan's eighteenth birthday yesterday. You'd think they'd have been out celebrating wouldn't you?'

In contrast to the Paul family's home, this house appeared well kept and clean. The doorbell was answered by a small woman with tidy black hair and alert brown eyes, who looked to be in her sixties. Her face took on a resigned expression when she saw their warrant cards.

'You'd better come in,' she said, stepping back and leading the way into a small sitting room. 'I suppose you want to speak to Ethan about last night.'

'What about last night?' Anna asked.

'The ruckus at the *Bullnose*. John from next door told me he and his mates were chucked out for causing a disturbance.'

'Really? That wasn't why we came, but I'm very interested to hear it. We're investigating an incident that took place round about closing time outside the *Blackbird*. You don't happen to know where Ethan and his mates went on to after the *Bullnose Morris*?'

'No. All I know is that he wasn't back until after midnight.' Patsy Roberts shook her head. 'I'm sorry. I do my best with him, but it's not easy. I'm getting too old for all this.'

'You're Ethan's grandmother – is that right, Mrs Roberts?' Anna asked, looking down at her notes. 'How long has he been living with you?'

'Since he was ten. Well, since he was eight, I suppose, but his dad was living here too, until he was ten. It was his dad going off and leaving him that …,' she sighed. 'Well, it's no wonder he's not right, when he knows his mum and dad both don't want to be bothered with him, is it? Shall I get him for you? He's out the back, messing with some old motorbike he's got hold of.'

'Why don't we go out and see him there?' Anna suggested, thinking that it might be a good idea to have a discreet look at the motorbike in case it turned out to have been stolen.

Patsy Roberts led the way through the kitchen into the back garden. Sure enough, the small paved area behind the house was almost filled with a large, powerful-looking motorcycle. Bending over it was a tall, lanky teenager with greasy black hair flopping over his eyes. His blue-and-white tee-shirt was smeared with oil, which also covered his hands and arms, almost obscuring the tattoos with which his entire body appeared to be covered. The ground around him was strewn with various metallic components, which Anna took to be parts that Ethan Roberts had already removed preparatory to re-building the bike.

'Hi!' Anna greeted him, in what she hoped would be taken as a friendly tone. 'That's an impressive machine! Where did you get it?'

Ethan looked up, eyeing them both suspiciously.

'Bought it on Ebay, didn't I?' he mumbled. Then louder and rather defensively, 'It's legit, OK? I'm gonna do it up and sell it.'

'I see.' Anna wandered round the bike, making a mental note of the registration number as she did so.

'Your gran's just been telling us that you were out with your mates last night,' she went on. 'We were wondering if you know anything about the accident outside the *Blackbird*. Were you over that way at all?'

'No,' Ethan grunted, bending over the motorbike again and making a show of being intent on unscrewing one of the bolts that held the engine in place. 'We were over in the *Bullnose*.'

'Until you got chucked out,' Alice put in. 'Why was that?'

'Some fucking fascists started dissing one of my mates. I told them where to go and, next thing I know, the fucking landlord says we've got to get out.'

'Fascists?' Anna enquired. 'What makes you call them that?'

'The things they said.'

'Such as?'

Ethan shrugged and resumed the business of removing the engine from the bike.

'Never mind. Where did you go after that?'

'Can't remember.'

'You didn't, by any chance wander along Watlington Road and pinch a car from Hoo Down Farmhouse?' Alice suggested.

'No!'

'OK,' Anna took over again. 'We'll leave that for the time being. Tell me about your mates. Who were you with?'

'Just mates. We weren't doing nothing.'

'Maybe not, but you were out in the estate last night. I'd like to talk to them, in case they saw anything that might help us find out who was driving a car that hit a pedestrian and may have killed him. What about you? Did you see a silver BMW driving at speed at around half ten, quarter to eleven? It probably came past the *Bullnose*. What time was it you got chucked out?'

'Dunno,' Ethan shrugged.

'Never mind, we can ask the landlord. Now what about the car? Did you see it?'

'I may have done. I don't remember.'

'Then, can you tell us the names of the mates that were with you?' Alice chipped in. 'So we can ask them if they saw anything.'

'Come on Ethan,' Anna urged, when he did not reply. 'Just give us their names and then we'll go and leave you to finish mending your bike.'

'It was Jason Paul and Callum Lee.' Ethan said grudgingly.

'Thank you.' Anna perched one of her business cards on top of the motorbike, before turning to go. 'If you do remember seeing anything, get in touch.'

'Callum Lee is another of the names on our list,' Alice said as they walked back to the car.' According to this, he lives just over the road.'

'Let's pay him a visit then,' Anna replied. 'I'm starting to suspect that Ethan, Jason and Callum could well be our joy-riders – all tanked-up and looking for trouble after being chucked out of the *Bullnose* for kicking up a shindy.'

Callum Lee turned out to be an inoffensive-looking young man, with a spotty face and a stammer. Unlike at their previous ports-of-call, his mother insisted on being present while they interviewed him. She appeared to have a strong personality and to be fiercely protective of her son. Anna decided to avoid making any suggestion that Callum was under suspicion. Her opening gambit set the tone for the interview.

'I gather you and your friends experienced some harassment in the *Bullnose Morris* last night. Is that right?'

Callum did not answer, looking to his mother for reassurance.

'Go on, Cal,' she urged. 'Tell the officer about it. I said you ought to report it to the police, didn't I?'

'Y-y-yes,' Callum confirmed. 'Th-that's right.'

'You were subjected to verbal abuse – is that right?'

Callum nodded. 'Y-y-yeah. They c-called me a-a-a f-f-f-f-,' he stuttered.

'A faggot,' his mother finished for him. 'They're always doing it. They're always picking on him.'

'So these were people you know?' Anna seized on this information eagerly. Alice, who had been about to jump in with a declaration that this constituted anti-gay hate speech and carried serious penalties, closed her mouth again. 'Do you know their names?'

'It was Gordon Redfern and his mates, wasn't it Cal?'

Callum nodded. 'Y-yes. G-Gordon and Rob Fry and some other guy. I th-think they called him Ian.'

'You don't happen to know where any of them live?'

'Gordon's house is just across the way,' Mrs Lee answered. 'Number sixteen.'

'Thank you.' Anna noted in her mind that this was next-door to the house where Ethan Roberts lived with his grandmother. Perhaps he and this Gordon had some history between them. 'Now, after this unpleasant incident, you and your friends left the pub. Do you remember what time that was?'

'What does that matter?' Callum's mother asked quickly.

'It's just part of our routine,' Anna assured her. 'We need to have all the details in case there's any dispute later. Callum?'

'Dunno. Half ten, maybe.'

'Thank you. And what did you do after that?'

Callum shrugged his shoulders.

'Could you have still been near the *Bullnose Morris* at ten forty-five?'

Callum shrugged again.

'We think that a car may have turned off Watlington Road into Cuddesdon Way at about that time, travelling very fast. Did you see it?'

'N-no.' Callum shook his head.

'Alright.' Anna closed her notebook and put it away. 'We'll leave it there.'

'If you get any more of that abuse, be sure and tell the police right away,' Alice added. 'You have a right to be protected from that sort of thing.'

CHAPTER 4: SATURDAY EVENING

Saturday high tea was always something of an event in Bernie's house. On this occasion, it was very much a Johns family affair, with Peter's son Eddie, Eddie's wife, Crystal, and their two children all present. Eddie had brought two-year-old Ricky and his little sister Abigail to spend the afternoon playing in their grandfather's large garden, while their mother was on duty as a nurse at the hospital. Now her shift was over and they were all sitting expectantly around the large table in the kitchen, watching Peter slicing a new loaf and Bernie pouring boiling water into a large teapot.

'How is your friend doing?' Crystal asked. 'The boy who was knocked down, I mean. Have you heard any more about his condition?'

'Sally rang,' Bernie answered. 'She said he's being brought out of the coma, but he was still unconscious when she left.'

'Do you think they'll find the driver of the car?' Crystal asked. 'It makes me frightened to think there are people out there who can do that sort of thing. It seems so random – as if it could happen to any of us. Was it kids joy-riding do you think?'

'It's looking like that,' Peter answered. 'The Blackbird Leys estate has a bit of a history of it, although, I must admit, I thought we were getting on top of the problem.'

'Anna's been talking to some of the usual suspects,' Jonah put in. He had telephoned his colleague for an update a short time earlier. 'But so far she hasn't got anything to suggest they were responsible. I'm not convinced it was just random. It could be a targeted attack.'

'You've got no evidence for that, you know,' Bernie cut in quickly, hoping to head him away from any mention of a connection with the series of homophobic attacks. She was unsure whether Eddie and Crystal were aware of Wayne's sexuality. Jonah, however, was in no mood to take the hint.

'Nothing definite,' he admitted, 'but it does seem a bit of a coincidence, doesn't it?'

'What does?' Eddie asked, puzzled.

'I'm investigating a series of escalating attacks on people who appeared in newspaper pictures of the Oxford Pride parade, and now Wayne is mown down in the street and left for dead.'

'Don't take any notice of him,' Bernie urged. 'He's just looking for an excuse to take over the investigation. He can never accept that someone else might be just as capable as him of solving a case.'

'I can't see how it *can* have been deliberate,' Peter chimed in. 'It was dark and the car was travelling at speed. There's no way the driver could've recognised Wayne.'

'They could've been stalking him,' Jonah insisted. 'I've been worried for some time that he and Dean might become victims. Most of the other people in that Oxford Mail article have done.'

'What article?' Crystal asked innocently.

'The Oxford Mail put a big picture of this year's Gay Pride parade on its website, and an article highlighting several local businesses that are owned by or run by members of the gay community,' Jonah explained. 'It was supposed to be showing how they make a positive contribution to life in the city. The day after it appeared, some of the business premises were vandalised and then, later, the people who were featured started suffering various forms of homophobic abuse. It was little things at first, which they didn't bother to report. They described it as *only the sort of thing that happens all the time*. Then it escalated. I got called in after there had been death threats sent to people's places of work and excrement pushed through their doors.'

'Are you saying that Dean and his friend are ...?' Crystal asked, wide-eyed. In her native Jamaica, homosexuality was still illegal and not something that people talked about.

'They've been married for nearly six years,' Lucy told her.

'But Dean goes to our church,' Crystal protested weakly, looking round at her husband for reassurance.

'Things are a bit different over here,' Eddie began, but Lucy interrupted him.

'What's that got to do with anything?' she asked scornfully. 'Loads of people from church were at the parade. Sally was there and lots of others. We were trying to show-'

'Wasn't that all about taking a stand against hate crime?' Eddie cut in. 'I mean Sally's got a husband and kids. She wasn't promoting their lifestyle, just saying that they have a right not to be molested.'

'Yes, Crystal agreed,' looking across at Eddie gratefully. 'I can see why we ought to stand up for – for ... or rather take a stand *against* people who do the sorts of things Jonah was talking about to ... ,' she hesitated over the unfamiliar words, 'gay people. Nobody ought to feel that they're not safe living here. But I don't see how people can call themselves Christians if they're not sticking to what the Bible says.'

'But what *does* the Bible say about same-sex marriage?' asked Jonah combatively. 'Nothing as far as I can see. It wasn't something that anyone had ever thought of in those days.'

'Well, there's Sodom and Gomorrah for a start,' Eddie answered defensively, feeling that his wife was under attack. 'That's where the word comes from, after all.'

'If you actually read the story, you'll see that the act that gave rise to the word *sodomy* was one of homosexual rape,' Jonah argued. 'It has no bearing on same-sex relationships of the sort that people have today.'

'And Lot offered them his virgin daughters in place of the men they wanted to rape,' Lucy added forcefully, 'which sort of suggests that they weren't gay at all.'

'I'm sure my father told me the Bible forbids homosexuality,' Crystal insisted quietly.

'Well there is a verse in Leviticus that forbids men from *lying with other men as man lies with a woman*,' Jonah conceded, 'but it's sandwiched between rules about not eating blood and not weaving different fibres together. Anyone who's eaten black pudding or worn a polyester-cotton shirt has broken just as many Levitical commands as Wayne and Dean have.'

'The prophet Ezekiel says that the reason that God destroyed Sodom was that they were wealthy but didn't help the poor,' Bernie added.

'But ...,' Crystal looked round, puzzled and disturbed. This was the first time that she had found herself at odds with her husband's family. 'But, it's not natural.'

'It would be unnatural for me or Peter or Eddie,' Jonah argued, 'but it's not unnatural for someone who's born gay. What *would* be unnatural for Wayne or Dean would be pretending to be attracted to a woman in order to fit in with society's expectations.'

'It's not a life-style choice, you know,' Lucy chipped in. 'It's the way they're made. And what's wrong with that?'

'I – I don't know,' Crystal did not know how to

respond to this onslaught. 'I suppose, if it really is something they were born with ... but how can we be sure?'

'Science does seem to back the idea,' Peter said gently, concerned about Crystal's evident discomfiture but determined to hold the line in support of their young friends. 'All the stuff that I was told when I was growing up – stuff like it being a phase that a lot of boys go through or that it was some sort of mental illness – has been debunked now.'

'But even so,' Crystal looked round at them all again before screwing up the courage to go on. 'Even so, isn't it still wrong to ... I mean, just because you have certain feelings and desires, you don't have to act on them, do you? Isn't saying that homosexuals should stay celibate just the same as telling teenagers to wait until after they're married?'

'Except that you're telling them they've got to wait forever,' Lucy retorted. 'How's that fair?'

'Some heterosexual people have to wait forever too,' Eddie came to his wife's defence, 'if nobody happens to fancy them.'

'It's not the same,' Lucy insisted.

'And Wayne and Dean *are* married,' Jonah added. 'Or at least in a civil partnership, which was all that was available to them at the time. And it's none of our business what they may or may not do in the privacy of their own bedroom.'

'Nobody's saying you don't have a right to your point of view,' Peter hastened to add, very aware of how beleaguered Crystal must be feeling. 'It's just that we've known Wayne and Dean a long time and it's just impossible not to think that they belong together.'

'Try to imagine what it would be like for you if it was Eddie lying in the ICU,' Bernie suggested. 'That's how it is for Dean now.'

'Bernie's right,' Peter agreed. 'That's the only thing that

matters at the moment.'

'Yes, of course,' Crystal said earnestly. 'You didn't think I would say anything to him about … you know, do you? I was just … surprised, that's all.'

'And there's something else you need to know about Dean,' Bernie added. 'While he was a student, some over-zealous members of the CU[8] got to him and convinced him that he was beyond redemption because of his sexuality and he did his best to kill himself.'

'He's still got the scars on his arms where he slit his wrists,' Lucy chimed in. 'If Mam hadn't got there in time, he might have bled to death.'

'And if he hadn't had Wayne there to look after him afterwards,' Jonah added pointedly.

'I'm so sorry. I didn't know,' Crystal sounded shocked.

'Of course you didn't,' Peter tried to pour oil on the increasingly troubled waters. 'And we're not suggesting that you would ever say anything as insensitive as those students did. But you can see now – can't you? – why we can't agree with the traditional line on same-sex relations and we don't want Dean exposed to that sort of talk.'

***

Back in the ICU, Dean was still waiting anxiously for Wayne to wake up.

'Did you see his eyelids flicker just then?' he asked suddenly, looking round at Barbara and Graham.

'I'm not sure,' Barbara said cautiously. She had not noticed any movement, but did not want to quash Dean's hopes. She bent down closer and studied her son's face. Perhaps Dean was right. There did seem to be a slight

---

[8] Christian Union. Each college at Oxford University has its own society for Christian students to meet together. Most of these are affiliated to a university-wide organisation called the Oxford Intercollegiate Christian Union (OICCU).

movement in the muscles around his eyes. His lips also seemed to be moving slightly, almost as if he were trying to form words.

'Wayne!' Dean called softly. 'Wake up! We're all here – me and your mum and dad.'

The movement was unmistakeable now. Wayne's lids lifted to reveal the grey eyes beneath. They moved towards the sound of Dean's voice and he seemed, briefly, to be attempting to focus on his eager face. Then they glazed over and appeared to be staring unseeing into the distance.

Dean turned to this mother-in-law.

'Did you see that?'

'Yes. I think maybe he is waking up. What do you think, Gray?' Barbara Major said, turning to her husband.

Graham, however was already off in search of a member of the nursing staff. Soon he was back with Megan Gould, who had returned to the unit for the night shift. She quickly ran through a sequence of tests to assess his responsiveness to stimuli before looking round at them all and nodding.

'Yes, I think he probably is starting to come round,' she said. 'Just carry on talking to him so he knows you're there. Try to be upbeat, if you can.'

Dean nodded eagerly, taking Wayne's hand in his and bending closer to speak into his ear.

'When he does wake,' Megan added, looking seriously at Barbara and Graham, 'he'll probably be quite confused; so don't worry if he doesn't recognise you at first or says some strange things.'

***

While Wayne's family were anxiously waiting for him to wake, Jessica Davenport was struggling with the opposite problem. Her baby sister, Donna, was refusing to settle after her evening feed. In vain, Jessica tried all the tricks that she had seen her mother employing: rocking, singing, carrying the infant around in her arms. Nothing had any effect.

'Why don't you take her out in the pram?' Marcus suggested, partly through genuine concern and partly with a view to giving himself some respite from the distracting noise. 'That usually sends her off.'

'OK. Can you hold her for a minute while I get it ready?'

'No thanks!' Marcus backed away. 'I'll get the pram. You keep hold of her.'

He went down to the hall and retrieved the folding buggy from under the stairs. He had just finished putting it up and arranging the blankets inside when the telephone rang. It was his mother, checking that all was well.

'Don't you worry,' he told her, hoping that she could not hear Donna's continued crying in the bedroom above. 'We're doing fine. The chips were ace and Jess made one of her sticky toffee puddings. There's some left for you when you get in.'

'Good. I'll leave you to it then,' Anna replied, ending the call and putting her phone back in her pocket. She was alone in her car outside an ordinary-looking house in a suburban street. Alice's shift had finished and she had presumably returned home to whatever accommodation she and Monica shared. It had been a day off for Monica. Would she have prepared a meal for Alice on her return, as Anna's husband Philip, used to do when they lived together?

She looked down at her notebook to refresh her memory. She was here to interview two witnesses to the incident the previous night. Simon and June Broadhurst were friends of the victim, who had been with him in the pub only a few minutes before he was run down. June had been the person who called the ambulance. But what exactly had they seen?

'I'm sorry,' June said a few minutes later, as they sat together in their small front room. 'I really didn't see anything. I was looking for my keys in my handbag and the next thing I knew there was this engine roaring and this screeching of tyres and everyone was shouting. Simon called to me to ring 999, which I did, and that was about it.'

'So you didn't see the car at all?'

'Not really. Simon and Gary were ahead of me – between me and the road.'

'What about you?' Anna turned to Simon. 'Did you get a clear view of the car?'

'I saw it OK, but it had its headlights on full, so I couldn't see much until afterwards when it headed off up the road.'

'You couldn't see what the driver looked like?'

'No,' Simon shook his head. 'I couldn't see inside at all. I can't even tell you how many people there were in it.'

'OK.' Anna looked down at her notes and bit her lip pensively, wondering whether to ask her final question. 'You saw the car mount the pavement – is that right?'

'Yes,' Simon answered confidently.

'Was that just because it was coming too fast round the bend – or could it have been deliberate?'

'How d'you mean?'

'Is it at all possible, in your opinion, that the driver could have been deliberately trying to hit the pedestrian?'

'Like them terrorists in London you mean?' Simon's jaw dropped open at this suggestion.

'Something like that, but maybe aimed at your friend Wayne specifically.'

'Murder you mean?' June gasped.

'Something like that,' Anna repeated.

'I don't see how it could,' Simon said decidedly. 'It was dark and the car must have been going at over seventy. There's no way they could've seen who it was they hit.'

'That's what we thought,' Anna nodded. 'We just had to be sure.'

***

'Look! I think he really is coming round now.'

Wayne's head moved towards the sound of Dean's voice and his eyes seemed to be looking round, as if searching for something. Dean bent across the bed and kissed him tenderly on the lips.

'Don't worry,' he told him. 'We're all here – me and your mum and dad. You've had an accident, but you're in hospital now and everything's going to be alright.'

Wayne's lips moved and he grunted something inaudible.

'Don't try to talk,' Barbara said gently from the other side of the bed. 'You need to rest.'

Wayne shook his head slowly and made another attempt to speak, but the sounds that came out of his mouth were incomprehensible. His face took on a look of alarm as he realised that he was unable to make himself understood. Seeing this same expression mirrored in Dean's face, Barbara looked towards her husband and spoke with authority.

'Go and fetch the nurse, Gray. We ought to let her know that Wayne's awake.'

Graham got up to go, but Megan was already there. She had been keeping a close watch on her patient and was already aware that a change had occurred. She spoke softly to Wayne and examined him carefully.

'He's still quite groggy from the medication,' she told them. 'So it's hard to tell, but I think his speech may have been affected by the trauma to his brain. Don't be too alarmed, though,' she added hastily, seeing the colour drain from Dean's cheeks. 'That's quite common immediately after a brain injury, but it's often only temporary.' She turned back to address Wayne. 'Try to relax and get some rest. The doctor will come to see you in the morning. You've had a nasty bang, but you're in good hands now.'

***

Gary Drinkwater, the other witness who had been with the victim in the pub, told Anna the same story as she had heard from the Broadhursts. He had only seen the car from behind while he was standing in the road trying to read the number plate as it sped away. He could not describe the driver or say whether there could have been more than one person in the car. He laughed at the suggestion that it could have been a deliberate attack on Wayne.

'That's ridiculous! How could anyone tell who it was, coming at that speed, in the dark? Whatever put that idea in your-?' Then he broke off and paused to think, remembering the way that the white lettering on the back of Wayne's jacket had shown up so clearly in the glare from the headlights. 'I suppose, if they knew he was wearing that jacket with his company name on the back … What are you saying? Has someone threatened him or something?'

'No, no. We're not aware of any threats,' Anna said hastily. 'We just have to look at every possible angle, that's all. Thank you for your time. Let us know if you remember anything else that might help us to trace the driver of the car.'

***

'You'd better have our bed,' Dean said to Barbara as they got out of her car. He had reluctantly agreed to return home to get some much-needed sleep, leaving his father-in-law to watch over Wayne during the night. 'I can use one of the bunks that we got for Carl and Harry.'

'Don't be silly. Graham and I will be fine in the bunks,' Barbara insisted. 'We don't want to turn you out of your room, and you'll sleep better in your own bed.'

She locked the car and then followed Dean up the

drive. As she passed the van, she noticed that there seemed to be some marks on the paintwork. She traced one of them with her finger. It was a deep scratch. In the fading daylight, it was several moments before she worked out that this was not just random accidental damage. Was Dean aware of it? Should she tell him?

She looked up and saw that he had the door open and was waiting for her to come in. She hurried after him. The van could wait. First, she would see him safely to bed.

***

'Yes,' said the bar-tender at the *Bullnose Morris* when Anna asked him about the conflagration that had occurred the previous night. 'I did have to ask those youngsters to leave. I was a bit sorry for them, actually, because it wasn't them that started it, but once that Jason Paul started throwing punches, I had no option.'

'And who *did* start it?'

'Hard to say. Gordon Redfern shouted out some choice remarks at young Callum, but it was Robin Fry who went over to them and started really goading him. Poor Callum couldn't say b-b-b-boo to a goose, but Jason was up on his feet right away calling Rob and Gordon all the names under the sun and swinging his fists. So I reckoned the best thing was to see them off the premises.'

'Did you know that Jason is only seventeen?'

'It was Callum and Ethan bought all the drinks.' The barman looked a little shame-faced. 'I checked their ID. It was Ethan's eighteenth and he was celebrating. He bought most of the rounds.'

'Even so …?'

'Look – the place was full. I didn't know who they were buying for, and I didn't have time to go round checking the ages of everyone in the bar. I never even saw him there until the trouble kicked off, and he's big enough and brazen enough to be well over eighteen. Look officer, if he's under-age, I'm sorry. I didn't realise. It was an oversight, OK? I'll be more careful in future.'

'OK. I've got more important things to do than worrying about Jason Paul having a few drinks a week or two before his eighteenth birthday. I'm more interested in knowing more about this Gordon Redfern and Robin Fry.'

***

'Hello?' Peter was the first to reach the telephone in the hall. Bernie and Lucy stood close by, in their pyjamas, watching anxiously, waiting to discover who could have been ringing so late at night. 'No, no,' he assured whoever it was, 'don't worry about that.'

There was a long pause. Bernie fought off the impulse to wrest the receiver from her husband's hand to speak to the caller herself. Nobody rang at this time to impart good news.

'No, we didn't know. It was fine on Thursday evening.'

Bernie and Lucy exchanged puzzled glances. What was this all about?

'Thanks. Yes, I'm sure you've done the right thing. I'll let Jonah know.'

Jonah! The ringing would be bound to have woken him. He would be even more anxious and perplexed than they were.

'Good ... Try to get some sleep yourself too ... Goodnight!'

Peter put the phone down and looked round at the enquiring faces of his wife and stepdaughter.

'That was Barbara Major,' he told them. 'She's at Wayne and Dean's house. She-'

'Hang on!' Bernie interrupted. 'Come into Jonah's room and tell us. He'll be having kittens wondering what's going on.'

'Barbara finally managed to persuade Dean to go home and get some sleep,' Peter resumed a few minutes later, after they had reconvened, standing around Jonah's bed. 'When they got there, she saw that their van has been vandalised. Dean didn't seem to notice and she hasn't said anything to him because he's got enough on his plate already.'

'Is that all?' Lucy demanded. She had been seriously worried by the late-night call, imagining all sorts of distressing scenarios. This news came as a bewildering anti-climax. 'Why couldn't she have-?'

'She waited until Dean was asleep before ringing,' Peter went on. 'She didn't want to worry him, but she's clearly got the wind up seriously herself.'

'I don't see-,' Lucy began again.

'It was the message that had been scratched on the van that upset her,' Peter continued. 'And she thought you ought to know about it, Jonah – in case it has anything to do with ... well, it looks as if you may be right about it being more than just a random hit-and-run.'

CHAPTER 5: SUNDAY MORNING

Jonah insisted on going round to inspect the damage to the van first thing the following morning. Bernie drove him there, grumbling all the while that he was off-duty and ought to have delegated the task to one of his subordinates. In reality, she was pleased that they were looking into to the incident personally, but she felt obliged to put up a token resistance in her role as guardian of his welfare.

Dean and Barbara had gone back to the hospital, but Graham was waiting for them, having been sent home by his wife to get some sleep after his overnight vigil.

'How is he?' Bernie asked at once.

'Awake, but very confused and frightened,' Graham told them. 'I'm worried that he still doesn't seem to be able to talk, but the nurse keeps saying that it's early days yet and his speech will probably come back spontaneously after a while. A more senior doctor is supposed to be in later this morning. He'll be able to give us a better idea of what to expect.'

Jonah meanwhile had been looking at the words scratched across the paintwork of the van.

'Someone really has a problem with a couple of gay

men running a successful business,' he observed. 'This fits in exactly with the sort of thing we found at the hairdressing salon and the taxi company.' He turned to Graham. 'Presumably you don't know when this was done?'

'Barbara talked to Dean about it this morning. He said it happened sometime on Friday, while the van was outside their office in the Science Park.'

'Why didn't they report it?' Jonah asked sharply, although he already knew the answer.

'They didn't think the police would take it seriously. They might've done if they'd realised you were investigating other incidents like it, but …,' Graham shrugged. 'It's the sort of low-level harassment that they've got used to by now.'

'It's a pity. I'll get a forensics team round tomorrow to go over the van, but I doubt there'll be anything for them this late in the day. If we'd known right away, there might have been a chance. Do they have CCTV at the Science Park?'

'I should think they must.' Graham brightened up a little. 'It's all very modern and hi-tech. Of course that's what the boys should've done – reported it to their security people and got them to check the CCTV tapes.'

'Never mind. I expect they'll still have them. I'll get on to one of my officers right away and tell them to go over there.' With a few small movements of his fingers on the keypad beneath his left hand, Jonah put through a call on the mobile-phone attachment and gave orders to Anna to organise the checking of the CCTV recordings.

'I'm glad you rang,' she said, after listening to his account of the damage to the van and promising to send someone over to the Science Park that morning to inspect the videos. 'I had an interesting conversation last night with one of the staff at the *Bullnose Morris*, which is a pub on the edge of the Blackbird Leys estate, if you didn't know.'

'Go on.'

'I went there, because that's where some of the lads on my list of likely joy-riders spent Friday evening. He told me that they had an altercation with a couple of older men who used homophobic language about them. I don't think any of them actually are gay. I got the impression it was more just supposed to be generally insulting. One of them is a bit of a mummy's boy and talks with a stammer, so maybe that's what set them off. Anyway, it all got rather heated and the bar-tender took the line of least resistance and chucked the young lads out.'

'And?' Jonah asked when Anna paused to gather her thoughts.

'The boys went off – probably angry and looking for trouble – and it's quite possible that they did steal the car and go on the rampage after that.' She paused again. 'But the more interesting thing may be what the bar-tender overheard later from the other men.'

'Which was?' Jonah asked impatiently.

'He wasn't very precise and he said that he only heard bits and pieces of their conversation, but I gather it was all very aggressive towards gay men. One of them in particular seemed to bear a grudge. I've got their names. Do you want me to follow up on them today or …?'

'Just see that you leave me all the details and I'll deal with it tomorrow.'

'Thanks. I've got plenty to keep me occupied with this hit-and-run. The owner of the car is kicking up a stink because he wants it back. I'm going to have to go over there in person and try to pacify him.'

'OK,' Bernie intervened the moment Jonah ended the call. 'You've seen the damage and you've set the wheels in motion; now it's time we let Graham get some sleep and headed back to get ready for church. How many times do I have to tell you you're not on duty today?'

***

Anna put down the phone and turned back to the task in hand, which was studying the images from a speed camera on Cuddesdon Road, which had picked up the BMW as it left the village of Horspath and headed for the open country beyond. It was difficult to be sure, but it looked as if the driver was the only occupant. That did not really fit in with the hypothesis that the three boys had taken it and gone on a spree.

And then there was the dog. It had led her handler to the home of the abandoned car's owner. Didn't that rather suggest that he had been driving that night; and that the theft had been invented in order to avoid prosecution for speeding, failing to stop and report an accident, and quite possibly also, in view of the time of day, driving while under the influence of alcohol?

She looked up at the clock on the wall. It was still early for a house call on a Sunday morning, but Ian Boulton had wanted to know what they were doing with his car. She would take Alice over there with her to give him a progress report and ask a few questions.

***

Sally Pearson was at the door when they arrived at the church on Cowley Road. She immediately asked after Wayne. While Jonah related what Graham had told them earlier that morning, Bernie, Lucy and Peter looked round the foyer at the colourful pictures displayed of the Cowley Road Carnival, which had taken place the previous weekend. This was a community event, which was supported by many local organisations and the church had played a prominent part.

'Look Mam!' Lucy called, pointing at one of the large photographs. 'There's Stella in her police cadet uniform.'

Stella Gilbert was one of very few girls of Lucy's age who attended the church.

'And there are Wayne and Dean showing off some of

their gadgets to some kids,' Bernie murmured, studying another picture. 'I wonder …,' she added thoughtfully. 'It's all good publicity for the business, but …'

'But what?' Lucy asked.

'I was just thinking: if there is someone out there who's got something against gay businessmen, then maybe having a high profile isn't such a good idea.'

'I'll pop in and see Wayne again this afternoon,' Sally was saying to Jonah. Bernie turned quickly to address her.

'I'm sure Dean will appreciate it,' she said, 'but you need to be aware that Wayne and his parents aren't … Well, I don't know what they'll think about a minister coming round.'

'Don't worry, I won't pray over them or anything,' Sally assured her. 'Not unless they ask me to. You'd be surprised though, how many people seem to appreciate a few words from a minister in this sort of situation, even if they would say that they weren't religious.'

'And be careful what you say about it to people in the church,' Bernie went on, remembering how shocked Crystal and Eddie had been to learn that Wayne and Dean were more than business partners and old university chums. 'I don't think everyone is aware that Dean has a husband.'

'I hadn't thought of that,' Sally reddened at the realisation that her well-intentioned plans for spreading the word among the congregation and encouraging them to offer help and support to Dean could have resulted in embarrassment, or worse, all round. 'Yes. I'll take care to explain properly, and I won't make a public announcement or anything like that. People are bound to ask after him,' she went on, 'because he was supposed to be playing today. It's lucky you told me about the accident when you did, so that I could find someone else to step in.'

Dean was an accomplished musician and had been organ scholar at his college. On his move back to Oxford a few months earlier it had not taken long for members of the congregation to discover his talent and to persuade him to join the rota of pianists who accompanied the hymn singing.

'I assume that I'm right not to expect Dean to come to church this morning?' Sally asked, after a moment's hesitation 'Or …?'

'Yes. Absolutely,' Jonah confirmed. 'Wayne's mum persuaded him to go home to bed last night, but he's back at the hospital again now.'

'The other thing you need to be aware of,' Bernie said in an urgent undertone, 'is that Dean once tried to take his own life. It was eight years ago and he's been OK ever since, but …'

'I understand,' Sally nodded. 'I'll be careful.'

***

'I'm DI Davenport and this is DC Ray,' Anna said briskly, holding up her warrant card. 'Are you Mr Ian Boulton?'

'That's right,' answered the thickset, red-faced man who opened the heavy oak door of Hoo Down Farmhouse to admit them to his home. 'I suppose you've come about the car. You'd better come in.'

Anna gazed round at the irregular black beams supporting the ceiling and the wood panelling that covered the walls. The door opened into a large rectangular hall with an enormous fireplace and a heavy wooden table and chairs. The flagstone floor had a long strip of carpet running from the front door to another door at the opposite end of the room. Ian Boulton led them through that door into a passageway. They continued to follow him down two shallow steps and through another door.

'Please – take a seat.'

Anna looked round in surprise. This room was in stark contrast to the dark hall and passageway, which seemed to belong to an earlier era. There were large windows along one side, letting in the strong July sunshine. The floor was covered with a deep-pile carpet; the furniture was new and of a modern design; the walls, painted in an attractive pastel shade of blue, were adorned with large photographs of dogs and horses.

'This is the new part the of house,' Boulton explained, seeing Anna's eyes moving round the room and detecting her surprise. 'We had it built on when we moved here. The original farmhouse dates back to the seventeenth century. It wasn't much more than a ruin when we bought it, but we restored it all and added this room and an office at the back for me with the master bedroom on top.'

'Very impressive,' Anna murmured, seeing that some sort of response was expected of her. 'Now, can we talk about your car?'

'By all means,' Boulton sat down in a large chair upholstered in black leather. 'But what more is there to say about it? I'm impressed that you found it so soon, but can't we just leave it at that? I mean, I'm not interested in pressing charges. Boys will be boys and all that.'

'I'm afraid it isn't as simple as that,' Anna explained patiently. 'As Sergeant Burton told you on Friday, we have strong reasons to suspect that your car was involved in a near-fatal hit-and-run incident. We have to keep it for forensic examination. I'm very sorry, but it may be quite some time before you can have it back.'

'I see. Of course I understand.' Boulton paused briefly as if thinking and then appeared to recollect himself with a jerk. 'How is the young man who was run over? It was a young man, wasn't it?'

'That's right.' Anna confirmed. 'He's still in a serious condition in hospital, but stable, I think.'

'Good, good.' Boulton's expressions of concern seemed insincere somehow, as if he were merely conforming to what he thought was expected of him. 'So, what was it you wanted to talk about?'

'I'd be grateful if you could take me through the sequence of events leading up to the theft of your car. I have it here in Sergeant Burton's notes that you left it on the drive on Friday evening and then you discovered it was missing some time later, when you went out to put it away in your garage just before you were planning to go to bed. Is that correct?'

'That's right. I very foolishly left the key in the ignition, which will have made it easy for anyone to come in and drive it away.'

'That explains something that had been puzzling us,' Alice commented. 'When our officers found the vehicle, the alarm and immobiliser were still in working order and there was no sign of the ignition system having been tampered with.'

'So you're telling us that the thieves simply walked up the drive, got in the car and drove it away?' Anna asked.

'Yes,' answered Boulton, looking a little shamefaced. 'I'm not usually so lackadaisical. The thing is: when I got back, one of the dogs was loose. She came running at the car and almost got under it. So I got out and went after her and took her inside. My wife heard me coming in and she came out of the kitchen and asked me to do something for her – getting a jar down off the top shelf of the dresser I think it was – and after all that I just completely forgot that I'd never parked the car properly.'

'I see,' Anna nodded, unsure whether she believed him, but taking care not to allow him to realise this. 'And about what time was this?'

'About quarter past six,' Boulton answered promptly. 'I went upstairs and changed for dinner; we ate in the kitchen; and then after that we sat in the back sitting room. So we were at the back of the house for the whole time, which is why we didn't see them take the car.'

'I see,' Anna repeated. 'So you're telling me that you didn't see or hear anything at all – not even sounds that you ignored at the time but which could have been significant in retrospect?'

'No – nothing. You see, the walls of this house are two

feet thick. Sound doesn't get through them.'

'And your wife? Is she in? Can we talk to her?'

'No. I'm sorry. She's taken the dogs out.'

'You and your wife are both insured to drive the car, I take it?'

'Yes. She has her own car, but we have both of them insured for both of us.'

'OK.' Anna glanced down at her notes. 'Now, we have a call logged at 23.24 reporting the stolen car. You made that, I take it?'

'Yes.'

'Did you telephone the police immediately that you discovered your loss?'

'Yes – well, perhaps not *right* away. I went back upstairs to talk to my wife first. I did tell you we were getting ready for bed, didn't I? My first thought was that she must have moved it. I thought I'd look like an idiot if I reported it missing and then it turned out that she'd taken it round the back or put it away in the garage.'

'But it will have been after eleven when you realised that the car was gone?'

'Yes.'

'And it could have happened any time after, say, six-thirty?'

'Yes.'

'Have you had any trouble before? No attempted burglaries or vandalism or trespassing?'

'No.' Boulton shook his head. 'I think the alarm deters burglars and we're a bit out of the way to attract vandals. There was a spate of fly-tipping a couple of years back. That's why we installed the gates at the end of the drive, but the nuisance stopped after a while and now we never remember to close them.'

'OK.' Anna closed her notebook and got to her feet. 'I think that's all for now. We'll be in touch when we've finished with your car.'

Boulton hurried to open the door for them and

escorted them back along the passage and through the hall.

Once she was sure that the door was closed behind them, Alice looked up at the house. There was a date engraved in the stonework above the door: 1697. On the wall next to it was an incongruous bright yellow box with the name of a local security company on it. Her eye was caught by a small movement in one of the windows above. Wasn't that a face looking out from behind the curtain in one of the bedrooms?

'I reckon he's lying when he says his wife isn't in,' she said to Anna, as they drove back. 'I'm sure there was someone watching us from upstairs when we left, and there wasn't time for him to have got up there.'

'But why would he lie about that?'

'If he's afraid that his wife might tell us a different story from the one he's given us?'

'But how could he be sure she wouldn't come down and speak to us? What could he have said to make her stay up in the bedroom?'

'He could have threatened her.'

'I suppose so.' Anna thought for a while. 'But, rather than keeping her out of the way, wouldn't it have been more convincing to have forced her to back him up?'

'Maybe he didn't trust her? Or he was afraid she'd forget what he'd told her and get it wrong.' Alice gripped the wheel tighter and her expression became more determined. 'I bet *he* was driving and he's made up this story about the car being stolen to protect himself. He's got his wife under his thumb through domestic violence or coercive control or whatever you like to call it, but he's afraid that if she speaks to the police she'll let something slip. So he tells her to stay out of the way and she's too frightened of him to disobey.'

'There was no sign of the dogs,' Anna pointed out. 'He said his wife had taken them out. If she was still there, what had happened to them?'

'Out the back somewhere, 'Alice answered promptly.

'He said the walls are so thick you can't hear through them. And that's assuming that they really do have dogs. Mel and Tracy never mentioned seeing any – and you'd have expected Q to have noticed if there were any about.'

'Q?'

'PD Q – Mel's dog.'

'Yes, of course.'

'And you said yourself that the trail wouldn't have led back to Ian Boulton's house if he hadn't been driving on Friday night.'

'OK,' Anna conceded. 'I agree it's a good working hypothesis that Ian Boulton was driving when the car hit Wayne Major. However, it's going to be quite difficult to prove that, if he persists with his story about the car being stolen – especially if his wife backs him up. I'll try and find an excuse to go round again this afternoon in the hope of getting to speak to her. Meanwhile, I want you to write up a report of this interview and then check out Ian Boulton's driving record – and Mrs Boulton's too,' she added as an afterthought. 'She may have been taking points for him to avoid him losing his licence.'

CHAPTER 6: SUNDAY AFTERNOON

'Excuse the clutter,' apologised the young woman who answered the door of the flat on the seventh floor of the tower block, bending down to move a small pink bicycle from behind the door in order to open it fully. Anna judged that she was of Afro-Caribbean origin, but her accent suggested that she was most likely a second or third generation immigrant, born in Britain. 'I suppose you want to talk to Leroy. He told me about the crash on Friday night. I hope that poor guy who was hit is going to be OK?'

'It looks like he's out of danger,' Anna told her, but the doctors are afraid he may have permanent brain damage.'

'That's awful! Did you hear that Leroy?' she turned to address her partner, who had come out from the living room carrying a small girl dressed in a sparkly pink tutu. 'It looks like you were right when you said it looked bad.'

'Is it OK for me to come in?' Anna asked. 'Or would you rather we went somewhere else?' she added, looking at the child in her father's arms and at a second, older girl, who had appeared from behind him.

'You're welcome, so long as you don't mind the mess,' Leroy answered. He put his daughter down and took her hand in his. 'Come on, Izzie. You and Serena are going to have to play nicely for a bit while I talk to the police officer.'

'Are you really a police lady?' Serena asked boldly, after Anna had taken her seat in the cramped living room. 'Why haven't you got a uniform on?'

'She's a plain clothes officer,' her mother told her. 'Like the detectives on the TV.'

'Are you detecting now?' Serena wanted to know.

'I suppose I am,' Anna smiled. 'I need to ask your daddy about a car accident that he saw a couple of days ago. He helped a man who had been knocked down. He looked after him until the ambulance came.'

Serena's eyes grew wide and she looked towards her father with renewed respect.

'Come on, girls,' their mother cut in. 'Come and sit up to the table and I'll find those colouring books that Granny gave you.'

Anna turned to address Leroy.

'I'm DI Davenport. And you're Mr Leroy Gilbert – is that right?'

'Yes. I'm Leroy and this is Olivia and our two girls Serena and Isabelle.'

Anna smiled round at them each in turn. Olivia, looking up from the drawer in which she was searching for the promised colouring books, nodded back.

'I've seen the account of the incident that you gave to Sergeant Appleton. He says that you were in the bus shelter when the car mounted the kerb, is that right?'

'Yes.' Leroy leaned back in his chair resting his hands on top of his head. 'I was having a last cigarette before going to bed.' He glanced across at his partner. 'Ollie's very strict about me not smoking in the flat, because of the girls.'

Anna smiled encouragingly.

'There was this massive roaring of a car coming round the corner out of Cuddesdon Way,' Leroy continued, 'and the next thing I know, it's up on the pavement, headlights blazing at me and this poor guy's down on the floor with his head banged up against the corner of the bus shelter.'

'Did you see the driver? Would you be able to describe them?'

'No. I couldn't even describe the car to be honest. I was dazzled by the lights.'

'You didn't even see how many people there were inside the car?'

'No. Sorry.'

'Don't worry. It can't be helped. So, you went to help the man who was knocked down. Did you notice anything about him particularly?'

'How d'you mean?' Leroy creased his brow in perplexity.

'Was there anything distinctive about him? Anything that might make him easily recognisable?'

'Not that I noticed.' Leroy continued to look puzzled. 'Should I have done? Why does it matter?'

'We just want to be sure that it *was* just a freak accident. It's been suggested that the victim could have been targeted deliberately. It sounds as if you think that's unlikely.'

'I suppose it depends if whoever it was knew he was going to be there.' Leroy thought for a moment or two. 'There were some big white letters on the back of his jacket. I suppose they'd have shown up bright in the car's lights. Apart from that …'

'Thank you. That's very helpful. Now, going back a bit. You said the car came round from Cuddesdon Way. Are you sure of that? Did you see it turning out?'

'Yeah, well, I saw the lights I suppose.'

'And you mean it came from the …,' Anna paused and studied a map of the area which she had brought with her. 'It came from the left – from where you were looking? I mean from the direction of the park rather than the shops?'

'Yeah. That's right. It came round the corner at ninety miles an hour and nearly hit one of them bollards in the middle of the road. Seems to me that was why it came up on the pavement, swerving to get round it.'

'That's interesting. Thank you.' Anna smiled at Leroy. 'Now is there anything else you can think of that could help us to find the driver of the car?'

'No.' He shook his head. 'It drove off up the road heading for the by-pass. There was this guy jumped out from the other side of the road and stood there watching it. And then he came over to see how the guy who was knocked down was. I think he knew him. And then it wasn't long before the ambulance and the police came.'

***

'Your turn to punt!' Bernie called out to Lucy, who was walking on the towpath alongside Jonah in his wheelchair.

She held the pole in the water at the back of the boat, skilfully guiding it towards the riverbank. They had debated whether they should abandon their planned outing in view of recent events, but, as Peter pointed out, there was nothing that any of them could do to help at present and there was no point curtailing their own activities out of a misplaced desire to show solidarity with Wayne, Dean and their family.

Jonah had argued that he, at least, could have been helping Anna to pursue the motorist responsible for the incident; but Bernie had overruled this suggestion telling him that it was about time that he learned how to delegate.

'Too late for that,' Peter had snorted, 'with retirement only three weeks away.'

So, now here they all were, enjoying an archetypal Oxford summer afternoon on the river, with a hamper stowed in the prow of the punt, containing cucumber sandwiches, scones and strawberries and cream in readiness for a picnic in some secluded place away from the town.

Jonah had refused the offer of being lifted into the boat, preferring the independence of his all-terrain wheelchair, which easily kept pace with the punt, however much energy the person wielding the pole expended. His friends took it in turns to walk with him, making conversation, which he often ignored, his mind being occupied with making plans for taking forward his investigation as soon as he was back at work the following day.

'I wonder if Anna's got those CCTV pictures yet,' he murmured, as he waited while Lucy and Bernie changed places. 'I think perhaps I'll just give her a ring ...'

'Oh no you don't!' Bernie grasped his hand firmly in hers to prevent him from using the phone. 'You're off-duty, and Anna doesn't need you checking up on her every five minutes. She is perfectly capable – provided you don't undermine her confidence by questioning everything she does.'

Their eyes met and, for a moment or two, it was a standoff, with neither willing to give way. Then, with a sigh, Jonah conceded defeat.

'OK. You win. I don't suppose it'll make much difference waiting for tomorrow.'

'That's better.' Smiling, Bernie released his hand and fell in beside him as they started off again along the path. 'Don't forget, Anna's had good teachers: first Peter and then you.'

'And I suppose you think I ought to be getting ready to hand over to the younger generation? Anna and Andy Lepage and the others?'

'I don't know about *getting ready*' Bernie laughed. 'With your retirement only three weeks away, I'd say you ought to have got ready by now!'

Jonah's only reply to this was a grunt. To him *retirement* still felt like a dirty word. They walked on together in silence for several minutes.

In the punt, Peter lay back luxuriously on a pile of pillows, reflecting to himself that there were some advantages in being surrounded by strong, independent women determined to prove themselves equal to every task. He was confident that he would finish the day without ever having to take a turn at propelling the punt or getting any water up his sleeve while doing so.

'This is the life!' he called out to Jonah on the bank. 'Aren't you looking forward to more days like this, instead of constantly chasing your tail trying to solve more crimes with less resources?'

'It's all very well for him,' Jonah muttered, only just loud enough for Bernie to hear. 'He's got his grandkids and the house to look after. This time next month I'll just be a useless-'

'Rubbish!' Bernie cut him off. 'That's just stupid nonsense. And we've been through all this before. You've just *got* to stop defining your identity entirely in terms of your work. You're a whole lot more than just a police officer. You've got your own grandchildren for a start, and-'

'Fat lot of use I'll be to them!' Jonah interrupted. His frustration at not being able to take forward the investigation into the attack on his friend was making him unusually peevish. 'You know perfectly well that when I go to stay with Anne and Reuben it's like them having an extra baby to look after; and Nathan and Georgia don't need anyone else to help them now that Georgia's mum has given up work – not that I wouldn't be a liability for them too.'

'Well there's one important role that you'll be needed for,' Bernie retorted, determined to deflect her friend from falling into the low mood that seemed always to accompany any mention of his impending retirement. 'And that's keeping me out from under Peter's feet at home. Remember – when you retire, I retire and he's so into this house-husband business now that I can foresee all sorts of trouble if I'm around all day trampling mud over his clean floors and untidying his freshly tidied rooms!'

'Wouldn't you rather take the opportunity to see the back of me? Settle me in a nice Care Home somewhere and *spend more time with your family*, as they say?'

'You *are* family!' Bernie squealed indignantly. 'We didn't take you in just because you're a DCI, and it won't make the tiniest difference when you become a retired DCI.'

'Still, you and Peter aren't getting any younger. I can't expect you to go on looking after me forever.'

'Let's cross that bridge when we come to it. We're not in our dotage yet!' with a sudden impulse, Bernie bent down and gave Jonah a quick peck on the cheek. 'It's no good. You can't get away from us that easily.'

***

'So this hasn't got us a great deal further,' Anna said to Alice, relating her interview with Leroy. 'He confirmed that the car came along Cuddesdon Way from the direction of Watlington Road, which fits with our idea that it could have been Ian Boulton driving from his house. But why would he be in such a tearing hurry?'

'It could equally be coming from the *Bullnose Morris*,' Alice pointed out. 'That's on the corner of Cuddesdon Way and Watlington Road. He could've been drinking in there first, and something got him going and he got in his car and headed off in a rage to do something about whatever it was.'

'But he'd have been seen,' Anna objected. 'It'd be a big risk for him to claim he was at home all evening, if he was really in the pub.' She sighed, 'Anyway, I'd better let you get off home. Can you bring Monica up to speed in the morning? She'll have to lead on this until next weekend. Oh! And make sure she keeps DCI Porter in the loop. He's convinced that this may be somehow connected with those attacks on gay business people that he's investigating, and you know what he's like – always wants everything done yesterday!'

'No problem,' Alice grinned. 'I doubt she'll let me wait until tomorrow. She's convinced she'll be able to crack this one. It was all I could do to stop her coming in this morning.'

'Oh yes! I forgot you and she were …,' Anna coloured in embarrassment. 'I mean Jonah told me you've moved in together.'

'Don't worry. We won't let it affect our work.'

'No, of course not. I didn't mean to imply …,' Anna said hastily.

'I know you didn't, but your face! Surely you must've realised that there are a lot of us in the police.'

'So you are …? I mean, it *is* more than just a couple of girls sharing a flat?' Anna asked awkwardly.

'Mm-mm,' Alice nodded, getting up and putting on her jacket. 'And, like you said, I'd better be getting back there now. We've got a couple of friends coming for dinner and I promised I'd take charge of the dessert.'

***

'Dean?' Wayne looked up enquiringly into his husband's eyes. Then with a great effort, he added, slowly and deliberately, 'Is … that … you?'

'Yes.' Dean, overjoyed at the first signs that Wayne was properly conscious and able to speak, struggled to think of anything to say. 'Your Mum and Dad are here too.'

'Wha … wha,' Wayne continued to struggle to form the words. 'What …?'

'You were knocked down by a car.'

'You had a bang on the head,' Graham added. 'That's why everything's probably a bit strange.'

'Don't try to remember,' Barbara added gently. 'It'll all come back over time. Don't try to force it.'

'W-when … How long …?'

'Two days ago. The doctors kept you asleep to help you recover,' Dean tried not to allow the fear that he felt to become apparent in his voice. 'Like your mum said, it'll take a while. Try to relax and give it time.'

'Ma … ma …,' Wayne faltered, breathing hard with the effort of speaking.

'Yes?' Barbara encouraged, but Wayne shook his head.

Dean squeezed his hand gently.

'It's OK. Everything's going to be OK. We'll get through this.'

CHAPTER 7: SUNDAY EVENING

When Jonah rang Dean's mobile phone in the hope of getting an update on Wayne's progress, it was Barbara Major who answered.

'Dean's having a shower,' she explained. 'We're all back home now and I'm determined to make him get an early night.'

'Is that good news?' Bernie asked, leaning over Jonah's shoulder so that the microphone would pick up her voice. 'I mean, it sounds good that you're able to leave him.

'I think so.' Barbara's voice sounded weary. Then, with an effort to strike an optimistic note, 'His speech seems to be coming back – I think.'

'That's good!' Lucy chipped in eagerly.

'Yes.' Barbara paused, undecided whether to voice her reservations. The hesitancy and long searching for words was so unlike her son's usual exuberance that it almost felt worse than when he had been unconscious and she had been able to hope that, once he awoke, everything would be back to normal. 'Yes, it is.'

'Presumably he can't tell us anything about what happened?' Jonah asked, unable to resist the urge to take every opportunity to further the investigation.

'No. He doesn't remember anything, and anyway …,' Barbara tailed off. Then, when nobody else spoke, she took a deep breath and continued. 'And anyway, he's still really struggling to talk. The nurse says they'll get one of the Speech and Language therapists to assess him tomorrow. And the consultant neurologist will be in tomorrow too. After he's seen him we should have a better idea …'

Everyone waited in silence as she swallowed hard before going on.

'He'll be able to give us an idea of – of the prognosis, and maybe even how long it's going to take before he's …,' she swallowed again. 'Anyway,' she continued with a rather forced brightness in her voice, 'we know it's going to take a while, so Graham's organised to look after the business for them. I think he's rather looking forward to it. He's been feeling at a loose end ever since he retired.'

'That's good,' Bernie said to fill the pause that followed. 'I mean, it's good that Graham's there to help. I can't imagine Dean's thinking of the business at the moment.'

'No,' Barbara agreed. 'I don't know whether to push him to take more interest – to give him something to take his mind off … or … I mean, he can't just … suspend his whole life for ever.'

'It's only been two days so far,' Peter pointed out. 'I know it feels far longer than that. If Graham's happy to look after the business, I'd give Dean at least a month to adjust to whatever he's got to face.'

'And if there's anything we can do to help, you will let us know, won't you?' Bernie added.

'And try to remember to be kind to yourself too,' Peter urged.

'That's right,' Bernie agreed. 'Don't feel that you have to be strong for the sake of everyone else. Allow yourself time to grieve too.'

'Can I go to see Wayne?' Lucy asked. 'Mam said we

weren't to all go at once, but now that you don't need to stay all the time, do you think I could? Or would it just confuse him having different people there?' she added warily.

'Yes, of course.' There was a note of relief in Barbara's voice. 'I'm sure he'd be pleased to see you, and ...,' she hesitated, 'I'm sure it will be good for Dean to see that it's not necessary for him to be there all the time. I can understand why he doesn't want to leave him, even for a minute, but if this is going to be a long-term thing ...'

'Yes. Jonah was in hospital for nearly a year,' Lucy agreed.

'And while there's no reason to think it'll take that long for Wayne,' Bernie put in quickly, 'you're right that Dean needs to realise that he can't put everything on hold until Wayne's back on his feet again.'

***

Anna stared at the fuzzy pictures on the screen in front of her. When was someone going to design a CCTV camera that took pictures from which a suspect could reasonably be identified? Detective Sergeant Andy Lepage, whom she had sent over to the Science Park earlier in the day, had noted down a list of times during Friday when people not known to the security personnel appeared in view at each of the cameras positioned around the campus. She looked at each figure carefully, trying to work out if any of them were familiar or appeared to be acting suspiciously. No. They all looked like innocent people going about their legitimate business.

Annoyingly, the *Design Ability* van, which she had seen arriving in a video time-stamped 8.43, had been parked out of the line of vision of the camera in the car park outside the building where Wayne and Dean had their offices. The two young men could be seen entering the building at 8.47, but there was no way of telling if anyone had approached the van during the course of the day or at what time.

She ejected the memory stick containing the final recording and dropped it into the bag with the others. This was not really her case, she reminded herself. The chances of the damage to the van having any bearing on the hit-and-run that she was supposed to be dealing with were slim at best. She picked up the bag of data sticks and carried them through to Jonah's private office, leaving them on his desk with Andy Lepage's list and a note to say that she had reviewed them and found nothing.

Then she returned to her own desk and wrote a brief email to Monica and Alice, summarising what she had done over the weekend and suggesting lines of enquiry for them to pursue. It was time to make tracks for home. She sighed. It had been a frustrating two days, with very little to show for her efforts. Was part-time working ever going to be practical in her current role? Should she consider applying for a civilian post with more regular hours and less responsibility?

***

'Time we turned in too,' Bernie declared as soon as Jonah had concluded his telephone conversation with Barbara. 'I can foresee that it's going to be a busy day tomorrow, so we could do with an early night almost as much as Dean does.'

'I'll do the honours,' Peter volunteered, meaning that he would prepare Jonah for bed, 'seeing as you're going to be on duty all day tomorrow.'

'I'll help,' Lucy added eagerly, seeing an opportunity for finding out more about Jonah's plans for taking the investigation forward.

Jonah led the way through his sitting room and into the bedroom. The electrically powered doors opened automatically in response to a signal from the control panel on the arm of his wheelchair.

Peter and Lucy worked systematically, following the familiar routine that they had established over the almost eight years since Jonah had been first a regular guest and later a permanent resident in their home. Peter reached inside Jonah's trouser-leg to detach the urine bag from its tube and took it into the bathroom to empty it. Lucy spread a waterproof sheet over the bed and topped it with an oversize bath towel. While she was doing this, Jonah manoeuvred his chair alongside the bed and made it recline so that Peter could roll him gently from the chair on to the bed. Then he moved the chair, which now resembled a hospital trolley, out of the way, so that he could help his stepdaughter with the task of undressing their friend.

'Do you think it's too late to ring Anna to find out where she's up to?' Jonah asked as Peter lowered the hoist to lift him from the bed and transfer him to the shower. 'I'd like to be able to keep an eye on Monica when she takes over tomorrow. She isn't always as thorough as she could be – always cutting corners and not bothering with the routine stuff.'

'That's rich coming from you!' Peter retorted, guiding the hoist along its track in the ceiling and through the open door into the bathroom. 'You're a world-class corner-cutter and hunch-follower and I don't remember you ever having the patience to do the routine stuff.'

'Well, I had the advantage that you were always so good at it that I didn't need to,' Jonah smiled complacently, remembering the time when he and Peter were both officers working under the direction of Lucy's father, Superintendent Richard Paige. 'And you house-trained Andy Lepage so well that I still don't. But that's got nothing to do with it. I still maintain that Monica is too slapdash. She always wants to be out and doing instead of thinking things through or trawling the files.'

'She models herself on you,' Peter told him with a grin, lowering him on to the seat inside the shower cubicle and stepping forward to settle him safely and remove the hoist. '*And* she had the most tremendous crush on you back in the day. Anna told me that she was all for applying for a transfer, she was so keen on the idea of working under you.'[9]

'That's a rather unfortunate way of putting it!' giggled Lucy directing the shower to rinse Jonah's back.

'All very understandable,' Jonah smiled back at Peter, ignoring Lucy's remark. 'And if what you say is right, that explains why Anna was so taken aback when she discovered that Monica and Alice are an item.'

'Doesn't she know what the *B* in *LGBT* stands for?' asked Lucy scornfully.

'I'm quite sure she knows perfectly well,' Peter answered, coming to the defence of an officer for whom he had considerable respect. 'But knowing things doesn't make it easy to throw off our preconceptions.'

'But we shouldn't have any preconceptions about people,' Lucy argued. 'We ought to take them as they come – treat them all as individuals.'

'It's all very well you saying that,' Peter argued, 'but it's harder than you think – especially about something where ideas have changed so fast over the last few decades.'

'How do you mean?' Lucy stepped back, holding the shower nozzle away while Peter soaped Jonah's genital area and legs.

'When I was your age, homosexuality had only just been legalised. And even then, the age of consent was set at twenty-one. That was because everyone – well the majority of people anyway – thought that it was a deviancy brought on by sexual experience during adolescence.'

'Not forgetting the theory that it was a natural stage of development that most boys went through,' Jonah added.

---

[9] Anna imparts this information to Peter in "Grave Offence" the 3rd Bernie Fazakerley Mystery, © Judy Ford 2017, ISBN 978-1-911083-30-6

'So?' Lucy asked.

'So I grew up with a completely different mind-set from the way you did,' Peter replied. 'Much more like the way Crystal thinks – or probably even more so, except that we weren't encouraged to think about such things at all. You saw how shocked she was. And you know it's not because she's not a very caring person; it's just the way she's been brought up. My sex education at school, for example, didn't even touch on any of that. It was all just about reproductive biology. And, of course, anyone of my generation who was bisexual would have kept jolly quiet about it and got on with dating members of the opposite gender.'

'But Anna wasn't brought up in Jamaica and she's nothing like as old as you,' Lucy protested. 'She isn't even as old as Jonah,' she added, seeing the amused expression on Peter's face at her reference to his advancing years. 'I bet she had proper sex education.'

'That's right,' Jonah cut in brightly. 'She will have gone through school under Section 28 – a very enlightened era!'

'Section 28?' Lucy asked, a puzzled frown on her face.

'Section 28 of the 1988 Local Government Act prevented local authorities from "promoting homosexuality".' Peter explained. 'It made everyone very cautious about what they said in schools. It was only repealed in 2003; so you see, your generation is the first not to have grown up effectively being told that anything other than one man and one woman is some sort of perversion.'

Lucy stepped forward again and began showering down Jonah's legs in silence. She had not realised how recent the shift in public attitudes towards sexual minorities had been.

'So, before 2003?' she asked at last. 'What would have happened to Wayne and Dean? I mean …?' she trailed off, not exactly sure what she did mean.

'Well, civil partnerships came in in 2004,' Jonah told

her, 'which gives you an idea of which way the wind was blowing even before 2003. It was all a very gradual shift, so there was a wide range of opinions – as there still is. The point that Peter was making is that, however much we may revise our ideas intellectually, we often fall back on instincts that were developed when we were growing up.'

'Is that what you think made someone write all that stuff over the van?' Lucy asked, suddenly remembering that she had been hoping to pump Jonah on his plans for investigating the homophobic attacks.

'Well, it's obviously someone with a bee in his bonnet about gay men,' Jonah agreed, 'which probably points to some ingrained prejudice. But most people don't work out their prejudices like that; they just avoid whichever group they don't like. So I reckon there must have been something more – some sort of trigger that made it more personal for whoever it is.'

'The thing is,' Peter added, 'most homophobic abuse – and racist and sexist abuse too, come to that – is opportunistic, rather than planned. But here we have someone who's seen the article in the Oxford Mail – or found out from some other source that Wayne and Dean aren't just business partners – and has taken the trouble to go along to their office and vandalise their van.'

'It's the same with the other incidents,' Jonah added. 'That's the main reason that we're taking them seriously, to be honest. We don't have the resources to hunt down every drunk who mouths off at a member of some minority group in the street, but this is different – it's premeditated and it seems to be escalating.'

Lucy turned off the shower and reached for a towel. Together, she and Peter wrapped Jonah snugly in two bath sheets and transferred him back into the hoist for the return journey to the bed.

'Do you really think that Wayne could have been run down deliberately?' Lucy asked while they gently patted Jonah's skin dry.

'No he doesn't,' Peter said before Jonah could answer. 'He's just looking for an excuse to butt in on someone else's case. How could anyone have picked him off like that, in the dark when they couldn't even have known he was going to be there? The damage to the van is different. It was outside the offices at an address that was even included in that Oxford Mail article.'

'I never said they hunted him down in the way you're suggesting,' Jonah protested. 'I'm saying that it could be that they just happened upon him and recognised the logo on the back of his jacket and saw red.'

'Too much of a coincidence.' Peter remained unconvinced. 'You're just determined to get involved and you're letting it cloud your judgement. You ought to be concentrating on the damage to the van and leave Anna and her team to investigate the hit-and-run.'

'What's the next step?' Lucy asked as she inserted Jonah's right arm into his pyjama sleeve. 'How're you going to find out who scratched the van?'

'Well, we've got a couple of possible suspects for some of the other attacks. So, we can start by seeing if either of them were hanging around the Science Park on Friday – which probably means going through hours of grainy CCTV footage.' Jonah sighed and then grinned. 'Peter's right, I'm afraid. That tedious stuff isn't my favourite part of the job.'

***

'You'd better try to make sure his nibs takes plenty of rest breaks tomorrow,' Peter told Bernie when he joined her in their bedroom after settling Jonah for the night. She was sitting on the bed in pyjamas and dressing gown, answering emails on her phone. 'That broken skin on his backside isn't healing. I've put another dressing on it, but the key is going to be keeping the pressure off it for a while.'

'I'll do my best,' Bernie sighed, 'but you know how he is when he's got the bit between his teeth with a case; and he's determined to get this all done and dusted within the next three weeks, which is making him even worse than usual. Not that any of us would dare to mention the R-word,' she added. 'He's still in denial about that in many ways. I just don't know how he's going to cope, to be honest. I have a horrible feeling we could be in for a re-run of the way he was back in 2009, when he thought he was going to be pensioned off on medical grounds.'

'I really don't think that's likely,' Peter tried to reassure her. 'He was still coming to terms with becoming disabled then. It's different now. He knows what a lot he can still do.'

'Yes, but he's still thinking in terms of it all being about what he can do *as a police officer*,' Bernie argued. 'Once he's lost that, I'm afraid he'll go back to thinking there's no point in him being here – that he's just a burden, and …,' Bernie's vice dropped to a whisper, 'I'm not ready to lose him.'

'None of us are.' Peter drew his wife into his arms and held her tightly to him. 'And I'm sure he knows that. Don't worry. He'll come round.'

'He very nearly didn't last time – when he was starving himself to death on the rehab ward.'

'Like I said – it was different then. He was confined to bed with nothing better to do than brood on everything. Now he can get out and about in his chair and do all sorts of things for himself with all the gadgets that Wayne and Dean have designed for him. Once he gets used to not having to fit his life around the job, he'll start appreciating the benefits of having more time to do the things he enjoys.'

'I hope you're right.' Bernie stood up, took off her dressing gown and hung it on a hook on the back of the door. 'And, talking of Wayne and Dean, I hope we don't have the same sort of thing to go through with poor

Wayne. I don't know how either of them is going to manage if he ends up seriously disabled. Dean relies on him so much.'

'I'm not so sure about that,' Peter continued his efforts to be reassuring. 'I know Wayne always appears to be in charge, but I think that's only because he's big and loud. I get the impression that Dean makes a lot of the decisions on the quiet. And they've got Wayne's mum and dad. Barbara won't let any harm come to Dean.'

'No. You're right there. I sometimes think she's fonder of Dean than she is of Wayne.' Bernie climbed into bed, arranging the pillows so that she could sit comfortably while she waited for Peter to make his own preparations for sleep. 'OK. I'll shut up and stop trying to fix everyone's lives for them.

CHAPTER 8: MONDAY MORNING

To Jonah's delight, when he arrived at work the following day, Detective Sergeant Andy Lepage greeted him with his notes on the CCTV pictures and an assurance that there was no need to look at more than a few selected clips. Anna had left a note saying that none of the unidentified visitors to the Science Park resembled any known criminals. All that was left for Jonah to do was to make a final visual check to satisfy himself that the video footage told them nothing.

'Do you want to look at the videos right away?' Andy asked. 'I don't think they tell us anything, but I know you always like to see things for yourself.'

'Maybe later. I've been told that I ought to put more trust in my subordinates, and, after all, you'll have to manage without me in a few weeks. I want to start by cross-checking with that hit-and-run that came in over the weekend. Get Monica Philipson in here will you?'

'Yes sir.' Andy fell back into formality, as he always did when taken by surprise. It was the first time that he had known Jonah to mention his retirement unprompted, even in this oblique fashion. 'I'll fetch her right away.'

While he was out of the room, Bernie filled the kettle,

which stood on top of one of the filing cabinets in Jonah's office, and made tea for all of them. Maintaining his fluid intake was important for Jonah's well-being – something that he had a habit of forgetting while busy at work. Having a case conference was an opportunity for Bernie to see that he drank enough during the day without seeming to nag.

'We've got several leads to follow up,' Monica said briskly, determined to demonstrate her capabilities to a senior officer who might have influence over her future promotion. Being left in charge of a potentially serious case – and one that she knew Jonah was taking a personal interest in – was a good opportunity for her to show her mettle. It would be a feather in her cap if she could identify the driver of the car before Anna's return at the end of the week. 'I've been going through Anna's interviews with the boys from Blackbird Leys and none of them has a convincing alibi. I've got it in mind to follow up on them this morning.'

'Good. Keep me informed. And I'd like a list of their names and addresses, so I'll know if we happen across them in our investigation into these homophobic attacks.'

'We've got people going over the car with a toothcomb,' Monica continued. 'I'll get on to them later to check if they've found anything. And our guys found some silver paint on the litterbin near the bus stop on Blackbird Leys Road. They've sent a sample to the lab for confirmation that it came from the car when it scraped past it.'

'Right. Let me know when the results come back. Not that it's very likely that we've got the wrong car, but we'll look very stupid if it turns out that there were two silver BMWs with similar numbers on the loose that night.'

'I don't think there's much chance of that,' Monica assured him. 'A BMW answering the description of our car was caught on a traffic camera coming off the by-pass and going right round the Littlemore roundabout and back on to the by-pass at 22.48. It looks clear to me that it joined the by-pass from Blackbird Leys Road, by going down Sandy Lane West. You can only get on in the southbound direction there. So to go north, they turned round at the roundabout.'

'Which suggests that, by the time they got to Littlemore at any rate, they had a definite plan for where they were going,' Jonah mused, 'rather than just being intent on getting away from the scene of the accident.'

'Yes. Well Alice has a theory about that.' Monica replied. 'She's not convinced that it was joy-riders at all. She reckons the owner was driving and he only reported the car stolen in order to shift the blame.'

'And that's because ...?'

'The dog that tracked the driver of the abandoned car landed up at the house where the owner lives.'

'Hmm! I can't see that standing up in court. Who is this owner? Does he have form at all?'

'Nope!' Monica shook her head. 'As far as I can tell, he's a respectable local businessman. His name's Ian Boulton. He owns a printing company. It seems to be doing well – which probably explains the brand new BMW.'

'I don't know about that. If the business was in trouble, he might want the car to create a façade that would prevent shareholders and creditors getting worried. Does he have an alibi?'

'He claims to have been at home with his wife all evening.'

'And does the wife back him up?'

'She wasn't in when Anna called round – or at least, he *said* she was out.'

'But?'

'But Alice is convinced that she saw someone at one of the upstairs windows as they left the house. So ...'

'So her theory is that the wife was upstairs all the time and the husband didn't want the police questioning her –

is that it?'

'That's right,' Monica nodded.

'Interesting.' Jonah pursed his lips in thought. 'Yes. I think this Ian Boulton warrants more investigation. Have a look into his background. In particular, look out for any links to right-wing organisations or any incidents of homophobia. Find out if he has a Facebook account or is on Twitter – that's the way a lot of people give away their prejudices.'

'Right you are, sir. I'll get on to it. And talking of homophobia, Anna left a note asking me to tell you about a couple of guys who were drinking in the *Bullnose Morris* on Friday night. One of the staff told her that they were using homophobic language against some of the boys from the estate.'

'Really? Did he know their names?'

'Yes. They were a Gordon Redfern and a Robin Fry. '

'Any idea where they live?'

'We've got an address for Redfern but not Fry. Do you want me to follow up on them?'

'No. Leave that with me. Andy Lepage is good at finding out that sort of thing. I'll get him on to it. It's more likely to be relevant to my investigation than yours – unless the two really are linked. Do you happen to have photographs of either of them – or of Ian Boulton?'

'Only the one off Boulton's driving licence. I can let you have that, if you like.'

'Yes please. It's a long shot, but one of the victims in my case saw his attacker's face and gave us a description – albeit a rather sketchy one – so it'd be useful to compare that with those three, just in case we've managed to strike gold there.' Jonah glanced down at the computer screen attached to his chair, checking the notes that he had made in preparation for this briefing with Monica. 'Now, I suppose, in fairness, I ought to share my suspects with you – just in case they crawl out from under any stones that you lift in the course of your enquiries.'

Monica nodded and turned to a new page of her notebook.

'Top of our list,' Jonah continued, 'are a lovely couple called Craig Jones and Tanya Lumley. They've been cautioned for homophobic verbal abuse and threatening behaviour. That was a while ago now and they seem to have kept their heads down since. There's not really anything to connect them with these more recent incidents except that one of their targets was Mark Brown, who owns *Antonio's*, the posh hairdresser's on Turl Street.'

'If you can give me the details, I'll keep a lookout for them,' Monica promised.

'Andy Lepage is looking after all that. I'll get him to give them to you. They both live in Blackbird Leys. She drives a till in one of the big supermarkets – I forget which one, but Andy'll be able to tell you – and he's a self-employed taxi driver. That was another reason he's on my list. One of the businesses that was attacked is a taxi company. I did just wonder if there could be an element of resentment, if he thought it was stealing customers from him, but it's a very tenuous link. The trouble is, we don't have anything better than tenuous at the moment. Clutching at straws is the metaphor that comes to mind where this case is concerned.'

'OK.' Monica noted down this information. 'I think I'll have a wander round Blackbird Leys and call in at the pubs. It'll be a good way to get the gossip about what happened on Friday night and there's a chance I may run into these two or else Redfern and Fry.'

'The only other suspects we've got – and these are *so* tenuous that they can hardly be described as suspects – are a rather sad couple of religious dinosaurs, who are trying to wipe out sodomy by calling gay people to repentance. Here they are at the Pride parade.'

With a small movement of his forefinger, Jonah brought up a photograph on the screen in front of him. Monica leaned closer to view two grey-haired people – a man and a woman – standing at the side of the street attempting to hand out leaflets to passers-by who were ignoring them.

'These are Susie and William Cunliffe. He's pastor of a House Church based in Summertown.'

'House Church?' Monica queried. She had not come across the term before.

'As the name suggests, they are churches – i.e. groups of Christians – who meet in each other's houses, instead of in a church building. They are mostly small and independent of any denomination and, because they're self-selecting, they are sometimes prone to getting bees in their bonnets. This one seems to be a bit fundamentalist and, in particular, to have very dogmatic views on homosexuality.'

'I see.'

'Personally, I think they're fairly harmless – except perhaps to any gay youngsters who actually believe the nonsense that they're peddling. There's never been any sign that they would resort to violence either against property or people. They just hang around gay bars and clubs with placards and leaflets hoping that someone will stop and listen to them.'

'I see,' Monica repeated. 'And is there anything specific to link them to the attacks?'

'Mainly just that they were at the Pride parade and they approached most of the people who have subsequently been attacked.'

'Dean had a long debate with them,' Bernie put in, suddenly remembering a conversation that she had had with her young friend after the parade. 'He'd done his homework and had a long list of counter-arguments for all the usual clobber texts that these people use. I think he quite enjoyed himself – didn't convince them though!'

'Clobber texts?' Monica looked round at them both in puzzlement.

'Verses from the Bible that can be interpreted as

condemning gay relationships,' Jonah explained. 'Depending on just *how* fundamentalist they are, some people also have texts that prove that women must be subservient to men and that unbelievers will spend eternity being toasted in Hell. You pays your money and you takes your choice.'

'The point is that it's all a matter of taking words out of context and ignoring the situation in which they were written,' Bernie added.

'Anyway,' Jonah concluded, 'that's all the suspects we've got. And I'm pretty convinced that none of them are the real culprits. So if you happen across any more in the course of your enquiries I'll be delighted to hear about them.'

***

'I've assessed your son,' Dr Meshach Mutambara said to Barbara and Graham, who had been waiting anxiously with Dean outside the cubicle where Wayne lay, while the neurology consultant made his examination. 'He's had a small bleed in the left-hand side of his brain. The damage caused by that is not extensive and he may well make a full recovery – in time.'

'That's good!' Barbara said in a tone of relief, looking towards Dean.

'How much time?' Graham was more suspicious of these words. Was the doctor trying to let them down gently with optimistic predictions that would always be looking towards some unspecified future date?

'I'm afraid it's impossible to say.' The doctor's deep brown eyes looked at him with compassion. 'You need to be prepared for a lengthy recovery period – certainly months, perhaps years.'

'But he's out of danger at least?' Barbara asked, seeing the anxiety in Dean's face and stepping in with a question calculated to prompt a positive response from the doctor.

'Yes. His condition is stable and improving,' Dr Mutambara confirmed. 'In fact, I've already authorised for him to be moved out of the ICU on to the main neurology ward.'

'Oh that's good!' Barbara looked at Dean again, smiling reassurance.

'As I said,' the doctor continued. 'I've assessed his condition. His speech is affected, but according to the nurses' notes, it appears to have been improving since he woke up on Saturday. I've arranged for a full assessment of both speech and swallowing by a Speech and Language Therapist later today. If his swallowing is OK then he can start taking food by mouth and we may be able to remove the nasogastric tube.'

'And if not?' Graham was still suspicious that they were being given a sanitised version of the true prognosis.

'Then we'll continuing tube feeding and reassess his swallowing in a few days.' The doctor held Graham in his gaze for a second and then looked across at Barbara before continuing. 'He has moderate to severe right-sided weakness. Again, this will probably improve over time, but he may be left with some permanent disability.'

'When you say *weakness*, what do you mean exactly?' Graham asked, his anxiety making him sound more aggressive than he intended. 'Are you saying he's paralysed down one side?'

'No, not exactly,' Dr Mutambara answered patiently. 'He has some movement, but not full control. From his point of view, his limbs feel heavy and some muscles don't respond at all. As I said, there will probably be improvement over time. Also, his whole body has suffered trauma. Some of the apparent weakness may be due to bruising and other damage locally.'

'So it's possible that he could eventually get back completely to normal?' Barbara asked, still trying to focus on the positive for Dean's benefit.

'It's possible,' Dr Mutambara agreed. 'But I would

sound a note of caution. While a full recovery is possible, it is also possible that he will be left with some residual disability – perhaps significant disability – and recovery will certainly be a lengthy process. However,' he looked round at them both again, 'you are doing the right thing talking about recovery. He will need your help to keep positive over the weeks and months ahead.'

'But you *do* think he may …? Is there anything we can do to help? Or …?' Dean's voice faltered to a halt as he struggled to express the mixture of relief and despair that he was feeling. Wayne was not going to die, but returning to the rugby field seemed unlikely and their hopes of becoming adoptive parents were fast disappearing.

The doctor looked towards him for the first time, as if he had not previously noticed that he was there.

'Dean is Wayne's husband,' Barbara explained.

'Yes. Of course.' With a conscious effort, the doctor made eye contact with Dean. 'It's going to be a long process, but I'm confident that there will be significant improvement in both his speech and motor function over the next few weeks. After that, with hard work and therapy, he may continue to make progress. It will require considerable effort from him and from those around him to maintain that progress, so anything you can do to keep him focussed and feeling positive will help.'

'Thank you,' Dean breathed, holding the doctor's gaze for a moment and then looking towards Barbara, who nodded and smiled.

***

Monica left the room and Jonah went in search of Andy Lepage and the video clips from the Science Park. He had them all ready to view with times and camera positions carefully documented. It did not take Jonah long to ascertain that, as Anna had indicated in her note, it did not appear that any of their known suspects had visited the

Science Park that day and none of the people caught on camera appeared to be acting suspiciously in any way.

'OK Andy,' Jonah said, rapidly becoming bored with this pointless exercise. 'I've got something much more promising for you to look into. Anna has uncovered a couple of guys expressing their views of gay men using somewhat colourful language in a pub in Blackbird Leys – not the one where Wayne was drinking, the other one on the corner of Cuddesdon Way and Watlington Road.'

'You mean the *Bullnose Morris*?' Andy queried.

'Yes. That's the one. Their names are Gordon Redfern and Robin Fry. I've got an address for Redfern. I want you to find out as much as you can about them. Even if they've got nothing to do with our case, they're worth keeping an eye on. According to Anna, they frightened one young lad half to death and nearly provoked a fight.'

'OK. I'll get on to that right away.' Andy got up to go, but Jonah called him back.

'Has the lab got back to you about that sample of paint from the van yet?'

'No. They don't work weekends – not unless it's an emergency. I rang them this morning and they said probably Wednesday. They've got a backlog.'

'Hmmph!' Jonah pulled a face. 'I suppose that will have to do. It probably won't tell us much anyway. It's bound to be just some bog standard spray paint that you can buy anywhere. Go on then – get cracking on Redfern and Fry.

CHAPTER 9: MONDAY AFTERNOON

Baby Donna was fractious after her midday feed. As Anna walked round the room with the infant's head resting on her shoulder, patting her rhythmically on the back, she pondered on the case. Had Alice really seen a face at the window of Ian Boulton's house? If so, who was it? Alice had been convinced that it was Mrs Boulton and that Mr Boulton was lying when he told them that she was out. But it could equally well have been a maid or a cleaning lady. They had not asked if anyone else lived in the house or if they had visitors staying or a cleaner who came in daily. What possible motive could Boulton have for pretending that his wife was out when she was not?

Donna continued to cry and to bang her head against Anna's shoulder. Anna decided to take her out for a walk, in the hope that the motion of the pram would send her off to sleep. She got the buggy out from the cupboard under the stairs and settled Donna into it. At once, the baby seemed to relax, as if relishing the prospect of an outing. Anna collected some essential items: a bottle of water, a spare nappy and wipes in case Donna needed changing, a teething ring and a few toys. She stuffed them hastily into the storage space at the back of the buggy, hurrying to get off before the novelty of wore off and Donna began to cry again.

Once out of the house, she set off at a brisk pace, walking with no particular aim in view, other than to keep Donna occupied with new sights and sounds until she dropped off to sleep. Without thinking about where she was going, she turned into the footpath that led through a tunnel beneath the by-pass. A few minutes later, she found herself standing by the bus stop opposite the *Blackbird*, staring down at bunches of flowers, which had appeared overnight, propped up against the end of the bus shelter where Wayne had fallen.

A car pulled up on the other side of the road and the driver wound the window down to speak to her.

'Hi there!' It was Peter Johns. What was he doing here? 'I'm taking the kids to the park. Shall we go together?'

'OK.' Anna hardly knew what to say. This was so completely unexpected.

'Hang on then. You wait here. I'll just park the car.'

Peter turned into the small road that ran down the side of the *Blackbird*. Anna crossed over and waited on the corner for him to return. It was not long before he was back, pushing a baby buggy, with a small boy trotting beside him. Anna recognised the dark skin and curly black hair of Peter's grandson Ricky. He seemed to have grown a lot since the last time she had seen him.

Peter stopped and stood looking round, estimating the distance from the corner of Cuddesdon Way to the bus stop, sizing up the space between the litterbin and the bus shelter, gazing along the road in the direction of the by-pass and noting that the view was blocked as it rose up to pass over the railway line. He turned to speak to Anna.

'As I said, I'm taking the kids to the park, but I have to confess that's just cover for having a look at the crime scene. Those flowers are where he hit his head, I assume?'

'Roughly,' Anna answered. 'As far as we can tell, he must've just stepped on to the pavement when the car hit him. Then it swerved back on to the road and its back end scraped against the bin. We should be able to establish for certain that we've got the right car once the guys in the forensics lab are back at work after the weekend. We've got paint from the car on the bin and paint from the bin on the car, which seems pretty conclusive to me. The big problem is proving who was actually driving the vehicle.'

'Come on grandad!' Ricky called out, pulling at Peter's arm. 'Want to go horsey!'

'Alright Ricky, we're going.' Peter turned the buggy and started walking down the road, past the pub to the corner of Blackbird Leys Road with Cuddesdon Way. Ricky tried to run on ahead, but he was constrained by the reins attached to a harness around his chest, which Peter held tightly in his left hand.

'The car came round from here – is that right?' Peter asked, as they skirted round the Church of the Holy Family, a modern grey-brick building standing on the corner, and viewed the road ahead.

'Well, we can't be sure,' Anna admitted, 'but that's our current hypothesis. 'All of the witnesses seem sure that it didn't come out of the road by the Windrush Tower, and I'm inclined to agree with them that it couldn't have got up so much speed if it had just turned that sharp corner. One of them was adamant that they'd *seen* it turning out of Cuddesdon Way, but I'm not convinced that the corner is really visible from back there; so I don't think we can be absolutely certain that it didn't come along the continuation of Blackbird Leys Road to the South of here. It wouldn't look that much different to someone standing outside the *Blackbird*.'

'But could they have been closer to the corner than that?' Peter queried. 'If they'd started walking home towards the estate and then came back to see what had happened after they heard the crash?'

'Yes, I suppose they might. I don't know that anyone asked them where they were when they saw it. Anyway,

Cuddesdon Way fits in with where we think the car came from. The owner claims that it was stolen from outside his house on Watlington Road.'

'Claims?'

'We have our doubts about that. He only reported it *after* the incident took place. And then there was the dog.'

'The dog?'

'By some sort of miracle, there was someone from the Dog Section in the area when they found the car abandoned on Cuddesdon Road – that's the road that goes east out of Horspath,' she added, seeing Peter about to ask another question. 'It's terribly confusing, I know, having a Cuddesdon Road *and* a Cuddesdon Way. Anyway, as I was saying, the dog tracked the driver from where they found the car, across the fields to the owner's house on Watlington Road.'

'So you're thinking that the owner was driving and he or she made up the story of the theft to shift the blame?'

'That's right. Alice is totally convinced that's what happened. I'm trying to keep an open mind, because it doesn't make a lot of sense a respectable businessman going on the rampage in a brand new, expensive car, whereas teen-age joy-riders ...'

'Yes,' agreed Peter. 'It's hard to see how anyone would be driving that fast unless they were just doing it for kicks – especially when they'd just come through that.' He pointed towards a narrowing of the road where traffic-calming measures were in place to make it safer for pedestrians crossing between the Children's Centre on the left and the entrance to the park on the right. If I owned an 18-reg BMW, I wouldn't be risking knocking its exhaust off going at ninety over those speed bumps!'

They turned in at the park and strolled along the path towards the children's playground.

'Unless, of course, Jonah's right and it was a deliberate attack,' Anna suggested. 'I don't suppose the witnesses would be able to swear that the car was already travelling at speed when it came round the corner. It could have speeded up when they saw their victim and decided to go for him.'

'You're not taking that idea seriously are you?' Peter laughed. 'That's just Jonah trying to get a slice of the action – and jumping to conclusions with even less evidence than usual. Mind you stand firm and don't allow him to take over! This is your case and he's got to learn to keep out of it.'

'I suppose it's understandable that he wants to find out who injured his friend.'

'Of course. But that only means that he's got a conflict of interests and needs to back off. Besides,' Peter added with a brief smile before becoming serious again, 'I would hate him to be right about that – and not just because I resent the way his hunches do seem to work out so often. I really don't want there to be someone out there who's got it in for Wayne and for all we can tell for Dean as well.'

'Yes,' Anna agreed. 'It doesn't bear thinking about, does it? I have to admit, my heart sank when Jonah told me about the spray paint on the van. It seemed just a bit too much of a coincidence. Oh well! I suppose I'll just have to wait and see what Monica and Alice come up with.' She sighed. 'I never thought that this part-time working would be so frustrating. I was just beginning to think I might be getting somewhere, when there I am having to wait for the best part of a week to see how it's going to pan out.'

'Are you still having no luck finding childcare?' Peter asked. 'My offer's still open if you change your mind about taking me up on it.'

'That's very kind of you, but you've got your hands full with these two,' Anna began.

'Which is exactly why it would be no bother for me to take on Donna as well,' Peter put in quickly. 'One more little one won't make much difference to me and it would mean you could up your hours a bit, and Jessica wouldn't have to give up all her weekends.'

'Jess has it in mind that she could take over completely during the summer holidays.' Anna sighed again. 'It worries me sometimes how seriously she's taking it all. Before Phil left, she never seemed interested in helping out at all, but ever since she knew that Donna was on the way she's been fussing around me like a mother hen.'

'Youngsters usually do rise to the occasion when they need to,' Peter observed. 'Look at the way Lucy insists on looking after Jonah.'

'But I'm determined not to allow it to take over her life,' Anna continued, refusing to be deflected. 'I've got Donna's name down for half a dozen nurseries. Something's bound to turn up soon – I hope! It makes me realise just how lucky I was having Phil staying at home to look after Jess and Marcus when they were little.'

Philip, Anna's estranged husband was an architect, who had combined working freelance from home with caring for their two children. Donna's unplanned arrival had come just as he was looking forward to relinquishing his childcare responsibilities and concentrating on developing his career.

'I think he was completely mad running out on you like that,' Peter said bluntly. He could not imagine any inducement that could possibly compensate for being separated from his own family.

'Well, he had put his career pretty much on hold for about fifteen years,' Anna pointed out, trying to be fair. 'So I suppose he thought it was my turn – and it's not as if we planned to have another baby.'

'That's not the point,' Peter insisted. 'What I'm saying is that I can't understand why he would want to run off to Devon like that. No job, however wonderful, can be important enough to be worth leaving your wife and kids for.'

'He was expecting the kids to go with him,' Anna told him. 'He thought they'd think of it as being like a permanent holiday, because they always used to have such a great time staying with their gran down there. I think it came as a shock to him when they both insisted on staying here with me. I have to admit it was a bit of a surprise for me too,' she added wryly.

'If he'd had any sense, he'd have changed his mind then,' Peter said decidedly, 'instead of pigheadedly going through with a plan that was coming completely unravelled like that.'

'I suppose he'd made commitments to his mum and his friend – the one who'd offered him a partnership in his business – and didn't like to back down. Anyway ...,' Anna sighed, 'we are where we are. I don't want Jess to think I'm not grateful, but I absolutely *must* find some proper childcare before September. I don't want it to affect her A' Level grades.'

'Well, like I said, the offer's still on the table.'

***

'I've got some info for you on Redfern and Fry,' Andy greeted Jonah when he returned from the lunchbreak, which Bernie had insisted he take. 'Would you like me to go through it with you?'

'Yes. Fire ahead.'

Andy flicked through his notebook, calculating the best place to begin.

'Gordon Redfern is forty-seven and married with one son. He lives in Horspath, but the house is up for sale at the moment. I think they're probably looking to downsize. He used to own a small construction company, which went bust after Carillion[10] collapsed, because it was a

---

[10] Carillion was a large UK company, which specialised in taking on government contracts for a wide range of outsourced services and construction projects, including building hospitals and maintaining prisons. It went into liquidation in January 2018.

subcontractor and was owed hundreds of thousands.'

'Hang on!' Bernie interrupted. 'Didn't Anna's notes say he lived in Blackbird Leys?'

'He grew up there,' Andy confirmed. 'And his mum still lives there, but his address is this big place in Horspath.'

'What's he doing now?' Jonah asked.

'Not a lot, as far as I can tell. Still licking his wounds, I think.' Andy consulted his notes. 'Fry used to work for Redfern. He's younger – only thirty-one, and he's got a reputation as a bit of a hothead. He's also got a criminal record.'

'What for?' Jonah asked sharply.

'Arson, assault and criminal damage.'

'Aimed at whom?'

'When he was fourteen, he set fire to his school. A couple of classrooms were gutted. That was while he was excluded following an incident in which he attacked one of the teachers with a knife. He spent some time in youth custody, which is where he did a course in bricklaying, which got him his job with Redfern's company. Or ...,' Andy paused to check his notes again. 'Yes. That's right. Fry's late father worked for Redfern and they were friends. I think his dad probably put pressure on him to learn bricklaying and then he wangled him a job with Redfern.'

'And the assault?' Jonah queried.

'Against his ex-girlfriend's new boyfriend – and he also set fire to their car while it was parked in the road outside their flat one night. She gave evidence that he was obsessed with fire, as well as being insanely jealous. There's evidence of him setting fire to various sheds and garages just for the hell of it, but those incidents were never followed up.'

'Not a pleasant person to have around,' Jonah observed drily. 'And yet, Redfern appears to relish his company, judging by the fact that they were drinking together on Friday night.'

'Going back to Redfern,' Andy continued, 'there's something that you may find interesting. Back in 2008, he led a protest trying to get a gay teacher removed from his son's primary school.'

'Yes, that *is* interesting,' Jonah agreed. 'And judging by his behaviour in the pub last Friday, he hasn't changed his opinions much over the last ten years. How old is the son now? Is he still living with his father?'

'That's something else that may be interesting. The son, Jack, died quite recently – on the 27th of May.'

'You mean, the week before the Pride march?'

'That's right. It's probably just a coincidence. I just thought you ought to know.'

'You're probably right, but check it out, will you? What did he die of? Was it sudden or expected? That sort of thing.'

***

'I'm Detective Sergeant Philipson,' Monica introduced herself to Barbara Major. 'I'm sorry to intrude, but now that your son has regained consciousness, I need to speak to him to see if he can remember anything that might help us to find out who was driving the car that hit him.'

'Can't it wait?' Dean asked from the other side of the bed. 'He's not up to it yet.'

'You must be Dean O'Brien,' Monica smiled across at him, 'Mr Major's partner. I do understand your concern, but we do need to know anything he can tell us about what happened, so that we can apprehend the person who did this. I'm sure you don't want them to get away with it.'

'I'm not honestly that bothered,' Dean shrugged. 'It won't help Wayne, will it?'

'Well, not exactly,' Monica was taken aback. She was more used to victims and their families making loud demands for justice and accusing the police of failing in their duty to catch the criminals responsible for whatever had befallen them. 'But it could stop this sort of thing happening to someone else.'

'What Dean's trying to say is that Wayne's speech has been affected by hitting his head,' Barbara intervened. 'The doctor says that it will improve, but it'll take time. Couldn't you come back in a few days?'

Monica hesitated. She did not want to cause distress to the family, but she was keen to make progress in the case. If Wayne were able to describe the driver of the car, she might even be able to have the culprit safely in custody before Anna returned on Saturday.

'I do understand,' she repeated, 'but I've spoken to his doctor and he said that it would be OK for me to try.'

'What … what …?' Wayne looked round at them with a puzzled expression. 'Who …?'

'This is a police officer,' Barbara explained gently.

'My name's Detective Sergeant Philipson,' Monica added, addressing Wayne, speaking slowly and carefully. 'I'd just like to ask you a few questions about what happened to you, if that's alright?'

'O-K,' Wayne nodded, speaking slowly and in a rather robotic way. Dean took hold of his left hand where it lay on top of the sheet and held it tight.

'You were hit by a car,' Monica said, still speaking slowly and distinctly and looking Wayne in the eyes. 'Do you remember that?'

'N-no.' Wayne turned his head and looked to Dean for reassurance. Dean gave a half-smile and squeezed his hand.

'Don't worry. It doesn't matter. Let's go back a bit then. You were with some friends in the *Blackbird*. Do you remember that?'

'The … blackbird?'

'Yes. It's a pub – on Blackbird Leys Road. You were having a drink with …,' Monica looked down at her notes, 'Simon and June Broadhurst and Gary Drinkwater.'

'Gary? … Yes.' Wayne seemed to be pondering on this name. Monica waited in silence to give him time to collect his thoughts. He creased his brow as if puzzling something out. Then his eyes opened wider and he looked round in agitation. 'The ... kids!'

'Yes?' Monica said encouragingly, but Wayne was floundering now, desperately trying to get out words that would not come. His agitation grew as he tried to convey the meaning that was so clear in his mind but which his voice was unable to express.

'The kids ... rugby,' he got out at last. 'What ... about ...?

'It's OK,' Dean cut in, anxious to alleviate Wayne's evident distress. 'Gary's got that all sorted. They've got some more guys from the club who're going to help out until you're ready.'

'He's worrying about the rugby training sessions that they were planning to put on for the local kids,' Barbara explained. 'That's what they were talking about in the pub on Friday night.'

'That's good,' Monica encouraged Wayne. 'You were in the pub last Friday, talking about the rugby training, and then you went out to get the bus. Do you remember crossing the road?'

'Friday?' Wayne looked round again, apparently appealing to Dean for information.

'Yes.' Dean understood, by some sort of intuition, what was bothering him. 'It's Monday now. You were out cold for a couple of days.'

'But ...,' Wayne lay back on the pillows, deep in thought. 'But ... Saturday? The ... boys?'

'Your dad went to see them – to explain.'

'Don't worry,' Barbara added. 'Of course they were disappointed, but there'll be other times.'

'Getting back to Friday night,' Monica intervened. 'Can you remember what happened after you came out of the pub?'

'Carl ...,' Wayne continued to struggle to find the words that he needed. 'Carl ...'

'Yes?' Monica prompted, hoping that this new name would turn out to provide an important new lead. 'You saw Carl? Is that it?'

'No!' Wayne shook his head vigorously.

'It's OK,' Dean assured him, flashing an angry look at Monica across the bed. 'Like Barbara said, your dad explained why we didn't go on Saturday.'

'Not ... Saturday ...,' Wayne trailed off unable to formulate the message that he wanted to convey into speech.

'You mean Friday?' Monica suggested, still hopeful that this was new evidence about to be revealed.

'Wen ... Wen ... Wednesday,' Wayne got out with a supreme effort. 'Carl ... Carl's ...,'

'Carl's birthday!' Dean exclaimed, torn between triumph at having finally understood and guilt at not having remembered this important occasion sooner. 'I'd forgotten – what with you getting yourself in this mess and everything,' he continued, trying to make light of the situation. 'Don't worry. We'll see that he gets his present. Maybe by then they'll even let him come and see you.'

'Well, perhaps not quite that soon,' Barbara cautioned, mindful of the effect that seeing her son in his current state might have on a child of seven. 'We'll have to see how things go.'

'But getting back to Friday,' Monica persisted. 'Did you see the car coming – before it hit you, I mean?'

'Car?' Wayne looked at her as if he hardly recognised the word.

'You were hit by a car,' Monica reminded him. 'You crossed over the road to get to the bus stop and a car came round the corner and knocked you down.'

'A car?' Wayne repeated, shaking his head. He looked round in confusion at Dean and Barbara.

'Yes. Do you remember anything about it?'

'You can see that he doesn't!' Dean exploded in an uncharacteristic burst of anger. 'Why can't you just go away and let him be?'

'I think that would be the best thing,' Barbara backed him up, speaking calmly but firmly.

'Yes. Alright,' Monica agreed, abashed. 'I'm sorry to have …Well, thank you for talking to me, anyway. Maybe in a few days …?'

***

'Horsey!' Ricky shouted, tugging to get away as the playground came into view. Peter looked round, checking for any hazards, and then bent down and unclipped the reins from Ricky's harness.

'OK Ricky,' he said. 'You can go and find the horsey, but go straight there; don't go running off now.'

The little boy set off happily across the grass, stumbling in his haste and then righting himself and running on. Peter and Anna followed with the buggies. The outer play area was deserted – the older children, for whom this was designed, were all in school – but there were several pre-school children in the inner playground, which was separated from the rest of the park by a metal fence.

Ricky reached the fence and stood holding on to it with both hands, looking in. When Peter came up behind him, he turned and looked up at his grandfather.

'Horsey!' he said in a tone of deep disapproval, pushing his hand through the railings to point at a small white-painted horse with a black mane and a bright red saddle. A small girl in a pink tee shirt and electric blue leggings was sitting on it, rocking vigorously back and forth.

'That's right,' Peter agreed. 'There's the horse. I expect that little girl will have finished her ride soon and then you can have a go.'

'Want my go now!' Ricky complained. 'Tell her to get off.'

'No. I can't do that. You've got to learn to share. The horse is for everybody, not just you.'

Peter opened the gate and allowed Ricky to go through before following with the buggy. He pushed it to a corner of the playground out of the way and put the brake on. Then he bent down to undo the harness that fastened baby Abigail safely into it.

'Hello Peter! I haven't seen you here before.'

He looked up to see Stella Gilbert, Leroy's younger sister, smiling down on him.

'Young Ricky here is a great fan of the horse,' he explained. 'There's nothing quite the same in the park near where we live.'

'He'd better have a ride then,' Stella replied, turning her head to call across to the girl in the pink tee shirt. 'Budge up, Izzie! Ricky here wants to come on too.'

Then, re-directing her smile towards Peter's grandson, she bent down and held out her arms, intending to pick him up and lift him on to the horse. 'Come along young man, there's room for two!'

Ricky shrank back against his grandfather's legs, unsure of this stranger who seemed to be addressing him.

'It's alright Ricky,' Peter told him. 'This is Stella. She's a friend of mine. She won't bite!' He turned towards Anna. 'Anna, I think you interviewed Stella's brother, Leroy the other day. Stella – DI Anna Davenport, who used to be one of my sergeants back in the day.'

Anna and Stella exchanged polite greetings while Peter lifted his granddaughter out of the buggy and set her down next to Ricky. Fourteen-month-old Abigail had not been walking for long. She took a step, wobbled and grabbed her brother's arm to steady herself. They made an odd pair, her bright ginger hair and pale face contrasting markedly with his tight black curls and brown skin. It had been a surprise to everyone to discover that Abigail had inherited her grandfather's colouration, which was so different from that of both her parents.

'You must be Abigail,' Stella said, 'I've heard a lot about you.'

Abigail looked up and smiled, displaying none of the suspicion of unfamiliar faces that her brother had shown. She was used to complete strangers coming up to them in the street and commenting on her hair and skin.

Urged on by his grandfather, Ricky allowed Stella to lift him on to the horse in front of Isabelle, who obligingly slowed down briefly while her aunt settled him securely in the saddle. Then a moment later, they were off again, rocking wildly and imagining that they were galloping across the countryside.

'Stella here has ambitions to be a police officer,' Peter told Anna as the three adults stood watching the children enjoying their ride. Peter held Abigail in his arms while Anna stood with her hands on Donna's buggy, watching for signs that she might be waking up. 'In fact, she's been a cadet for a few years now. She's just waiting for her A' level results to decide whether to do a degree first.'

'I wouldn't want to put you off applying right away,' Anna said seriously, 'but I'd say getting a degree is a good idea, so you have something else to fall back on if things don't work out.'

'People keep saying that,' Stella sighed, 'but nine thousand a year is such a lot of money!'

'You don't have to pay up-front,' Anna reminded her. 'You can get a student loan and then you only start paying back when you're earning more than whatever the minimum amount is by the time you graduate.'

'Yes, I know, but no one in my family has even had a mortgage before, and it seems a lot to take on when I know what I want to do anyway. I've got my interview next week. If I get offered a place I'll take it, but I'm afraid they'll think I'm too young or they'll want me to do the CKP first.'

'CKP?' Anna asked, not recognising this acronym.

'Certificate in Knowledge of Policing,' Peter explained. 'Thames Valley has a policy now that all recruits have to have done it. But I'm sure you'll be OK,' he added to

Stella. 'Everyone knows how keen you are, and there'll be plenty of time for you to do the course after you start work.'

'I do hope so. I want to have a proper job. I feel like I've been sponging off my gran these last two years. I've done a bit of bar work and then I've been helping out with Izzie and Serena, but …,' she tailed off as she looked across at her small niece who was still riding furiously over the prairies in her imagination.

'I think you've done plenty for your family,' Peter told her firmly. 'And if you don't get offered a training place with Thames Valley, I'll go round and have it out with the Chief Constable personally!'

'Granddad!' Ricky wailed suddenly. 'Want to get off!'

'Poor kid,' Stella said, stepping forward to speak to Isabelle, who, rather reluctantly, slowed down and allowed Stella to lift Ricky off and set him down next to Peter. She looked at her watch. 'It's time to go now, anyway,' she told Isabelle. 'Serena will be out of school soon and we'd better be there to meet her.'

Isabelle pulled a face, but consented to get off the horse. Stella took her firmly by the hand. 'Say bye-bye to Ricky now!' she instructed.

'Bye-bye Ricky,' Isabelle repeated obediently, raising her hand and waving regally towards him.

'Bye-bye,' Ricky replied, giving a quick glance in Isabelle's direction before turning away and racing off towards the slide.

Stella led Isabelle towards the gate. Then she stopped and turned back. 'I forgot to ask: how's he doing? The man who got knocked down, I mean?'

'Conscious and out of danger,' Peter told her, 'but …,' he paused, unsure how much more to divulge. 'We don't know yet if there'll be any permanent damage.'

'Oh. … Well, I hope he gets better.' Stella opened the gate and left the playground. Peter, turning back to Anna saw that she was engaged in lifting Donna out of her buggy. The baby was now awake and looking round excitedly at the novel sights and sounds that met her eyes and ears. Abigail was standing next to them, steadying herself with a hand on the side of the buggy, staring down at the baby. Then, without warning, she turned and toddled off towards the slide in search of her brother.

'Abbie's walking very well now,' Anna said to Peter, reflecting silently that it would be a long time – if ever – before Donna would be able to achieve such a feat.

'Yes,' Peter agreed, hurrying after his granddaughter. 'She's got a very determined streak has our Abbie – and she expects to be able to do anything Ricky can do. I suppose it's not surprising, with them being so close in age and girls growing up quicker.'

'Stella seems a nice girl,' Anna murmured a few minutes later, catching Donna at the bottom of the slide for the fifth or sixth time. 'I should think she'll make a good officer.'

'Yes. I'm sure of it,' Peter agreed. 'She's just the sort we need more of. Apart from anything else, we don't have enough officers from ethnic minorities. She's had a tough life. Her mum "didn't have much luck with men", as her mother put it, and Stella spent most of her childhood with her gran. Leroy's her half-brother – same mum different fathers – and she's got a younger half-brother too. Leroy was a real tearaway when he was younger, but he's settled down now. It'll be a real travesty if Stella's application is turned down.'

'But you can see the argument for an all-graduate police service, can't you?' Anna countered. 'Especially now that such a large proportion of eighteen-year-olds go to university.'

'Of course, I'm biased,' Peter admitted with a smile, 'seeing as I never got a degree – neither did Jonah, and you can't say he's not bright enough! But then there are people like Gav Hughes. There's no way he'd ever have even got A' levels, but look at what he's achieved with the homeless people around Oxford! And all off his own bat too. And I can't think of any officer as reliable as him.'

'I suppose so.' A Cambridge graduate herself, Anna often struggled to relate to old-school coppers such as PC Hughes. 'But these days, don't you think people like Gavin would be better as Community Support Officers[11]?'

'Maybe you're right.' Peter paused in thought. 'But that doesn't alter the fact that there's something wrong with a system that deters people like Stella from applying. Nobody disputes her brains or her ability, so why put up barriers that make her think it's not for the likes of her?'

---

[11] A Police Community Support Officer (PCSO) is a uniformed civilian member of police support staff in England and Wales. The role was created in 2002.

CHAPTER 10: TUESDAY

Jonah called Monica into his private office the moment he arrived at work the following morning.

'I've received a complaint from Wayne Major's father,' he told her. 'He says that your questioning of his son in the hospital yesterday was insensitive.'

'But he wasn't even there!' Monica protested, without thinking. Then, seeing Jonah's implacable expression, she toned down her indignation. 'I'm sorry, sir. I'm afraid I misjudged it. The doctor said that he was conscious and communicating and I thought it would be a good idea to ask him what he could remember.'

'Which I gather was nothing at all – as anyone with an ounce of sense would have known.'

'Yes sir, but-'

'And then, even after it must have become apparent, even to you, that he could tell you nothing, you persisted in questioning him,' Jonah interrupted, unprepared to listen to any excuse, 'causing distress not only to Wayne but also to his family. This just isn't good enough. You're supposed to be an experienced police officer. I've seen probationers showing more sensitivity and insight!'

'I'm sorry sir.' Monica wisely opted for abject humility.

'I should've waited. I realise that now.'

'Yes, well ...,' Jonah muttered, unreasonably annoyed at her capitulation when he had not yet exhausted the store of cutting remarks that he had composed in his head during his journey to work. 'Go back to your desk and write an apology to the family and you can take it round to them in person after work this evening.'

'At the hospital?'

'No – at home. Your presence on the ward might upset the patient.'

'Yes sir.'

'And don't just stick the note through the door either – see that you tell them you're sorry personally.'

'Yes sir.'

'Your behaviour reflects badly on the whole police service. It just isn't good enough.'

'No sir.'

'Now get out of my sight, and send in Lepage. I want an update on the two guys he's been looking into.'

Monica hurried out, almost colliding with Andy, who was standing outside the office with his hand raised, about to knock on the door.

'Go on in,' she said to him with a wry smile. 'He's all yours.'

Andy slipped inside and closed the door behind him.

'I've found something rather interesting,' he said excitedly, sitting down without waiting to be asked. He knew that Jonah found it a strain having to crane his neck to speak to colleagues who insisted on standing over him. 'Ian Boulton – the guy who reported the car stolen – is a friend of Gordon Redfern!'

'Really?' Jonah's eyes lit up. 'You're right. That *is* interesting.'

'And what's even more interesting,' Andy continued, 'is that Ian Boulton was a signatory to the letter that Redfern wrote asking for a gay primary school teacher to be dismissed. It seems that they both had kids at the school and they both objected to the idea of their kids being taught by a gay teacher.'

'Where are the notes Anna took of her interview with the bar man at the *Bullnose Morris*?' Bernie asked suddenly. 'Didn't he say something about someone called Ian being there with Redfern and Fry?'

'I don't remember that,' Jonah said sceptically, 'but we'd better check.'

For several minutes, they all waited in silence as he scrolled through pages of notes on his computer screen.

'No ... no ... nothing here ... unless ...,' he murmured, opening a different file and resuming his search. 'Here it is!' he declared triumphantly at last. 'It wasn't the bartender it was one of the boys from the estate. Callum Lee said that there was a man called Ian sitting with Redfern and Fry.'

'What's the betting that was Boulton?' Bernie cried eagerly.

'It would make sense,' Andy agreed, more cautiously. 'It is his local. But it would mean that he was lying when he said he'd been at home all evening.'

'Which would explain why he didn't want Anna to speak to his wife,' Jonah put in. 'We were wondering about that – assuming Alice's hunch that she was there when they called is right.'

'So, what are we saying really happened?' Bernie asked. 'Boulton was drinking with his friends in the *Bullnose* all evening, and then he got in his car and went on the rampage? Why would he do that?'

'It could be as simple as having had too much to drink,' Jonah suggested. 'Or maybe there was more to the row with those kids than anyone's telling us. Maybe he got in his car to go after them for some reason.'

'Yes,' agreed Bernie. 'It always seemed a bit queer to me the way the men were the ones shouting abuse, but it was the kids who were chucked out.'

'I thought the bar-tender was probably taking the easy

option,' Andy said. 'Or else the men were good customers that he didn't want to upset.'

'But say the boys did give as good as they got – or more,' Jonah persisted. 'Boulton could have been angry enough – especially if he'd had a few – to go after them. That would explain him heading off into the estate, instead of going home.'

'And it might also explain his erratic driving,' Bernie added.

'But equally well,' Andy argued, 'if the boys had a set-to with Boulton and got chucked out because of it, they could've gone up to his house with the idea of getting their own back by causing some sort of damage.'

'And they found the car on the drive with the key in the ignition,' Jonah continued, 'and decided to take it for a spin.'

'Which would mean that the only thing Boulton was lying about was going for a few pints with his friends that evening,' Bernie finished.

'Hmmm,' Jonah frowned in thought. 'It looks as if we could do with speaking to *Mrs* Boulton,' he murmured. 'Although, by now, her husband will probably have got her briefed to back up his story. Maybe we'd do better talking to people from the *Bullnose Morris* to see if anyone remembers him being there on Friday night.'

'I suppose that's for Sergeant Philipson to decide, isn't it sir?' Andy suggested nervously. 'I mean, she's leading on the hit-and-run.'

'Yes,' Jonah sighed. 'You're right. We ought to be concentrating on establishing whether we really do have some sort of anti-gay conspiracy going on – maybe with Redfern, Fry and Boulton as the ringleaders – or just some random incidents that just coincidentally appear to be linked. Have you got any more info on how Redfern's son died?'

'No – or at least not anything official. There's a newspaper report saying it was suicide, but I'm not sure how accurate that is. I've put in a request for the coroner's report, but it hasn't come through yet. The inquest was only concluded last week.'

'OK. Let me know when you've got it. How old was this son when he died?'

'Twenty. He was doing a business studies degree at Oxford Brookes[12] and was still living at home.'

'And when was this letter sent about the teacher at his primary school?'

Andy consulted his notes. '2008 – October 2008.'

'When the boy was about ten. And Boulton had kids at the school too. That means they must be teenagers or at most twenty-one now. You'd have thought *they* would be still living with their parents too, wouldn't you?'

'Are you suggesting that could explain the face at the window?' Bernie asked. 'Rather than it being Boulton's wife?'

'It would fit, wouldn't it?' Jonah replied. 'And that would mean that Boulton doesn't need to have been lying. He may just have wanted to keep his kids out of the police investigation.'

'Or just not have thought they were relevant to it,' Andy suggested.

'Yes.' Jonah thought for a moment or two. 'You'd better pass that idea on to Monica – or Alice – but then I want you to find out more about Ian Boulton and his family. In particular, try to get to the bottom of that business with the primary school. How many children did Boulton have there and in what years? Were there ever any actual allegations of misconduct against the teacher or was it purely a matter of principle with Boulton and Redfern that they didn't want their kids taught by a gay man? And

---

[12] Oxford Brookes University is one of the so-called "new universities" created in 1992 by the Further and Higher Education Act, by which many polytechnics were awarded university status.

do we know the name of the man – presumably that will have been in the letter?'

'All the stuff I've managed to find so far has been redacted to protect his identity,' Andy told him. 'But I'll get on to it and find out. It shouldn't be hard.'

'The other thing that could be related to this, is Ian Lane's taxi firm,' Jonah went on. 'You remember he got a threatening note pushed through his door that seemed to be objecting to his company providing school transport? Find out if that includes any children from that primary school – or if Ian Boulton still has kids at school who could somehow be affected.'

***

'Hello,' Crystal said nervously, looking down at Wayne. Curious to know how he was faring, determined to try to understand her in-laws' views on his sexuality, and anxious that she might herself have been exhibiting prejudice, she had taken some time during her lunch hour to visit him on the ward. 'I'm Crystal Johns,' she added in response to his puzzled look. 'I'm married to Peter's son, Eddie. I work here. I came to see how you're doing.'

Wayne smiled and nodded. He opened his mouth to reply, but it was several seconds before he managed to formulate the monosyllable, 'Hi!'

Crystal smiled back, struggling to think of anything further to say. She had taken the precaution of asking the charge nurse on the ward for information about Wayne's condition and had been told that, as far as they could tell, his cognition was unaffected by the head injury, but that his speech was still very slow and laboured. Encouraging him to converse would be the best way to help this to improve, but what could they speak about? On the face of it, they had nothing in common.

'I've seen some of the things you made for Jonah,' she said eventually. 'You must be very clever to think of them all.'

Wayne smiled again, but did not attempt to speak. Crystal ran through in her mind all the topics that she usually brought up when making conversation with her patients. Mostly these revolved around home and family. None of them seemed appropriate here.

'Peter told me you were thinking of starting up a club for boys to keep them off the streets in the school holidays,' she ventured at last. 'I think that's a splendid idea.'

'Rugby,' Wayne nodded. 'Teach … them … teach … be a … team.'

'You want to teach them how to play as a team?'

'Yes.' Wayne smiled. 'Important … life skill.'

'Indeed it is!' Crystal agreed with a feeling of relief at having found some common ground. 'That's one of the first things I say to the student nurses when they come on the ward: we've got to all work together as a team.'

Time passed more quickly than she had expected and it did not seem long before a nurse approached to tell them that it was time for afternoon visiting. Crystal got up to go, smiling and saying a few words to Wayne as she did so.

Turning, she saw three figures on their way in. The tall, burly man in the front must be Wayne's father. The family resemblance was unmistakable. He was followed closely by a middle-aged woman, quite small – but perhaps that was only by comparison with her husband – with blond hair and soft blue eyes. That must be his mother. And the young man with the thick fringe and anxious brown eyes must be his partner, she supposed. He looked quite ordinary – but then, what had she expected?

'This – is …,' Wayne began, looking first towards Crystal and then towards his parents and Dean. He appeared to be struggling to locate the right words. 'Peter's … Peter's …,' he tailed off, unable to remember Crystal's name or to find words to describe who she was. Seeing that this was making him anxious, Crystal came to his rescue.

'I'm Crystal Johns,' she explained. 'Peter Johns is my father-in-law. I work here, so I just popped in to see Wayne while I was on my lunchbreak.'

'That was kind of you,' Barbara smiled.

'We've been talking about his plans for the boys,' Crystal went on. 'It all sounds very exciting.'

'It is,' Dean agreed, his eyes lighting up. He sat down beside the bed and took Wayne's hand in his. 'I've got some good news about the boys. I've been speaking to their case worker and she says not to worry. This is going to slow things down a bit, but once you're better, we can just pick up where we left off.'

'They were so worried that the adoption would be stopped,' Barbara explained to Crystal in a low voice, seeing her puzzled expression at the mention of case workers and correctly suspecting that they might have been talking at cross-purposes. 'They've invested so much in Harry and Carl. It would have been heart-breaking if this accident prevented them from taking them in. I just hope …' she turned and looked at the two young men, now with their heads close together, deep in conversation. 'I hope it doesn't all end in disappointment after all. I'm not sure that the case worker knows just how serious Wayne's head injury is.'

***

'I've got the forensics report on the car,' Monica told Jonah the moment he entered the room that afternoon. She was keen to redeem herself after the débâcle with Wayne and his family. 'Shall I take you through it?'

'Anything interesting in it?'

'Mostly confirmation of what we already thought. The silver paint on the litterbin came from the car and the black paint on the car came from the litterbin. So that confirms it's the right car.' Monica looked down at her notes. 'They've got fingerprints from the steering wheel, driver's door and rear-view mirror. I'm going to go over later and get prints off Boulton and his wife for elimination purposes. After that, we can run them through the database. We've got prints on file from almost all those kids that Anna interviewed over the weekend because of crimes they've been arrested for in the last couple of years, so …'

'So, if it's one of them who took the car, there's a good chance we'll be able to identify them,' Jonah finished for her. 'But if Ian Boulton was driving, there won't be any evidence, because his prints would be all over the interior of the car anyway.'

'There were some footwear prints in the field,' Monica said hopefully. 'We can try to match them with Boulton. The trouble is, in the dark, they all got a bit mixed up with the uniformed officers' prints. I doubt there'll be anything clear enough. If we had enough evidence for a search warrant, we might be able to find mud from the field on Boulton's shoes, but …'

'That wouldn't wash. He could always say it got there some other time – when he was walking the dog, for example,' Jonah cut in.

'Yes sir.' Monica got the feeling that the inspector was still annoyed with her and not inclined to give credence to any of her ideas. 'There was just one thing they found in the car, which *may* help. They've retrieved a human hair from the driver's head restraint. It's too long to be Boulton's – he's got his head shaved – but it could belong to one of the joy-riders.'

'Or to Mrs Boulton,' Jonah commented drily.

'Maybe. Anyway, they reckon there's a good chance it's got enough of the root attached that it may be possible to extract DNA from it. I've asked them to go ahead. I hope that's OK?' Monica added, suddenly remembering that laboratory tests cost money and thinking that perhaps she ought to have checked with a more senior officer before committing scarce resources to what might easily turn out to be a futile exercise.

'Yes.' Jonah looked up at her and smiled, recognising in the younger officer the same traits of impatience and enthusiasm for the chase that drove his own work. 'That's looking like the only likely prospect for pinning down who the driver may have been. We can't afford not to check it out.'

***

'I called in on Peter's friend at lunch time,' Crystal told Eddie that evening, after the children were both in bed. 'That young boy who was knocked down by the car, I mean.'

'How is he?'

'Not good. It's still early days, but the nurses on the ward think there's most likely going to be permanent disability. I think his mum realises that. I'm not so sure about his dad and his … partner.' The slight hesitation before this final word betrayed her continuing uneasiness with the concept of two men being married.

'I suppose they'll want to keep his spirits up by talking as if everything's going to be alright,' Eddie suggested. 'I know that's what I'd do.'

'Yes. I suppose I did too,' Crystal agreed. 'And I *have* seen patients recover better than anyone ever thought possible, when they're determined that they will.'

They sat in silence. Then Crystal plucked up courage to broach a subject that had been worrying her all afternoon.

'Did you know they were planning to adopt?' she asked tentatively.

'Adopt?' Eddie looked at her in surprise. 'A baby you mean?'

'No. Two brothers. It sounded as if it was all arranged, but I can't really believe … Do they really do that here? I thought only married couples would be eligible.'

'No. I do know that gay couples can apply – and single people too. I remember there was a fuss a few years back about some adoption agencies who had a policy of *not* accepting them. I think they had to change their rules or else close down.'

'It doesn't seem right to me.' Crystal continued to struggle with the alien concept of a family with two fathers and no mother. 'I mean – it's not natural, is it?'

'I suppose if there's nobody else who'll take them in …,' Eddie began.

'And it was all so strange.' Crystal pictured in her mind the scene around Wayne's hospital bed. 'The young man's parents both seemed to think it was … *normal*, I suppose. And his mum kept referring to the other one – Dean – as Wayne's husband, which seemed so odd.'

'She was probably trying to make you see that there isn't any difference,' Eddie suggested. 'That's what Dad seems to think – and Bernie and the others.'

'Yes. And in a way I can sort of see that,' Crystal said slowly. 'Seeing them together, it was like brothers. They seemed very close, but … but … even if it isn't doing any harm … even if … well, it can't be right to have children being brought up with it like that, can it?'

CHAPTER 11: WEDNESDAY MORNING

Jonah arrived at work with plans in his mind for interviewing the victims of the sequence of homophobic attacks to find out whether they had ever had any dealings with Redfern, Fry or Boulton. However, all plans had to be shelved when the custody sergeant informed him that she had Tanya Lumley and Craig Jones in the cells. They had been arrested the previous night when caught red-handed spraying graffiti on the wall of Antonio's Hairdressing Salon. This was excellent progress and potentially meant that the case would soon be closed. Jonah decided to interview them at once.

Jones was an unattractive individual with greasy black hair, a large beer belly and plump, tobacco-stained fingers. His eyes were bloodshot and there were traces of dried vomit on the tee shirt that he wore over grimy combat trousers. Jonah assessed him as being in his early to mid-forties and suffering from a severe hangover.

He had no choice but to admit to having sprayed obscenities across the front of the hair salon, since PC Ben Timpson had apprehended him in the act. He vigorously denied, however, any suggestion that he might be involved in any more systematic targeting of gay-owned businesses. He was also adamant that he had not made death threats either against the proprietor of the hairdresser's or anyone else.

'Look,' he said, leaning forward across the table to emphasise his point, 'So I painted a few home-truths on that paedo's window. OK. I admit it. I'll pay my fine or whatever, but why d'you have to keep on at me about all this other crap?'

DC Joshua Pitchfork, who was assisting Jonah with the interrogation, sat back further in his chair to avoid the stench of their suspect's breath. He stared across the table at him with a look of contempt, and had to make a conscious effort to continue the questioning in a measured tone.

'This isn't the first time that this business has been targeted,' he told Jones for the third or fourth time. 'And the paint you were carrying when PC Timpson arrested you last night is the same as was used on several other premises.'

'As was the colourful turn of phrase,' Jonah added. 'So, I must ask you again to account for your movements on each of those earlier dates.'

He looked towards Pitchfork who hastily thumbed through his notes.

'Let's start with Friday 22nd June,' he said, naming the date when graffiti had appeared on the premises of Ian Lane's private hire firm. 'Where were you between ten in the evening and seven the following morning?'

'I dunno, do I? Tucked up in bed most of the time. I tell you – you've got nothing on me – 'cept the paedo's window.'

'Why do you keep talking about "paedos"?' Jonah asked sharply. 'Who're you talking about?'

'That Antonio of course! Who d'you think?'

'You mean Marcus Antonio, the owner of the hairdressing salon?'

'Yeah. Who else?'

'But what makes you say that he's a paedophile?' Jonah pressed him.

'Everyone knows,' Jones shrugged.

'I don't. He doesn't have any convictions.'

'That's 'cos you lot are too busy running round arresting me and Tanya for calling people like that out, instead of getting his sort banged up.'

'Do you have any evidence for that accusation?' Pitchfork asked.

'Evidence that cops are soft on paedos you mean?'

'No.' Jonah said firmly. 'Evidence that Marcus Antonio has ever abused children.'

'Everyone knows,' Jones repeated. Then, after a short pause, 'He hangs around places picking up young boys.'

'You mean he has sex with under-age boys?' Pitchfork asked. 'Do you have any proof of that?'

'One of my mates told me his son went with him.'

'Does he have a name, this mate of yours?' Jonah asked.

'No comment,' Jones muttered. Jonah sensed that he had already said more than he had intended and was now determined not to reveal anything more.

Sure enough, although they continued the interview for half an hour more, their questions elicited nothing more than further sulky repetitions of "no comment". In the end, Jonah gave up and sent Jones back to his cell to wait while they questioned his girlfriend and accomplice, Tanya Lumley.

It did not take Jonah long to conclude that Tanya was the brains of the outfit. She had clearly sized up their situation and concluded that it would be to her advantage to appear contrite about their offence and keen to help the police with their further enquiries. She apologised for the damage that they – or rather, Jones – had caused to the salon and offered to pay for the removal of the paint. She explained his behaviour by telling them that he had consumed an unusually large amount of alcohol that evening, it being his birthday.

When Jonah asked her why they had targeted the hairdresser, she explained that Jones had recently heard about the death of some young man – no she did not know his name or the circumstances of his death – whose father was a friend of his. He – the father – blamed Antonio. No, she did not know why exactly, except that it was to do with Antonio being a predatory paedophile, so they could draw their own conclusions.

At the end of the interview, Jonah was left feeling distinctly dissatisfied. While there was every chance that Jones and Lumley had been responsible for most, if not all, of the homophobic attacks, it was impossible to charge them with anything more than the spray paint incident of the previous night. Gathering evidence against them for any of the earlier offences would be time-consuming and might prove impossible. Then there was this new accusation against hairdresser Mark Brown, AKA Marcus Antonio. Almost certainly, there was nothing in it, but could he afford to ignore it completely? He sent Lumley back to the cells with every intention of letting them both go with a police caution[13].

'Sir!' Andy Lepage accosted him as he came out of the interview room. 'I've found out something you ought to know. There's a link between those two that Ben brought in last night and Redfern and Fry – and Boulton too!'

Jonah's face brightened up and he immediately changed his mind about releasing Jones and Lumley.

'Come up to my office and tell me about it.'

---

[13] A *caution* is a formal warning given by the police to an offender who admits to having committed a minor crime. If they refuse to accept the caution, they can be prosecuted. Although a caution is not a conviction, it does contribute to a person's criminal record and may debar them from certain employment.

***

'You told me to find out everything I could about Redfern and Fry,' Andy began, when they were settled in Jonah's office with cups of tea, brewed by Bernie. 'I discovered that Redfern is one of the admins of a Facebook group called "Protect our Kids". It's ostensibly for parents who are worried about their children being preyed on by paedophiles, but some of the stuff they post makes them seem more like vigilantes.'

'What sort of stuff?' Jonah demanded.

'Veiled threats – and some not so veiled – *We know where you live!* That sort of thing. Looking back, one or two of the threats could have been referring to the attacks on Antonio's hairdresser's place and that private hire company. The posts are dated the same days as the attacks happened.'

'Before or after?' Jonah asked. 'I mean, were they predicting them or merely commenting on them after the event?'

'Before. That's the thing. And there's something that Fry's put up only this morning, which I think maybe we ought to do something about.'

'Oh?'

'He's named one of the gay-friendly nightclubs in a post that hints that he's planning some sort of attack on it tonight. Nothing definite, but something about the punters getting a *big surprise* tonight. Oh! And he illustrated the post with a link to a report of that school fire that he started back in ninety-one, including a photo of the burning building. And with Fry's history of arson and assault …'

'Hmmm,' Jonah pursed his lips in thought. 'It's probably nothing, but I agree we can't afford to take chances. We'd better organise a bit of extra police presence around the club tonight. But you haven't told me yet what all this has got to do with that pair down in the cells. Should I let them go or not?'

'I was coming to that sir. They're both members of the group too, and Jones is another of the administrators. Ian Boulton is a member as well. It's as though this is linking all of our chief suspects together.'

'Yes, but that doesn't necessarily mean that they're working as a group,' Bernie pointed out. 'Most likely, it's only one or two them who are actually doing anything. The others may be egging them on without knowing that it's not just all talk.'

'Yes,' agreed Jonah. 'We still don't have any evidence against any of them apart from Jones and Lumley – and even then only for this latest lot of graffiti. However,' he went on, smiling grimly, 'this does give us an excuse for keeping hold of Lumley and Jones for a bit longer so that we can talk to them again. I think we'll leave them in the cells for a few hours to give them a chance to worry about how much we've got on them and to work out that it would be better to come clean, and then I'll interview them again.'

There was a knock at the door. It was Monica Philipson with an update on the hit-and-run. Jonah dismissed Andy with instructions to carry on digging into the life-histories of Redfern, Fry and Boulton. Then he turned to Monica, treating her to a lop-sided smile intended to reassure her that her over-zealous questioning of Wayne the previous day was not being held against her.

'What can I do for you?' he enquired mildly.

'I thought you'd want to know that it looks as if the hit-and-run probably *was* joy-riders after all,' she told him. 'The lab has found forensic evidence to link both Jason Paul and Ethan Roberts to the car.'

'Oh?' Jonah asked. 'Come in and sit down and take me through it.'

Monica closed the door behind her and sat down in the seat recently vacated by Andy Lepage.

'You remember they'd found a hair on the driver's head-rest? Well, they reckon it came from Jason Paul. His

DNA is on file after he was arrested for burglary a couple of months back. There was insufficient evidence to charge him, but the sample hasn't been destroyed yet.'

'So it looks as if this Jason Paul could have been driving,' Jonah cut in eagerly. 'He's one of the group of lads who were ejected from the Bullnose Morris, is that right? What does *he* say he did after they left the pub?'

'We haven't managed to interview him yet. He wasn't at home when Anna went round, and nobody seemed to know where he'd got to. There was nothing other than his past form to link him to the incident, so we let it go, but this new evidence means we need to find him pronto. By all accounts, he was the ringleader of the group and was the one who started the fight. I guess he would insist on doing the driving. I gather he fancies himself as a tough guy and the leader of the gang.'

'And the other boy? Ethan.'

'There was a handprint on the bonnet of the car that matches his fingerprints.'

'I see. And do we know how long it is since the car was washed?'

'No, but I can find out.' Monica made a note to ask the car's owner about this. 'You think Ethan might claim it got there earlier than Friday night?'

'I'm just saying that it isn't proof that he did any more than lean on the bonnet while it was parked somewhere. Still, it gives you a reason for talking to him again. OK. Thanks for the update. I'd better not keep you any longer.'

'There was just one other thing,' Monica said as she got up to go. 'There were fingerprints on the steering wheel that we haven't managed to match to anyone – not any of the boys from the estate or Ian Boulton or his wife. We can't quite work out what to make of those.'

'So none of Jason Paul's prints on the steering wheel?' Jonah asked sharply. 'How do you account for that, if he was driving?'

'Gloves?' Monica suggested and then rapidly changed

her mind when she saw Jonah's sceptical expression. 'No. That doesn't sound like his style. Probably one of the others must have been driving – someone who hasn't done anything to get his fingerprints on the database – and the hair got on the headrest some other way. It still proves that Jason Paul was in the car. And it still gives me a good reason for arresting him and asking him to account for his movements on Friday night.'

She left the room, intent on finding the erring youth and bringing him in for questioning. Bernie looked towards Jonah.

'So now will you admit that this was just an accident, not a deliberate attempt to kill Wayne?' she asked.

***

Monica looked across the table at Jason Paul and his mother, trying to think of some way of eliciting a more useful response than the "no comment" with which he had greeted almost all of her questions so far. She had found him at home, still in bed although it was past ten in the morning, and brought him back to the police station with Lyn Paul accompanying him to act as the *appropriate adult* during the interview. Now, after nearly half an hour of questioning, he had admitted nothing and divulged next to no information.

'Look Jason,' Monica said wearily, 'we have witnesses that can confirm that you left the *Bullnose Morris* after ten on Friday night. Before eleven, a car that *you* had been driving smashes into a pedestrian. If you're expecting us to believe that you weren't responsible for the crash, you're going to have to tell me where you went after you left the *Bullnose.*'

'No comment,' Jason repeated in a bored voice staring ahead of him as if Monica were not there. Monica turned to address his mother.

'Mrs Paul, your son is suspected of some very serious

offences, including dangerous driving. He faces a custodial sentence. It's important that he co-operates with our enquiries.'

'What're you expecting me to do?' Lyn asked languidly, gazing across at Monica with a vacant expression. 'I can't *make* him talk if he doesn't want to.'

Monica looked from mother to son, thinking how alike they were in appearance. They both had pale blue eyes and a short, slightly up-turned nose set in an oval face surrounded by straight blond hair. The difference was that, while Jason looked sulky and defiant, Lyn's expression was more one of defeat verging on despair. She took another breath and tried again.

'Jason,' she said in a firm, matter-of-fact voice. 'We found your DNA in the stolen car. We know that you weren't the only person in it. It's even possible that someone else was driving. If we find them, and they tell us that you were the driver and you're still refusing to talk, then we're going to believe them, aren't we? So now's the time to tell me exactly what really did happen.'

'No comment.'

'You left the pub with Ethan Roberts and Callum Lee. Did you all stick together after that? Did you go together to steal the car?'

'No comment.'

'My guess is Callum was driving,' Monica continued, seizing on the one out of the three whose fingerprints were not on file. 'Is that right Jason?'

'No. None of us was. We didn't take any fucking car.'

'Then tell us what you *were* doing. If you can prove that you were somewhere else between ten and eleven on Friday night then you'll be in the clear.'

'No comment.'

CHAPTER 12: WEDNESDAY AFTERNOON

'OK, Ms Lumley,' Jonah said, watching Tanya's face closely across the table in the interview room. 'Tell us about your friends Gordon Redfern and Robin Fry.'

'What do you want to know?' she asked, staring back with wide-eyed innocence, which Jonah assessed as being a deliberate ploy to put him off his guard.

'Let's start with how you got to know them in the first place.'

'Craig and Robin were at school together, didn't he tell you?'

'He may have done, but I'm asking you. What about Redfern?'

'Robin introduced us. Robin used to work for Gordon – 'til his business went tits-up.'

'And when did you come up with the scheme for setting up this Facebook group of yours – *Protect our Kids?*'

'I'm sorry, I can't really remember,' Tanya smiled sweetly and fluttered her eyelids. 'A year or two ago, I suppose.'

'And whose idea was it?'

'Gordon's, I think – or maybe Ian's.'

145

'Ian Boulton?'

'That's right. He and Gordon were old friends.'

'Yes. That's what we heard too,' Jonah told her, hoping to put pressure on her to tell the truth by implying that he already knew the answers to some of his questions. 'They both seem rather ... antipathetic, shall we say ... towards gay men. Do you know why that might be?'

'They don't like queers, if that's what you mean.'

'Yes. That's what I meant, and I'm asking if you know why.'

'D'you know about Gordon's son, Jack?'

'What about him?'

'Gordon reckoned one of them turned him gay. He was a bit obsessive about it really. Kept going on about it.'

'Did he tell you who this person was?'

'No.' Tanya shook her head vigorously. 'He never told us his name. He did say he was still flaunting himself at the Gay Pride march a couple of weeks back – even after Jack topped himself. He kept saying it showed a lack of respect, but I dunno: would he even've known about it?' She shrugged and then leaned closer to speak to Jonah confidentially. 'I don't make any secret of not liking queers, but I'm not obsessive like Gordon. Look, I'm sorry about the spray paint. It was silly and childish of us. We wouldn't have done it if we hadn't been well pissed. But Craig and me – we never did anything more than that. It was Gordon who had this obsession about them all being a danger to kids.'

Jonah was convinced that Tanya's contrition and willingness to talk were largely a ploy to avoid being charged for criminal damage, but he decided to press his advantage in the hope of eliciting more information about the members of *Protect our Kids*.

'What about Fry?' he asked. 'Where did he fit in?'

'Like I said, he worked for Gordon.'

'I mean, what made him join the group? He doesn't have any kids, does he?'

'No. I don't think so. I …,' she leaned across the table again and looked round furtively as if she thought they might be overheard. 'To be honest, I've always been a bit afraid of Rob. He's a bit of a nutter, if you know what I mean.'

'Tell me about it.'

'He's like … always angry … and obsessed with setting things on fire.'

'Like he did to his school?'

'You know about that?'

'We know a lot of things, but carry on. You were telling me about Robin Fry and why he frightens you.'

'That's it really. He boasted about smashing things up and setting fire to things and he said he'd got stuff at home that would blow a building sky high if he wanted to.'

'But it didn't occur to you to report these claims to the police?' Jonah asked mildly.

'I didn't know if he was serious … and I didn't want people to think I was a grass, especially if it was just him shooting his mouth off about nothing.'

'I see. Now tell me – have you seen this?' Jonah rotated the screen attached to his chair so that Tanya could see the Facebook post from Fry threatening to set fire to a gay bar.

For a moment, he thought that she was going to pretend surprise at seeing the post, but she decided against it and instead opened her eyes wide and looked into his with feigned innocence.

'Yes, I saw it, but it never occurred to me that he was serious. He was always talking about setting fire to things – like I said before – but apart from his dad's shed, I don't think he ever did.'

'Tell me about the shed incident. Was that recent?'

'A year or so back, I suppose. I don't know why he did it – just for the hell of it I think.'

'OK. Now, getting back to Redfern and his son, are you sure he never mentioned the name of this man who was supposed to have turned Jack gay?'

'Positive.'

'Redfern and Boulton complained about a gay teacher at Jack's primary school. Did you know about that?'

'No. I didn't know Gordon back then.'

'They didn't talk about it then? I thought they might've done. I thought they might have held it up as an example of kids being in danger from gays.'

'Well they didn't.'

After several more minutes of questioning, Jonah was left with the feeling that, although Tanya had appeared co-operative, she had managed to avoid giving him answers to his key questions. Moreover, what she had told him might not be reliable, since it all seemed to be carefully calculated to direct his attention towards Redfern and Fry and away from Craig and herself. According to Tanya, she and her boyfriend were essentially harmless scamps who had got carried away while under the influence of alcohol. Fry, however, was a dangerous pyromaniac; and Redfern was an obsessive homophobe with a grudge against an unnamed gay man.

He decided to issue both Jones and Lumley with a formal police caution and to let them go. He had no evidence of their involvement in any of the other attacks, although it seemed likely that they were responsible for the earlier graffiti as well as this latest incident. There was even less reason to suspect them of the assault on Christopher Jackson, the manager of the bicycle repair company, or of the threatening notes.

***

Monica reviewed the situation. A single hair was not much evidence with which to charge Jason Paul. She had taken fingerprints and DNA from his younger brother Ryan, thinking that it was possible that he could have been the driver. Might it even have been his hair that had been found in the car? She would have to wait for the results on that to come back from the forensics lab. Meanwhile, what should they do next?

Eventually, she decided that Callum Lee was the most likely of the three boys to give way under questioning. According to Alice, he had appeared nervous and eager to please when she and Anna had spoken to him. In any case, as she had told Jason, there was a strong chance that he could have been the one who left the unidentified fingermarks on the steering wheel. Taking DC Joshua Pitchfork with her, she went to call on Callum at home, intending to take his fingerprints and a DNA sample, both for identification purposes and as a way of impressing upon him the seriousness of his situation and the benefits to him of co-operating fully with their enquiries.

There was no reply when they rang and knocked at the door of the Lee family home. A neighbour informed them that Callum had a job retrieving trolleys at a local superstore. They made their way there and tracked him down in the car park. Monica decided against arresting him then and there. To do so might jeopardise his job. She could hardly justify doing this when the evidence against him was entirely circumstantial. Instead, she made arrangements for him to attend the police station after work to give a DNA sample and have his fingerprints taken.

'I d-didn't d-do it,' he insisted, following them back to their car. 'We – we – we – n-never took any c-car.'

'If I'm to believe that,' Monica told him, seizing the opportunity afforded by his apparent eagerness to talk to her, 'I need you to tell me where you went after you left the Bullnose Morris.'

She opened the door of the car and made to get in, but Callum caught her by the shoulder. She turned and looked at him.

'Well?' she asked. 'Are you going to tell me?'

Callum looked round furtively, as if checking that there

was no one else listening. Then, speaking even more hesitantly than usual and twisting his hands together nervously all the time, he told her the whole story.

After leaving the pub, they had made their way, on foot, through the estate to the Evenlode Tower, which was the twin of the Windrush Tower where Leroy King and his family lived. There was a secluded space round the back there, near the bins, where they could sit undisturbed. Why had Jason refused to tell her about that? Callum supposed it was because he didn't want to admit to what they were doing there. Which was? Smoking cannabis. Ethan had somehow obtained some with which to celebrate his birthday. Monica wouldn't let on that he had told her about it, would she?

Monica assured him that she was much more interested in establishing whether the boys could have taken the BMW and driven it recklessly through the streets of Blackbird Leys than in getting him into bother with his friends. She would need to find some corroborating evidence before she could be sure that he was now telling the truth about their movements that night, but she was grateful to him for pointing her in the direction of where to look for this. She sent him back to his work with a reminder to come down to the station as soon as he clocked off, to have his DNA and fingerprints taken, and a warning about the dangers of using illegal drugs.

When she got back to the police station, she found Andy Lepage waiting to speak to her.

'DCI Porter told me you'd want to know that Ian Boulton has a daughter living with them,' he said without any preamble. 'He asked me to check up on the family because Boulton wrote a letter a few years back complaining about a local primary school employing a gay teacher. I checked the electoral roll and he's got a daughter aged seventeen listed at the same address as him and his wife. Jonah seemed to think you'd be interested to know that.'

'He's right – I am,' Monica smiled. 'Yes. That's very interesting indeed. That could very well explain Alice's face at the window. Thanks.'

She sat down at her computer, planning to record the interview with Callum Lee. Then she looked up again and called after Andy, 'does she have a name, this daughter?'

'Bethany. Bethany Grace Boulton.'

***

'Hi Wayne!' Lucy called softly as she approached him. 'Peter says I mustn't stay long in case it makes you tired, but I wanted you to know that we haven't forgotten you.'

'Hi … Lucy. Good … to … see … you.' Wayne's speech still sounded strangely robotic as he searched for each word in his frighteningly befuddled mind. He smiled to indicate the welcome that it would have been too much effort to put into words.

'It's good to see you out of bed,' Peter added, coming up behind Lucy and looking Wayne up and down.

He was sitting in a high-backed chair next to his bed on the rehabilitation ward. One side of his face was still swollen and purple and there were scabs on his right hand, which lay motionless on the arm of the chair. The nasogastric tube with which he had been fed during his first four days in hospital had been removed, leaving a red mark on his upper lip where it had chafed. There was a plastic beaker of water on the tray table that stood across his lap. That was good. It looked as if he must have passed the swallowing test.

'We brought you this to add to your collection,' Lucy said, holding out a pale blue envelope. 'Shall I open it for you?'

Wayne nodded and smiled again. Lucy tore open the envelope and took out a card with a humorous picture on the front of a man being fussed over by a voluptuous nurse.

'I couldn't find an appropriate one,' she told him with a grin. 'I don't think the card manufacturers have heard of male nurses!'

She held it out to towards Wayne, who took it rather clumsily in his left hand. He smiled at the picture and then, with some difficulty, opened the card and looked inside.

'We've all signed it,' Lucy told him. 'Even Jonah! But then he has you to thank that he ever learned to write again. It was your writing board gadget that got him started.'

'Looks like … I'm … going to … need … gadgets … myself,' Wayne said laboriously.

'Don't forget, the doctor said that it's still early days yet,' his mother intervened. 'They still think you could get back completely to normal in time.'

'Yes,' Lucy agreed. 'Remember when Eva had her stroke? She was completely paralysed down one side at first, but now she can walk with just a stick.'

'I … don't … think … I'll … be … coaching … rugger … this … summer.'

'Maybe not, but I wouldn't rule out next summer,' Graham said a little too heartily to be convincing. 'Think positive and we'll soon have you back on your feet again.'

'But it doesn't make any difference,' Dean added earnestly. 'I mean, you're still just as important to us all whatever happens.'

'That's right,' Lucy backed him up. 'You aren't any less of a person just because you can't do all the things you used to do. I mean – look at Jonah!'

'And if you do need any gadgets to help you, you could hardly be better-placed to get tailor-made ones designed for you, could you?' Peter added, sensing Dean's anxiety and trying to lighten the mood with gentle humour.

'Yes,' said Dean, picking up on Lucy's mention of Jonah. 'Nobody would ever suggest that Jonah wasn't making a valuable contribution, would they?'

'Hardly!' Peter broke in with a laugh. 'He'd soon put

them right if anyone suggested it!'

'And he's far more disabled than you, even now,' Dean continued. 'And, like Barbara says, it's early days and you'll probably get a lot, lot better than this.'

'Need ... get better ...,' Wayne began falteringly. Everyone waited on tenterhooks, fighting down the temptation to attempt to finish his sentence for him. 'Need to ... get better ... for ... Harry ... and Carl.'

The smile had left his face now and his pale eyes were anxious. Dean leaned over and put his arm around his shoulders hugging him to him.

'I spoke to their case worker,' Graham told him. 'She said they'd wait.'

'That's right,' Barbara agreed with a rather false brightness. 'Don't worry about that. Just concentrate on getting better and the boys will still be there when you're ready.'

'But ... what if ...?'

Dean tightened his arm around Wayne's shoulders, unable to think of anything to say. Lucy knelt down on the floor in front of his chair and took his right hand in hers.

'Try not to think about that,' she said earnestly. 'We're all here to help. I'm sure that whatever happens we'll manage to work something out for you and the boys. The main thing is for you to do whatever the doctors and physios and people say, so that you get better as quickly as you can.'

'But if ...,' Wayne continued to argue, 'if ... I ... stay ... like this ...'

'Which the doctors say isn't likely,' Graham intervened.

'Not fair on ... Dean ...'

'Never mind me,' Dean protested. 'I can manage. I'll do whatever it takes ...'

'... or the boys,' Wayne continued, flashing a sad smile up at Dean. 'Can't ... be ... a ... proper dad ... like ... this.'

'That's rubbish!' Lucy declared forcefully. 'Look at the

way Jonah plays with his grandkids. And – and there's my mam. Didn't she ever tell you about her mum having motor neurone disease? Plenty of parents have disabilities and it doesn't mean they're not proper mums and dads.'

'Not ... the ... same.' Wayne shook his head. 'And ... what ... about ... Design ... Ability? Too ... much ... for ... Dean ... Carl and Harry ... and ...'

'Don't you worry about that!' Graham broke in. 'I can help Dean with the business for as long as you need me. You chose the right time to get yourself knocked down. Here I am, just retired and looking for something to keep me occupied! And Mum'll be glad of something to get me out from under her feet during the day.'

'Oh!' Dean exclaimed at the mention of the business. 'I'd completely forgotten. We've got interviews for the new customer liaison post on Friday. We were going to do them together. I don't know now ... could we put them off, do you think?'

'No. I'll do it with you,' Graham said firmly. 'You don't want to lose all your decent candidates.'

'I'm not sure I'll be able to ...,' Dean began, struggling to explain his reluctance to commit to this important task. 'I mean ... I don't think I'd be concentrating properly, what with ...'

'Why not ask Jonah to do it with Graham?' Lucy asked with sudden inspiration. 'He'd be the perfect person to ask questions about customer liaison, and it's about time he started thinking about things he could do after he retires.'

'Won't he be busy?' Dean asked, his eyes lighting up at this suggestion nevertheless.

'Of course,' Peter smiled, delighted at Lucy's idea. 'but I happen to know that he's got three days' leave that he's got to take before the end of the month, so the HR department will be only too pleased if he takes the day off on Friday.'

'Is that settled then?' Graham asked in a tone that suggested that he would not listen to any objections.

'Jonah and I will do the interviews. I'll just need you to bring me up to speed on exactly what it is you're looking for,' he added to Dean.

'Yes, of course.' Dean turned back to Wayne. 'Is that OK with you?'

***

'Do you think they will still let Wayne and Dean adopt Carl and Harry?' Lucy asked Peter on the way home.

'I don't know,' Peter sighed. 'It does seem a pity to drop the idea after they've come so far, but, if I was their case worker, I can't help feeling that I'd be on the lookout for other parents for them. And not just for their sake. It's looking as if, for a good while at least, Dean's going to have plenty to do looking after Wayne, without having to cope with a couple of young boys with challenging behaviour.'

'That's what I thought,' Lucy agreed, 'and I think Wayne does too. It's just so unfair!'

CHAPTER 13: WEDNESDAY NIGHT

'All quiet so far,' Sergeant Appleton reported when Inspector Jordan Fox came up to him in his position outside the nightclub in central Oxford, which had been named in Robin Fry's threatening Facebook post. 'There's just those two stopping the punters and handing out leaflets, but I think they're harmless enough.'

Fox followed Appleton's pointing finger and saw a middle-aged couple dressed in rather old-fashioned clothes standing near the entrance with glossy pamphlets in their hands and earnest expressions on their faces. A group of young men walking past them into the club waved and called out cheerily to them, but did not stop to talk or accept the proffered reading matter. It seemed that the couple were well-known and tolerated as harmless lunatics.

'Their names are Mr and Mrs Cunliffe,' Appleton continued. 'Do you want me to move them on?'

'Not unless anyone complains. That's not what we're here for tonight. What we're looking out for is any sign that those threats to set fire to the place could have been genuine.'

'Well, as I said, there's no sign of anything of that sort so far. We've got officers stationed at strategic points all round the building and there's been nothing to report yet.'

As if designed to contradict this assessment, his radio crackled and the voice of PC Ben Timpson came through.

'I think there may be someone hiding round here by the bins,' he reported. 'Mel's here with PD Q. Shall we try to flush them out?'

'No,' Fox said before Appleton could answer. 'Just keep an eye on what they're doing.'

'OK sir.' The radio went silent and Fox turned to Appleton.

'I'm going round there to have a look for myself,' he told him. 'You keep watching here.'

He made his way stealthily round to the back of the building, narrowly avoiding bumping into Timpson and Stanton who were standing silently in the shadows. An almost imperceptible rumbling in Q's throat confirmed that she also was aware of his presence.

'It looks like a male in a dark-coloured hoodie. He's over there, between those two bins,' Timpson said in a low voice. 'The security light doesn't penetrate in there, so you can only see him when he moves. He seems to be crouching down now.'

Fox strained his eyes but could see nothing. Then, all of a sudden, a light flared and for a second or two he could see a man's face clearly, lit up by flames emanating from something that he was holding. Then he bent backwards and hurled the object, whatever it was, towards a window at the back of the building.

There was a sharp bang as the object hit the glass, but the sealed unit did not break and the missile dropped to the ground beneath the window. There was a sound of breaking glass and flames spread along the base of the wall. Timpson leapt forward and started to stamp them out.

'This is the Police!' Fox called out in a loud voice. 'We have a dog with us. Come out with your hands up.'

Q let out a volley of barks. Fox waited for a few

seconds before repeating the command. 'Come out or we'll send the dog in to find you!'

Suddenly the man broke cover, emerging from the other side of the bins and making off through a narrow alleyway on the other side of the yard. Stanton released Q, who raced after the fugitive barking eagerly.

In a matter of minutes – seconds almost – he was captured. Fox watched as the man emerged from the alley in handcuffs, followed by the dog handler with a jubilant Q on a short leash.

'Name?' he asked brusquely.

The man looked round sheepishly as if wondering whether to try inventing a false identity. Then he decided against it and muttered, 'Robin Fry.'

CHAPTER 14: THURSDAY MORNING

'Uniform did a good night's work last night,' Andy greeted Jonah when he arrived at work the next morning. 'They've arrested Fry in the act of attempting to set fire to that gay nightclub and they've brought in Susie and Will Cunliffe on suspicion of creating a diversion to help him do it.

'What did they want to do that for?' Jonah asked in a rather exasperated tone. 'What makes them think those two are anything more than harmless nutters?'

'Dunno,' Andy shrugged. 'You'd better ask Fox. It was his decision. Something about a bit of argy-bargy breaking out by the main entrance, just as Fry threw his petrol bomb at the back. Anyway, they're all in the cells waiting for you to decide what to do with them.'

'OK,' Jonah sighed. 'I'd better speak to the God-botherers first. Then we can send them home and concentrate on our arsonist. Find out if they've got a lawyer they want present and get that all set up while I apply for a search warrant for Fry's house.'

***

'So your story is that you were simply standing outside the

club as usual, handing out these nice friendly leaflets?'
Jonah said to the Cunliffes, while Bernie held up a
brightly-coloured document entitled "God, love and same-
sex attraction".

'That's right,' Susie answered, looking defiantly at
Jonah and Bernie across the table in the interview room.

'And that you have never met this man,' Jonah added,
inclining his head towards Bernie, who promptly put down
a photograph of Robin Fry in front of them.

'That's right,' they agreed, both nodding.

'We've never seen him in our lives,' Susie added. 'And
we don't agree with what he did. We want to *save*
homosexuals from their sin, not to hurt them.'

'God has given us a big heart of love for them,' her
husband added fervently. 'He saved me and now I want to
save all those men who go that place.'

'I see.' Jonah looked towards Bernie who replaced the
leaflet with another one. This was entitled "The Town that
was Doomed to Die", graphically illustrated on the cover
by a skull and crossbones printed across images of burning
buildings. Inside was a cartoon strip telling the story of the
destruction of Sodom, with a strong emphasis on the
message "God doesn't play games" when it comes to
destroying unrepentant homosexuals with fire and
brimstone. 'And these are just another way you have of
demonstrating that love, I suppose?'

'You may mock,' Susie answered in a rather high-
pitched nervous voice, 'but that's exactly right.'

'It *is* an act of love to warn those people that they have
set their feet on the path to hell,' William agreed. 'As you
would see, if you read the whole of that tract, God loves
sinners so much that He sent his Son to die to save them
from their sin. We are calling them to put their lives in the
hands of Jesus, who will enable them to turn away from
the sin of homosexuality.'

'And this one?' Jonah continued coldly, ignoring them
as Bernie placed another leaflet on the table. 'This one I

don't like at all.'

The Cunliffes looked down. This document was headed "Home Alone". The cartoon inside told the story of a boy who is left in the care of a male baby-sitter while his parents go out. The man tells him, 'it's cool to be gay.' The boy is tempted to adopt a gay lifestyle – just as his baby-sitter was made gay by an encounter with older gay boys when he was only a child himself.

'I don't like the implication that gay men are all paedophiles and out to change other people's sexuality.'

'But it doesn't say that at all!' Susie protested. 'All it's saying is that nobody is born gay and everybody can turn away from a gay lifestyle if they put their trust in Jesus as their Lord and Saviour.'

'That's not how it reads to me,' Jonah told her bluntly. 'And what's this bit about calling AIDS "Gay-related Immuno-deficiency Disorder" and blaming its spread on the promiscuity of gay men?'

'That's completely accurate,' William said defensively. 'That's what it *was* called originally, before the gay lobby forced the medical profession to change it. And it was spread by the promiscuity of gay men.'

'So you don't approve of promiscuity, and yet this same little gem of literature denounces gay marriage as an abomination?' Jonah commented caustically.

'Marriage is between one man and one woman,' Susie stated dogmatically. 'And all sex outside of marriage is fornication and forbidden by God.'

'And you think handing out this sort of stuff is going to convert people to your point of view?' Jonah sounded incredulous.

'It's the first step,' Susie said earnestly. 'It's to open up their minds – to convict them of their sin and to show them that, through Jesus they can change.'

'And what if they don't want to change?' Jonah asked with cold calm. 'If they're happy as they are?'

'They may think that they're happy,' Susie answered

promptly, 'but no one can be truly happy until they invite Jesus into their hearts. Tell them William! Tell them what it's like to be changed by Jesus.'

'I used to feel same sex attraction,' William told them, taking his wife's hand in his and giving her a long look before turning back to Jonah, 'but with prayer, and with Susie's support, I put all that behind me. The Lord defeated Satan, and washed me clean and enabled me to change my life. Are you a homosexual?' He asked suddenly, leaning forward with his elbows on the table and looking into Jonah's eyes. 'Is that why you find it so hard to listen to what we have to say?'

'That really takes the biscuit!' Jonah laughed. 'You two are absolutely obsessed, aren't you? It's alright. You don't need to pray for the redemption of my soul – or not on that account anyway! Bernie here can probably come up with a long list of unforgiveable sins that I've committed, but that isn't one of them. Firstly, whatever my inclinations, I'm not any longer in a position to commit fornication of any kind – erectile dysfunction is one of the consequences of my spinal injury.'

At this, Susie blushed very red and looked down at her hands, which were lying clasped together on the table.

'And secondly,' Jonah continued, smiling at Susie's embarrassment, 'I was happily married – to a woman – for thirty-three years, until my wife died. So now let's forget all this claptrap and concentrate on establishing what happened last night.'

'Do *you* know Jesus as your Lord and Saviour?' Susie asked leaning forward and gazing into Jonah's eyes.

'Evidently not,' Jonah said curtly. 'Not the cruel, judgemental Jesus that you seem to have in mind, but let's get back to last night. Just as Mr Fry is creeping round the back of the club with his incendiary device, you get into an argument with a couple of the punters. There's a lot of shouting and some pushing and shoving and the bouncer on the door asks you both to move off and stop annoying their customers. Is that right?'

'I suppose so,' William admitted grudgingly. 'Except we don't know anything about that fellow who was round the back.'

'We didn't start it,' Susie added defensively. 'They were drunk. One of them grabbed a whole pile of our leaflets and threw them up in the air, and then while we were on the ground picking them up, one of them drew a lewd picture on our "Jesus loves you" poster.'

'I protested to them about that,' William continued, 'and then this policeman comes up and arrests us for no reason. We've done nothing wrong.'

'I'm inclined to believe you when you say that you've done nothing illegal,' Jonah agreed. 'Whether you've done anything wrong is between you and your god. What you seem to be saying is that, although you're happy with the idea of gay people burning in hell for the whole of eternity, you do draw the line at burning them alive in a nightclub. That's not my idea of how God behaves, but my job is upholding the law of the land, not denouncing dodgy theology. I'll take you back to the custody sergeant to collect your things, and then you can go.'

As they walked together through the corridors to the custody officer's desk, Bernie leaned towards the Cunliffes and asked in a low voice, 'has it ever occurred to you to think about the likely consequences if anyone reads one of those leaflets of yours and takes it seriously?'

'I don't understand what you mean,' Susie answered in genuine perplexity. 'Of course we want people to take them seriously.'

'And it's never crossed your mind that some people might read them and then go out and try to punish all these wicked gays by setting fire to nightclubs where they carry on their licentious behaviour, for example?' Bernie persisted.

'Of course not! That's not what we're saying at all,' Susie said, shocked. 'We're just warning homosexuals of the consequences if they don't change their lifestyle – and we're doing it out of love.'

'But, don't you realise that the people that you're actually going to attract are homophobes who *want* to think that they're righteous and all those nasty gay people are damned to hell?' Bernie persevered.

'No,' William insisted. 'That's not the case at all. We don't judge you,' he went on generously. 'We realise that you've been brainwashed by exposure to pressure from the government and the media into thinking that sexual deviancy is something natural that can't be changed, but I know better. I *have* changed – or rather, I've *been* changed by God.'

'I won't tell you what I think you've been changed into,' Bernie muttered threateningly.

'Here you are!' Jonah announced, as Bernie opened the door and ushered the Cunliffes towards the desk, behind which custody officer Pamela Gregson was standing. 'I think we will have to agree to disagree,' he continued, darting a look at Bernie that told her not to say any more. 'But perhaps you might like to include in your prayers some thought for a young man who is fighting for his life in the John Radcliffe after being mown down by a maniac in a stolen car, and for his husband of six years who is watching and waiting to see if he will ever recover.'

***

Jonah's second interview of the morning was very different. Fry sat sullenly next to the duty solicitor, refusing to answer any questions about the incident at the nightclub. Jonah turned to another topic.

'Last Friday you were drinking in the *Bullnose Morris* with a couple of friends. Do you remember that?'

'Might do,' Fry shrugged. 'I go there most Fridays.'

'The bar man remembers you,' Jonah told him. 'And he says that you got into a bit of a barney with a group of young lads who were in there. Do you remember that?'

Fry shrugged again.

'I'm surprised you don't remember,' Jonah said conversationally. 'One of them aimed a punch at you. It's not the sort of thing that most people forget.'

'OK. Some boys were in there making trouble,' Fry growled. 'What about it? They were the ones that got thrown out.'

'We've spoken to witnesses who said that it started with you and one of your friends calling out homophobic abuse at the lads. Is that true?'

'No comment.' Fry sat staring down at the table in front of him.

'And then you went over to them and went into a little more detail about what you thought of gay men,' Jonah continued. 'And before you give me another "no comment" let me tell you that we have several eye witnesses who are quite clear about what you said.'

Fry, who had opened his mouth to reply, closed it again and sat in sullen silence.

'Which means that I don't actually need you to admit to your verbal abuse of a young lad whom you thought was gay,' Jonah continued. 'I was just telling you about it, because I thought it might help you to see why you are at the top of our list of suspects when it comes to scrawling unpleasant messages on walls and vans and sending death-threats and pushing excrement into people's letterboxes.'

'I never!' Fry burst out, looking up for the first time with an expression of alarm on his face. He looked round wildly, first at the solicitor, who raised his eyebrows but said nothing, and then at Bernie, Andy and finally back to Jonah. 'What's all that about? I never did none of that.'

'Really?' Jonah said smoothly. He seemed to be getting somewhere with this suspect at last. 'Let's get this clear: you are denying having sprayed anti-gay graffiti on *Antonio's Hair Stylist* shop, the offices of *Lane's Luxury Limos* or the van belonging to *Design Ability*? And yet, you have been seen speaking in a threatening manner to a young man whom you accused of being … let me see … yes! Here it is! A *faggot*.'

'Yeah, well, I may have said something like that,' Fry mumbled, 'but I never wrote death threats or any of that other crap you said.'

'No, I suppose not,' Jonah conceded, feeling satisfied that he had got the suspect talking at last. 'You don't go in much for writing, do you? You probably left all that to your friends. Your talents lie more on the practical side, don't they?'

'Not that you're even very good at that,' Andy put in, hoping to taunt Fry into a confession. 'I've been looking into your past. Three attempts you had setting fire to your old school. And after all that, only two classrooms affected. And now last night! Call yourself an arsonist! You couldn't even lob a petrol bomb straight!'

'I wasn't to know the window'd be so strong!' Fry protested, stung by the mockery in Andy's voice. 'And I'd got plenty more of them. If you lot hadn't come along, you'd have seen all them disgusting homos running for their lives alright!'

The solicitor put his hand on Fry's shoulder in a restraining gesture and signalled for him to stop talking, but Fry's pride had been wounded and he carried on regardless.

'You been inside that place?' he demanded, looking first at Andy and then at Jonah. They both shook their heads.

'Neither've I,' Fry admitted, 'but Gordon has. You know his son was a queer, I suppose?' Jonah nodded. 'He followed him in there one night. He told me there's rooms upstairs where the homos go, to … you know. It's disgusting. I wasn't aiming to hurt anyone, just to smoke 'em out like.' Fry laughed, apparently finding this idea very funny.

'Mr Fry,' the solicitor intervened as soon as his client

paused for breath. 'I really must advise you not to say any more at this stage.'

'That's alright,' Jonah said equably, smiling across at them both. 'I think we have all we need now. I'm terminating the interview. DS Lepage will take you back to the cells to wait while we make arrangements for you to be charged with arson. I have to warn you that, following the discovery at your home of various items of bomb-making equipment, we will probably also be charging you with various offences under the Terrorism Act 2006. Do you understand?'

***

Monica and Alice, meanwhile, had been following up on Callum Lee's story that the boys had walked through the estate to the Evenlode Tower after leaving the *Bullnose Morris* the previous Friday. Fortunately, the tower had security cameras fixed at strategic points, which provided fuzzy footage of the three boys wandering round to the back of the building and settling down in a huddle at the side of one of the garages.

'The pictures aren't clear enough to prove they're smoking cannabis like Callum told us,' Monica reported to Jonah when he called the whole team together to discuss progress in the two cases, 'but it's them alright.'

'Which means that they can't have taken the car from Boulton's drive and gone on the rampage with it, whatever forensics say about that hair on the headrest,' Alice added. 'Personally, I'd trust Q's nose ahead of a lab test any time!'

'You'd better get on to them to run the tests again,' Jonah told Monica. 'If we're hoping to charge Boulton with dangerous driving, we can't afford to have that DNA evidence casting doubt on whether it was him at the wheel.'

'I've already done it,' Monica assured him. 'I've told them to double-check the match and to look again at where the original sample from Jason Paul came from. It may be that there was a mix-up of some sort right back then.'

'Good man!' Jonah said approvingly. 'And meanwhile, let's consider what we've got regarding the attacks on gay businesses. Robin Fry was caught red-handed setting fire to the nightclub, but that doesn't actually fit the pattern of the other incidents. My own opinion is that he's not motivated so much by hatred of gays as by a compulsion for setting fire to buildings. I'd say he latched on to Redfern's obsession because it gave him an excuse for indulging in his pyromania and made him feel that he was doing it as part of something bigger and more important.'

'*I'd* say Gordon Redfern was the most likely instigator of the death threats,' Bernie ventured. 'Several people seem to have suggested that he was obsessed with the idea that his son had been turned gay by association with other gay men. And Jack Redfern died not long before the attacks started. Could that have been the trigger – rather than the Gay Pride article?'

'Or the two together,' Andy suggested. 'If one of the people featured in the article was also one of the men that Redfern held responsible for his son's sexuality – and maybe even for his death – then that could explain why he targeted them.'

'And it could either be because he held them all responsible collectively, in a weird sort of way,' Alice added, 'or as a way of putting us off his scent by hiding his real target in amongst a group of others.'

'Oh! I've just thought!' Monica exclaimed. 'You saying that made me think. What if you're right, Alice, and the threats and vandalism are a smoke screen for the actual attempted murder of Wayne Major?'

For a moment, there was a stunned silence. Then Jonah spoke in a measured tone.

'No. That won't wash,' he said firmly. 'We're all agreed that, if that was a deliberate attack, it must have been a spur-of-the-moment thing after a chance encounter. Nobody apart from Wayne and his friends, even knew he was going to be drinking in the *Blackbird* that night, never mind that he'd just left and was crossing the road.'

'I suppose so,' Monica admitted reluctantly. 'If not Wayne, then who else might be the real target?'

'Did any of our victims know Jack Redfern personally?' Alice asked.

'No,' Jonah answered, 'or at least not that we know of.'

'There *was* something Lumley or Jones said,' Andy said slowly. 'I can't remember exactly – have you got the notes of the interview there?'

Jonah immediately started fiddling with buttons on the keypad on the arm of his chair, searching for the transcript on his computer.

'One of them said that Mark Brown – that's Antonio of *Antonio's Hair Stylist* – was a paedophile who had abused the son of a mate of theirs. I was wondering if the mate might have been Redfern.'

'Yes,' Jonah agreed, looking up from his computer screen. 'Here it is: "You mean he has sex with under-age boys? Do you have any proof of that? … One of my mates told me his son went with him. … Does he have a name, this mate of yours? … No comment." Yes, you're right. It would all fit.'

'But, if Antonio's – or Marcus Antonio – is the main target, why didn't Fry try to set fire to the hairdressing shop, rather than the nightclub?' Bernie asked.

'I don't think it's as organised as a proper conspiracy,' Jonah replied. 'The way I see it, this Facebook group has attracted a whole lot of people who all feel vaguely antagonistic towards gay men and they've been feeding off each other's bigotry, stoking up feelings and then going off and doing their own thing. Craig Jones has a history of anti-social behaviour and vandalism – so he goes round spray-painting obscenities. Fry loves setting fire to buildings – so he turns to arson. But it's all just random, rather than planned and co-ordinated.'

'Jack Redfern used to go to that nightclub,' Andy pointed out. 'Maybe he used to meet Marcus Antonio there. Do you remember what Fry said about there being rooms upstairs and about Redfern following his son there?

'Yes. You're right,' Jonah said excitedly. 'That could be it! Redfern blames Antonio for his son being gay – and perhaps for his death as well – and he blames the club for making it easy for Antonio to prey on Jack, as he sees it. Then he pours it all out to the others in this Facebook group they've set up. They take everything he says at face value and that makes Jones turn his attention to the hairdresser's shop and Fry attempt to burn down the club.'

'And what about Boulton?' Monica asked. 'If we assume that he was driving the car on Friday night, was his hitting Wayne just a strange coincidence or do we go along with the idea that he recognised the logo on the back of his jacket and saw red? Either way, there doesn't seem to be any convincing reason why he drove so recklessly *before* he got to the *Blackbird*.'

'Drink?' Andy postulated.

'Monica's right.' Jonah shook his head. 'Drink could explain him driving erratically, but why was he there in the first place? If he was driving home after his drink in the *Bullnose Morris*, he wouldn't have gone anywhere near the bus stop where he hit Wayne.'

'Could he have been giving Redfern a lift home?' Bernie suggested suddenly. 'He lives on the estate, remember? Callum's mum said his house was just across the road from them. No! Bother! It was his mother that lived there, wasn't it? And Gordon had a house in Horspath.'

'But Boulton could still have been giving him a lift – to his mum's house,' Andy broke in eagerly. 'And it could've been Redfern who spotted the logo and thought Wayne was one of the gays that he blamed for corrupting his son. Maybe he grabbed the wheel and forced the car off the road.'

'Could Redfern have actually believed that Wayne was personally responsible for his son being gay or for him killing himself?' Monica queried. 'Did Wayne – or his partner for that matter – know Jack Redfern? Or did either of them visit that nightclub where Jack used to meet Antonio?'

'I shouldn't think so,' Bernie said dubiously. 'They've only been living in Oxford a few months, and they've been too busy doing up their house and sorting out the new offices to spend much time in clubs. And they're a very faithful couple,' she added defensively. 'There's no way either of them would be going upstairs with Jack Redfern, if that's what you were thinking.'

'That could've been the problem,' Alice suggested. 'What if Jack Redfern had a crush on one out of Wayne and Dean, but they told him to get lost?'

'Yes,' Monica agreed. 'They may not have meant to upset him,' she added quickly, glancing towards Bernie. 'They probably had no idea … They could've just told him they were already spoken for and assumed he'd just go away and forget it.'

'And Gordon Redfern tries to kill them for *not* indulging what he sees as his son's shameful perversion?' Bernie asked sceptically. 'That doesn't seem very logical to me.'

'No,' Monica answered. 'I'm saying he could've wanted to kill them for driving his son to suicide.'

'I don't suppose logic came into any of this,' Jonah commented drily. 'I think Monica's hypothesis *could* be right, but we still don't have any hard evidence to prove who was driving, never mind whether they intended to hit Wayne.'

There was a short silence while they all thought about this. Then Monica got to her feet.

'If there's nothing more, sir,' she said briskly. 'I want to go and have another little talk with Jason Paul. If we can't do him for dangerous driving we may be able to charge him with possession with intent to supply.'

***

'Isn't that ambulance stopped outside the Pauls' house?' Monica exclaimed as Alice drove carefully past the long line of parked cars that cluttered the narrow residential road.

'Looks a bit like it,' Alice agreed, backing carefully into a space that was only just large enough to accommodate their car. 'Better stop here I think. It doesn't look like we'll find anywhere closer.'

They got out and walked towards the small cluster of people standing on the pavement watching as two paramedics in green suits were let into the house by a scared-looking Ryan Paul. Monica hurried inside after them, leaving Alice to speak to the onlookers who had gathered at the sound of an ambulance approaching.

One of the ambulance crew turned as she entered and attempted to bar her way. She held up her warrant card and the man stood back to let her in before closing the door firmly behind her. His colleague was already kneeling on the floor beside Lyn Paul, who was lying at the foot of the stairs groaning and attempting to raise herself on one arm, while Ryan Paul sat on the bottom step staring down at her.

'Don't let me interrupt you,' she said to the ambulance crew, 'but I'll need to know what happened as soon as you've got a moment.'

'I slipped on the stairs,' Lyn said quickly. 'Tell them, Ryan.'

'That's right,' Ryan confirmed obediently. 'I was in my room. I heard her fall and I rang 999.'

'You've had a nasty bang on the head,' the paramedic murmured as she gently examined Lyn. 'And I'm afraid your collar bone looks as if it may be broken. We'd better get you to hospital where they can look at you properly. Just lie back there and try to relax, while we get you on to the trolley.'

'No!' Lyn protested, raising her head and looking round wildly. 'I can't go. What'll happen to my boys? I want to stay here. I'll be alright.'

'Don't worry,' the paramedic said soothingly, gently pushing her head back on to the floor. 'I don't expect they'll keep you in, and someone will see to it that your kids are OK. Your son doesn't look as if he needs a lot of looking after,' she added, glancing towards Ryan. 'He did great ringing for us and staying with you 'til we arrived. Now just relax while I check there's nothing else we need to do before we get you into the ambulance.'

Monica noted Lyn's concern for the welfare of her sons with some surprise. This was very different from the way in which she had shrugged off all responsibility for them when Monica last visited the family. She decided to attempt to take advantage of this new mood of maternal anxiety.

'Where's your other son, Mrs Paul?' Monica asked as the two paramedics transferred her carefully on to the low trolley. 'Does he know you've had an accident? Would you like me to tell him for you?'

'He's off out somewhere,' Lyn answered vaguely. 'He's been out all morning, hasn't he Ryan?' she added, twisting her neck to look up at her younger son.

'Yeah. That's right.' Ryan's confirmation did not sound very convincing to Monica. This was the second time that Lyn had appealed to him for confirmation after making a statement calculated to pre-empt any suggestion that Jason could be to blame for her accident.

'Can I come with you?' Ryan asked suddenly, seeing the paramedics opening the front door again and preparing to wheel his mother out.

'I'll take you,' Monica volunteered, seizing this opportunity to speak to Ryan out of his mother's hearing.

She had a strong suspicion that this "accident" might not be all that it seemed. 'Then I can wait with you while the doctors see to your mum.'

Ryan looked at her suspiciously and then down at his mother, who gave a slight nod and seemed to be trying to force a smile.

'Thanks,' she managed to get out just before the trolley disappeared through the doorway.

Monica turned to Ryan.

'Right! Let's go!'

She led him out to the car, collecting Alice, who was still chatting with the waiting crowd, on the way. Alice got back into the driving seat while Monica went with Ryan in the back.

'Now Ryan,' Monica said as soon as they were on their way. 'Let's have the truth. What really made your mum fall down the stairs?'

'She just slipped, that's all,' Ryan replied sullenly.

'Just slipped? Are you sure no one helped her? Gave her a little push?'

Ryan said nothing. Monica debated in her mind how to persuade him to open up. She was convinced that the fall was no accident and that Ryan could tell more if he chose. What was making him so reticent? Was it fear of what Jason might do to him when he found out? Or loyalty to his older brother? Or obedience to his mother, who seemed also to be determined to shield her violent son?

Monica felt hopelessly ill-equipped to get inside the mind of this truculent teenager. Her own upbringing – the only child of well-to-do parents, educated at an independent girls' school and then Oxford University – was so very different from the experience that these boys were having. With a father like his, was it any wonder that Jason Paul was violent towards his mother? He was only following the example that had been set to him.

'Where's Jason?' she asked at last. 'We ought to let him know what's happened to your mum.'

'She told you – he went out.'

'I was hoping you might be able to tell me where he went.'

'Well I can't.' Ryan took his phone out of his pocket and was soon absorbed in some game, which Monica did not recognise.

She pondered what to do next. There was not much time. They would soon be arriving at the hospital. This was her one chance of persuading Ryan to tell the truth. She decided to try a more direct approach.

'Look Ryan,' she began. 'I'm going to be honest with you. Those injuries your mum's got don't look like she just fell down the stairs. She's got bruises on her face as well as that big lump on the back of her head. Shall I tell you what I think happened?'

Ryan ignored her, continuing to stare down at his phone, absorbed in his game.

'I think,' Monica continued, 'that Jason had a fight with her and knocked her downstairs. I don't suppose he meant to,' she added, hoping to conciliate Ryan by hinting that his brother would not face serious charges if he were to support her theory with an eye-witness account. 'Is that what happened?'

'Mum slipped and fell,' Ryan repeated dogmatically without looking up from his phone.

'I know that's what she told you to say,' Monica insisted gently, 'but I think that's just because she doesn't want to get Jason into trouble. But in the long run, it'll be better for Jason, as well as for you and your mum, if you tell us the truth.'

'We did.' Ryan replied sulkily. 'Anyway, I was in my room. I told you. I didn't see what happened.'

'Are you sure, Ryan? Are you sure you're not just saying that because that's what your mum wants you to say? Or is it that you're frightened of what Jason will do if he finds out?'

'No. I told you. Jason wasn't there. Why don't you

believe me?'

Monica struggled to force down her rising irritation with his stubborn refusal to change his story. Alice had told her about the bruise that she had seen on Lyn Paul's face and her admission that it had been inflicted by her older son. She herself had – several years earlier – attended the post mortem of another woman who had refused to allow them to bring charges against her abusive boyfriend. The experience of looking down at the brutally battered remains of that pathetically young body had made a deep impression on her.

'Look Ryan, I know you think you're doing the right thing, but if you keep covering up for Jason like this, one day he may do your mum some really serious damage – even worse than what happened today. She needs you to tell us what really happened so that we can stop him doing it again.'

Ryan continued to ignore her. The car turned in at the hospital gate and headed towards the space near the emergency entrance reserved for the police. Monica made a final attempt to coax Ryan into changing his story.

'There are places for people like you and your mum,' she told him. 'We can take you to a Women's Refuge, where Jason won't be able to come and hurt you – either of you, and-'

'Shut your face!' Ryan shouted rudely, breaking off his game and stuffing the phone back into his pocket. He sat in silence, his face going very red. Monica thought he looked close to tears. What a pity the journey had not lasted a few minutes longer. She sensed that he was on the verge of letting down his defences, but now it was too late. He was reaching for the door of the car and anxiously looking round in search of the ambulance that had taken his mother.

CHAPTER 15: THURSDAY AFTERNOON

'This must be the place,' Bernie said, stopping the car outside a large detached house in the village of Horspath

Looking out from the back, Jonah noted a *For Sale* sign attached to one of the concrete gateposts that flanked the entrance to a wide drive. On that drive, were parked two cars: a sleek Jaguar and a small low-slung convertible. Both vehicles were new and shiny and bore personalised number plates featuring the initials *GWR*.

'It looks as if our Gordon is fond of fast cars,' Bernie observed as she released Jonah from the straps that held him, in his wheelchair, securely in the back of their people carrier. 'And I'm guessing *GWR* doesn't stand for *Great Western Railway!*'

They approached the front door together and Bernie rang the bell. They heard the sound of footsteps descending the stairs inside. A moment later, the door opened to reveal a large man with dark hair and a black beard with small flecks of grey in it. He looked down at Jonah with an expression of surprise, which rapidly changed to animosity. He was clearly not in the mood for visitors, and especially not strangers in wheelchairs who were probably on the scrounge for handouts.

'I'm DCI Jonah Porter and this is my Personal Assistant Dr Bernadette Fazakerley. We've got a few questions we'd like to ask you. Can we come in?'

'What's all this about?' Gordon Redfern stared unwelcomingly at them both as Bernie held up Jonah's warrant card and her own identification badge over Jonah's head. 'Are you accusing me of something?'

'We've arrested a friend of yours for arson,' Jonah told him. 'And we're hoping you might be able to throw some light on what made him do it.'

'It's not convenient right now. I'm busy.' Redfern attempted to close the door, but Bernie had her foot in it,

'Would it be more convenient for you to come down to the station and talk there?' Jonah asked mildly.

'What …?' Redfern stared round at them both again.

'I've been reading the things you and your friends have been writing in that Facebook group of yours – *Protect our Kids*. You seem to have something of a problem with members of the gay community. That, coupled with an incident of homophobic verbal abuse that's been reported to us, and the arson attack on a gay nightclub last night by a member of your group, gives us ample evidence to arrest you on suspicion of *intentionally stirring up hatred on the grounds of sexual orientation*. Would you prefer me to do that? Or are you going to invite us in for a nice friendly chat?'

'You're joking, right?' Redfern stared down at Jonah with an expression of disbelief. 'This is all just a wind-up – it's got to be!' his expression changed as Jonah continued to stare back impassively. 'Let me have another look at that warrant card! I don't believe you're a real policeman. They don't have cripples in the police force.'

Bernie obligingly held up the warrant card again, while Jonah dialled a number on the phone attachment on the arm of his wheelchair.

'I'm just calling a couple of uniformed officers to vouch for me,' Jonah told Redfern. 'Of course, having gone out of their way to get here, I can't promise they won't decide to arrest you. Are you sure you wouldn't prefer just to let us in so you can tell us your side of the story without a whole lot of formalities?'

'OK,' Redfern said grudgingly, hearing the ringing tone on Jonah's phone. 'Switch that thing off and come inside.'

'Thank you,' Jonah cancelled the call and reversed his wheelchair away from the door to make room for Bernie to set up the mobile ramp, which they carried with them to give him access to premises with steps at the entrance.

Redfern led the way into a large lounge with an impressive marble fireplace housing a much less impressive living flame gas fire, a three-piece suite upholstered in brown leather, and a range of display cabinets containing expensive-looking glassware. This was quite some home for a boy from the Blackbird Leys estate!

'Excuse the mess.' Redfern moved a large cardboard box out of the way to allow Jonah's wheelchair to enter. 'I'm having a bit of a clear out. You'll have seen the house is on the market.'

'Yes.' Jonah looked down at the contents of the box. There was a jumble of clothes – mostly jeans and tee shirts – topped by a pair of trainers. There was also a shoebox containing various documents, most of them bearing the name Jack Redfern: a gym membership card, two credit cards, a driving licence, a supermarket loyalty card and … a business card for Antonio's hairdressing salon. 'I was sorry to hear about your son. Is that what prompted the move?'

'It was a mixture of things,' Redfern grunted, pushing the box behind the sofa. 'But you didn't come here to talk about Jack. Let's get on and get this over with.'

'Very well. If you wouldn't mind sitting down.'

Redfern sat down on one of the large armchairs, perching on the edge as if he did not intend the interview to take long and was poised to leap to his feet the moment it was over. Jonah positioned his own chair so that he could look him in the eye. Bernie settled down on the sofa and got out her laptop to take notes.

'Last Friday night you spent some time in the *Bullnose Morris* with a couple of friends,' Jonah began. 'Do you remember that?'

'So what if I did?' Redfern demanded aggressively. 'It's a free country, isn't it? Or aren't I allowed to go for a drink with my mates any more without the polizei coming after me?'

'I'd like you to confirm the names of the two men that you were with,' Jonah continued calmly, 'to make sure that our witnesses are reliable. Will you tell me who they were?'

'What business is it of yours?'

'I gather some young lads were making trouble for you and your friends and the landlord had to ask them to leave. I need all the names in order to find out exactly what went on. My witnesses say that there were three of you together, and they gave me some names, but I'd like to hear it from you. Who were you with?'

'Rob Fry and Ian Boulton,' Redfern muttered. 'Is that all? Can I get on now?'

'Thank you. That's better. You and Ian go back a long way, don't you?'

'How d'you mean?'

'I was thinking about the letter you both signed demanding the dismissal of a teacher at your son's primary school. Do you remember that?'

Redfern did not reply, acknowledging the question by a scowl.

'Let me refresh your memory.' Jonah rotated the screen attached to his wheelchair to enable Redfern to see the image of a typed letter. The name of the teacher was blacked out, as were the signatures at the end. 'You used some quite intemperate language here. Do you regret any of it now?'

'Why should I?' Redfern growled. 'I believe in calling a spade a spade. It's not right having a bloody queer teaching young boys. The world's gone mad with all this political correctness. They should've removed him. If they had, maybe-' He stopped suddenly. Jonah wondered what he had been about to say – that if the teacher had been dismissed his son would not have turned out gay? Or perhaps that he would still be alive now?

'Getting back to Friday night,' Jonah resumed. 'I'm interested in knowing what time you each left the pub. Did you all go out together or did you leave one at a time?'

'Ian went first,' Redfern answered grudgingly. After his outburst, he now seemed to be trying to strike a more conciliatory note. 'He said he needed to get home. He had things to do. Myself and Rob had another drink and then we went out together. He went home and I went round to my mum's. I often stop off with her if it's late.'

'I see. And did you happen to notice what time it was when Ian left?'

'Ten on the dot. He'd got the alarm on his phone set to tell him when to go. We gave him a bit of stick about that,' Redfern smiled briefly at the recollection and then resumed his scowl.

'Good. That's useful. And did he have his car with him or was he on foot?'

'On foot, of course. What's all this about? You trying to do him for drink driving?'

'I'm just trying to get the sequence of events clear in my mind.' Jonah paused and consulted the notes of Anna's interview with Callum Lee. 'According to what other people have told us, the set-to with those lads wasn't until a bit later than that. Was Ian still there when it all kicked off or had he already left?'

'He'd already gone. He never saw them,' Redfern sounded strangely defensive. Jonah wondered why he considered it so important to emphasise Boulton's lack of involvement in the altercation. One might have expected him to have preferred to spread the blame as widely as possible.

'I see. So, just to confirm, it was just you and Robin Fry

who had the argument with the young men which led to them being ejected from the bar?'

'That's right. It was that Jason Paul started it – him and Ethan Roberts. It's them you ought to be talking to.'

'Don't worry; we've got our eye on them.'

'Is that it now?' Redfern leapt into the brief pause that followed while Jonah considered his next question, seizing the chance of bringing the interview to a close.

'Not quite.' Jonah remained calm. 'Now I'd like to ask you about your other friend, Robin Fry. What did you think when he put up that post threatening to set fire to a nightclub full of people? Didn't it worry you at all?'

'Post? What are you talking about?' Redfern blustered.

'On Facebook. He posted to your group yesterday morning "tonight's the night!" with the name of the nightclub and a picture of the school he set on fire when he was fourteen.'

'I never saw it!' Then, realising that Jonah did not believe him, he added, 'anyway, Rob was always saying that sort of thing. It didn't mean anything.'

'So you weren't aware of his little store of petrol bombs in his backyard?' Jonah asked, derisorily. 'Or his amateurish attempts at producing explosives from weed-killer?'

'No! I thought he'd got over all that years ago.'

'Ah! So you were aware of his history, then?'

'Yes, of course. He served time in a youth offenders institute for the school. His dad persuaded me to give him a job when he came out. I was being a good citizen, trying to rehabilitate an offender,' Redfern finished self-righteously.

'Getting back to his threatening Facebook post: you were an administrator for the group. Shouldn't you have been keeping an eye on what people were putting up there? Don't you think that one ought to have been taken down?'

'I can't watch what people put 24/7 can I? I've got

other things to do.'

'OK. We'll leave that. Tell me about Fry. You say you thought he'd given up on arson, but he was still rather inflammatory in other ways, wasn't he? Do you have any idea why he was so angry all the time?'

'He wasn't. Not all the time.' Redfern leaned forward so that his face was close to Jonah's and spoke confidentially. 'It's been a bad few months for both of us, what with the business going under and me having to let him go.'

'I suppose he will have known your son, Jack, too,' Jonah suggested. 'It's always upsetting when someone you know takes their own life. Do you think he could have blamed anyone at that nightclub for driving him to it?'

Redfern jerked back, his face registering first surprise and then anger.

'Too right he could!' he declared. 'It's a putrid cesspit of filth in there. Why haven't you closed it down? If it'd been girls in there, instead of boys, you'd have been in there quick enough, but you're all afraid of upsetting these perverts with their filthy carryings-on.'

'What exactly are you implying by that?' Jonah asked sharply. 'What do you mean by "boys"? Are you saying that there are under-age male prostitutes working there? Do you have any evidence for your accusations?'

'That's for you to find out, isn't it?' Redfern retorted. 'You're the police aren't you? Why don't you go in there and see what goes on, instead of coming round here harassing law-abiding citizens.'

'If there's any substance to your allegations, you need to tell us about it,' Jonah replied patiently. 'We can't just raid the place for no reason. Fry told us you'd been there with your son. Tell me about what you saw.'

'I wasn't *with* Jack,' Redfern protested. 'I followed him there, because I wasn't happy with the way he was carrying on.'

'When was this? Recently? Or when Jack was younger?'

'Just before Christmas.'

'So Jack will have been nineteen? – twenty?'

'Yes. He turned twenty in February. What's that got to do with anything?'

'I'm sorry – I thought you were alleging that he had been exploited for sex when he was a minor,' Jonah said innocently. 'Or was it that *he* was having sex with under-age boys at that club?'

'No, of course not!' Redfern was angry now. 'Jack never did anything wrong, he was just led on by those perverts.'

'I'm still rather at a loss as to who these "boys" are that you referred to. Did you actually see any boys in the club when you were there?'

'I just meant kids like Jack – too young to know their own minds – easily led by the likes of – of – that Marcus Antonio guy.'

'Ah! Now we're getting somewhere. Did you tell your friend Craig that Antonio needed teaching a lesson? Is that why he sprayed paint all over his hairdresser's shop?'

'I don't know what you're talking about.'

'He was caught red-handed on Tuesday night. Didn't you know? You really should keep better tabs on what the administrators of your group are getting up to.'

Redfern said nothing. Jonah considered what he had learnt from this interview. He now had a clear link between Jack Redfern and both the nightclub and the hairdressing salon. Should he push his luck and ask about the other businesses – or would it be better to conceal the fact that the police were linking the various incidents? He decided to leave Redfern still guessing as to how much they knew.

'Thank you, Mr Redfern,' he said politely, nodding to Bernie to pack up her computer. 'That will be all for now. We can see ourselves out.'

***

'Sir!' Andy greeted them excitedly when they arrived back at CID headquarters. 'I've found out something very interesting – about the teacher that Redfern and Boulton complained about.'

'Oh yes?' Jonah looked up at him, slightly amused by his young colleague's enthusiasm.

'He's Christopher Jackson – you know! The manager of *Bicycle Rehab* – the guy who was verbally abused by a male in a denim jacket. He got so much hassle from parents complaining about his sexuality that he gave up teaching and turned his cycling hobby into a business.'

'You're right,' Jonah agreed, smiling broadly. 'That is very interesting indeed. We now have a clear link between Gordon Redfern's son, Jack, and three out of our five gay businesses.'

'I may possibly have a fourth for you,' Andy said cautiously. 'Ian Lane's taxi company *does* provide transport for children attending the primary school that Jack Redfern went to, but the contract didn't start until well after he left – and, in any case, he wasn't eligible for local authority transport.'

'I suppose it could still have been a matter of principle with Redfern,' Jonah mused, 'or maybe he knew someone else whose kids were directly affected.'

'Or maybe it's like we said before – he's tarring all the businesses from the Oxford Mail article with the same brush,' Bernie suggested.

'I wonder if Wayne or Dean did know Jack Redfern,' Jonah went on, ignoring Bernie's remark. 'I've been trying not to hassle them, but it would be a simple enough question for Dean to answer.'

'You can ask him, when you meet for him to brief you about those interviews,' Bernie reminded him. 'You hadn't forgotten he's calling round this evening, had you?'

'No, of course not,' Jonah lied. 'Although I don't know why Lucy volunteered me for that. It isn't as if I haven't got plenty to do trying to pin down who's the ringleader in all this.' He turned back to Andy. 'I'm going to call on Ian Boulton next. I'd like you to come with us, seeing as you're the one who has all the gen on his background and in particular that daughter who lives with them, but that he didn't bother to mention to Anna or Monica.'

***

'Be sure to come to your physio appointment next week,' the nurse reminded Lyn before returning her to the safekeeping of Monica and Alice. 'And don't try to use that arm. Give the collarbone time to heal.'

Monica looked at her thoughtfully as they stood together in the waiting room. Her left arm was in a sling. There was a dressing on the right-hand side of her face. Her left eye was almost closed with purple swelling around it. She swayed slightly and then recovered her balance. Alice stepped forward quickly and took her by the right arm.

'Would you like to sit down for a few minutes before we go to the car?' she suggested. 'To get your breath back.'

'No, no. I'll be OK,' Lyn insisted, starting towards the door. 'I'd rather get home.'

Monica led the way outside. Lyn followed, supported by Alice, and Ryan brought up the rear, looking very anxious and subdued. When they reached the car, Monica held the door open while Alice helped Lyn inside. Ryan got in behind his mother, still looking very shell-shocked. Monica closed the front passenger door and joined Ryan in the back.

'Where to?' Alice asked from the driver's seat.

'Back home,' Lyn said at once. 'Just take us home.'

'You don't have to go back,' Monica told her, as the car moved off. 'We could take you to a refuge where you'll be safe.'

'I'm safe at home,' Lyn insisted. 'Just take us back there.'

'But what about Jason?' Alice asked sharply. 'You admitted the other day that he often hits you, and now he's pushed you downstairs. What if he does it again?'

'He never pushed me! I never said that. I told you – I slipped on the stairs. Jason wasn't even there.'

'That's not how it looks to-' Alice began, but Monica cut in before she could finish.

'I can understand that you want to protect your son, Mrs Paul,' she said, making an effort to remain calm despite her rising frustration, 'but it really isn't helping him – or you – to keep shielding him like this.'

'We'll be OK. Just take us home and stop going on at me.'

'But think of your other son,' Monica persisted, trying another tactic. 'He needs protecting too. And Jason needs help to stop his violent behaviour before he gets himself into serious trouble. It'll be much easier for us to help him if you and Ryan are out of the way for a while.'

'You! Help him? Don't make me laugh!' Lyn spat out bitterly, twisting in her seat in an effort to face Monica. The motion produced a sharp pain in her shoulder and she winced visibly, before slumping back into her seat. 'I suppose you mean "help him into jail" like you did with Dave!'

'He needs to understand that he can't knock you around and not face any consequences,' Alice argued dogmatically. 'A spell in custody might bring him to his senses.'

'Leave her alone!' Ryan protested suddenly from the back of the car. 'Can't you see you're only making things worse? Just shut up and take us home like you said you were.'

'OK,' Monica sighed. 'But I'm coming in with you when we get back, to check he's not waiting to punish you for getting yourself treated. I've seen this sort of thing before and I'm not prepared to take risks with your life, even if you are.'

***

Ian Boulton stared with undisguised astonishment at Jonah, when he opened the door to Hoo Down Farmhouse. He immediately re-directed his eyes towards Andy, who was deliberately standing well back behind Jonah and Bernie.

'What's all this about?' Boulton demanded. 'Are you collecting for something?'

'I'm Detective Chief Inspector Porter,' Jonah told him in his most authoritative tone. Bernie obligingly held up his warrant card as evidence. 'And this is Sergeant Lepage.' Andy stepped forward brandishing his own warrant card. 'We'd like to talk to you about a few things. May we come in?'

Boulton glanced at Jonah's identification and then looked up and addressed Andy again.

'I've already told that female detective everything I know. What more do you want? It's only a car theft after all – bloody inconvenient for me, but not exactly a major crime.'

'We're not here to talk about the alleged theft of your car,' Jonah informed him. 'This is to do with arson, threatening behaviour and stirring up hatred on the grounds of sexual orientation, as set out in Part 3A of the Public Order Act 1986. I hope that we can agree that those *are* serious crimes that warrant investigation.'

'What the hell is he talking about?' Boulton demanded, still addressing Andy over Jonah's head. 'I haven't got time for this sort of nonsense!' He made to close the door, but, once again, Bernie was there first, stepping over the threshold and forcing it open wide.

'Would you rather the sergeant arrested you and took you down to the station?' Jonah asked mildly. 'I'm sure he would be happy to oblige if that *is* your preferred choice.'

Boulton stared round for several seconds without speaking. Eventually he concluded that Jonah's threat was serious.

'Very well,' he muttered ungraciously, 'I suppose you'd better come in.'

Bernie stepped back out to set up the ramp, which she had put down outside. Soon they were all in the hall looking round at the beamed ceiling and wood-panelled walls. Boulton led the way through the passage to the large modern room where he had entertained Anna and Alice. As soon as they were settled in three of the cream-coloured easy chairs, with Jonah's wheelchair carefully positioned for interrogating Boulton, he began his inquisition.

'You belong to a Facebook group called *Protect our Kids*. What's that all about?'

'What it says on the tin – it's about trying to keep kids safe from paedophiles and perverts.'

'How exactly?'

'Campaigning mostly. Letting people know where they are. Getting them removed from places where they might come into contact with kids.'

'Demanding that a homosexual teacher be removed from his post, for example?' Jonah suggested, calmly but with a hint of menace in his voice. 'The way you and Gordon Redfern did with Christopher Jackson.'

'Yes,' Boulton replied unrepentantly. 'We weren't happy about his sort teaching our young kids and filling their heads with all sorts of perverted ideas.'

'You had children at the school too then? It wasn't just Jack Redfern?'

'My daughter was there too. She's a few years younger than Jack.'

'That would be Bethany, would it?'

'Yes.'

'According to the electoral roll, she's still living here with you. Where was she last Friday night?'

'She's at boarding school. Her term didn't end until last week. We collected her on the Saturday. We had to use my wife's car,' Boulton added in an aggrieved tone, 'seeing as the police have impounded mine.'

'We'll let you have it back as soon as the forensics team have finished with it,' Andy assured him. 'We've asked them to double-check some of their results. We don't want to make any mistakes.'

'Is your daughter in now?' Jonah asked.

'No. She and her mum are out shopping, why?'

'It's just that we could do with taking her fingerprints, in case any of the ones we can't identify in the car belong to her.'

'No point doing that,' Boulton said quickly. 'She's never been in the car. We bought it after she'd gone back to school this term.'

'You didn't take her out in it at half-term perhaps?' Bernie suggested, remembering the stories of life in a girls' boarding school, which she had read as a child. 'I thought parents were expected to visit.'

'No.'

'OK,' Jonah conceded, seeing that Boulton was determined not to allow them to involve his daughter in the investigation. 'Let's leave that for now. I want to go back to this Facebook group of yours. Did you see the post that Robin Fry put up threatening to set fire to a night club?'

'I saw it, yes,' Boulton admitted. 'But I didn't take it seriously. I was as shocked as anyone when I heard about it on the news. I never for a moment thought he meant it. As soon as I heard about the arrest on the radio, I got on to the admins to take down the post and exclude Rob from the group.'

'Really?' Jonah sounded surprised. 'And when was this?'

'Lunchtime today. I heard it on the lunchtime news and got on to them right away. I got a message from Gordon saying he'd taken the post down and excluded Rob just before you came.'

Jonah secretly wondered whether it was Boulton's message or his own visit that had prompted Redfern's belated attempt to distance the group from Fry's actions. However, he said nothing, merely nodding his acknowledgement of the information.

'OK. We're nearly finished – for now. There's just one other thing I'd like to ask you about. Bernie! Show Mr Boulton those leaflets will you?'

Bernie got up, placing her laptop on her seat, and went round behind Jonah's chair. Reaching into the storage space at the back, she got out several copies of the pamphlets that Susie and William Cunliffe had been attempting to distribute. She handed them to Boulton, who stared down at them, turning them over in his hands.

'Do you recognise these?' Jonah asked. 'They have your company name on them.'

'Yes. I remember printing these. What about it?'

'Do you know Mr and Mrs Cunliffe?'

'Who?'

'The couple who hang around gay bars and clubs trying to hand these out. I thought they were probably the ones who commissioned you to print these.'

'Oh them!' Boulton smiled as if he found the recollection of the Cunliffes amusing. 'No, I wouldn't say I knew them particularly. They're just customers. I do printing for all sorts of people. It's my job.'

'I see,' Jonah leaned back in his chair and sat for a moment in silent contemplation. 'So you don't necessarily agree with the sentiments expressed in these jolly little leaflets – God will rain fire and brimstone down on the wicked fornicators? Homosexuals will go to Hell? God loves you so much that he's going to torture you for ever?'

'No, of course not!' Boulton laughed out loud now. 'I don't have any truck with all that *God* stuff. Like I said, I'm just a printer. They pay me to print what they want – the same as all my other customers. I don't have to believe any of it.'

'No, of course not,' Jonah agreed coldly. 'But you ought to read everything you print. Are you familiar with Part 3 A of the Public Order Act 1986? If someone made a complaint that this material was threatening towards gay people or designed to stir up hatred against them, then you would be implicated in its publication.'

Boulton stared at Jonah in silence for several seconds, before exploding into indignant protest.

'Are you serious? What about freedom of expression? What about my right to make a living? You'd soon have me in court if I refused to print stuff advertising gay rights, wouldn't you? Why do they have the protection of the law to go round flaunting their perversions and I don't have the right to put the opposite view?'

'I'm not here to argue about that. My job isn't making the law, only upholding it; and I'm just warning you that you should take care over what you're being asked to print for people.' Jonah turned to look at Bernie and Andy. 'OK. Let's go. We're finished here.'

***

Peter found himself with time on his hands that afternoon. It was an off-duty day for Crystal, so Ricky and Abigail were with her, and Peter was alone at home. He decided to pay Anna a visit. Their conversation on Monday afternoon had left him feeling anxious for her and her family. A listening ear from someone who understood the special nature of a police officer's job and who had himself juggled its demands with those of a growing family might be helpful to her.

She smiled when she saw him standing on the doorstep clutching a large punnet of raspberries, which he had picked from the garden to provide an excuse for the call.

'Would you have a use for these?' he asked, holding them up. 'We've got far more than we can eat.'

'Thank you! They look lovely.' Anna took the fruit and

stepped back to allow Peter inside. 'Go on into the lounge, while I put these in the fridge and pop the kettle on.'

Peter found Donna sitting on the floor, propped up on cushions, surrounded by various plastic toys. She looked just like any other eight-month-old child, waving her arms around trying in vain to pick up one of the gaily-coloured plastic beakers that lay in front of her. It would be a few more months before it became obvious that she was not keeping up with her peers as they began first to crawl and then to toddle. He kneeled down beside her.

'Hello Donna! Do you remember me? I'm Uncle Peter.'

She turned her head at the sound of his voice and studied him gravely. For a moment, it looked as if she might be going to cry. Then she seemed to change her mind and returned to trying to reach the plastic beakers.

'Shall I help you?' Peter found the largest beaker and set it upside-down on the floor in front of her. Then he placed the next in size on top of it. Soon he had all twelve beakers stacked in a tower. Donna looked up at it and waved her arms in delight. Then, with a swift movement, she sent it crashing to the floor, letting out a delighted gurgle as she did so.

Peter raced on hands-and-knees to collect them together again and re-build the tower. Donna had just knocked it down for the third time when Anna returned with mugs of tea and a plate of biscuits.

'I see you've made friends,' she commented, seeing her daughter clapping her hands excitedly. 'You should consider yourself honoured. She's been a bit funny with people she doesn't know recently – especially men. Phil came to stay the weekend-before-last and it wasn't until Sunday evening when he was about to leave that she allowed him to hold her.'

Peter got up off the floor and sat down on the sofa. Anna handed her daughter a two-handled plastic cup with a lid and spout before sitting down next to him and holding out the plate of biscuits. Peter took one.

'Does Phil come often?'

'About one weekend a month. In fact, it's been a bit more than that recently. I think he misses the kids.'

'And you?' Peter suggested.

'Maybe,' Anna shrugged. 'I sort of miss him too, I suppose.' She sighed. 'I miss the way it used to be, when he seemed to be happy staying at home with Jess and Marcus and just doing freelance work around looking after them. But ...'

Peter sipped his tea in silence.

'Last time he was here, Phil started talking about coming back,' Anna resumed after a long pause. 'I was tempted to say "yes" but ... I don't know.'

'It must be difficult to forgive him for the way he reacted when you were expecting Donna,' Peter suggested gently. Anna's husband had been angry to discover that she was pregnant and had urged her to have an abortion, even before the second scan had shown up Donna's abnormality.

'Strangely, that's not the biggest thing. The thing that I really find hard to take is the way he organised the move down to Exeter behind my back like that. He never even so much as dropped a hint until after he'd got the partnership with Brian all arranged! And he told his mum we were all moving down there before breathing a word to me. He never stopped to think about me or my career or ...'

'Perhaps his friend was in a hurry for him to make a decision,' Peter suggested.

'But he never even told me he'd been talking to him. And if he could tell his mum all about it, why not me – or the kids? He simply took it for granted that we'd all go along with it, because they always liked the holidays we used to have down there with his mum.' Anna sighed again. 'Anyway, the thing is: I don't think I'll ever be able to trust him properly again. I'll always be wondering if there's something he isn't telling me. And If I did take him back, I'd always be thinking: did I do this just to get a child-minder for Donna?'

'Is that the deal then? He'd come back and look after Donna the way he did with Jessica and Marcus?'

'That's what he suggested,' Anna sighed again. 'And, with the trouble I've been having over finding childcare for Donna, it's very tempting in a way, but …. I'm afraid I'm only thinking of him as a cut-price nanny, which wouldn't be fair on him.'

'I don't know,' Peter argued gently. 'He ought to realise that he doesn't deserve anything more after the way he behaved.'

'I'm trying not to think of it that way. Anyway, it would still mean I was sort of living a lie.'

'But maybe only at first,' Peter persisted, ever the optimist. 'Don't you think that, after a while you might both manage to get back more to how you were before? I mean, it seems a pity to give up on so many years of marriage, if he's willing to have another go – on your terms, obviously.'

'That's just it – is it reasonable for me to expect it to be on my terms? And I'm not even sure what I want my terms to be! And then there's the kids. I'm sure Marcus would be pleased to have his dad back with us, but Jess? I really don't know. She's always civil to him – because I spoke to her about it – but I don't think she can forgive him for wanting an abortion. She sees everything in black-and-white and considers it to be the same as murder. I think she finds it hard to reconcile that with the father she thought she knew.'

'You said he's offered to look after Donna for you, doesn't that help her to see he's accepted her now?'

'If anything, I almost think that makes it worse! Jess seems to resent Phil's fondness for Donna – as if he's forfeited any right to a part in her. She's rather possessive towards her altogether. Donna is hers and mine – and maybe Marcus's, only he's not that interested, so it doesn't matter. Phil, I suppose, represents competition for Donna's affection, and Jess doesn't believe he deserves to get any of it, even if he is her dad.'

'Well, it's your decision,' Peter said as he drained his mug. 'And don't forget, the offer's still there for me to add Donna to my child-minding responsibilities if you're still struggling to get her into a day nursery when Jess's new term starts in September.'

***

Jason was waiting for them when they arrived back at the Paul family home. Alice helped Lyn up the drive, past the battered car, to the front door. Ryan stepped forward and put out his hand to unlock it, but it jerked open before he could touch it. Jason stood there, glowering down at them. He was tall and heavily built, with a shock of fair hair flopping over his eyes. Monica felt considerable sympathy with the bar tender who had assumed that he must be over eighteen – and some admiration for his skill in managing to eject him from the pub without a fight.

'Where you been?' he demanded, staring at his mother and brother. His speech was slurred and he seemed somewhat unsteady in his feet.

'Stand back please,' Alice said briskly. 'You mother needs to rest. Let her past.'

'Who're you?' Jason turned his attention to Alice, breathing beer fumes over her and belching loudly in her face. 'What're you doing here?'

'We are police officers,' Monica told him, while Alice helped Lyn past Jason and into the living room. 'We've brought your mother back from the hospital, where she's been treated for a broken collarbone and a variety of other injuries. She needs to take it easy for a few weeks while the bone mends – and she doesn't need any hassle from you, do you understand?'

'What you been telling them, Ryan?' Jason suddenly

reached out and grabbed hold of his brother by the arm. 'What does the bitch mean – hassle from me?'

Ryan, who had been attempting to slip past to join his mother, cowered away with an expression of terror on his face.

'I never said nothing,' he insisted. 'I told them Mum slipped on the stairs, just like you said.'

'I thought you said Jason was out all morning,' Monica cut in. 'What do you mean – just like he said?'

'Nothing!' Ryan's voice rose in panic as he realised what he had said. 'I didn't mean nothing. I was in my room. I didn't see nothing. Mum slipped on the stairs. That's all I know.'

Monica looked Jason up and down. She was now confident that he had been responsible for his mother's fall, but she was undecided as to the best way of securing his arrest. He was considerably taller and heavier than she was and, in his present belligerent mood, would almost certainly put up resistance.

'OK,' she said at last. 'Let's forget all that and go and see how your mum is, shall we?'

Jason released his brother, who immediately scampered away to join Lyn and Alice. Monica followed him. Jason put out an arm to stop her, but then changed his mind – or perhaps lost his balance – and used it to steady himself against the wall instead.

Lyn was lying on the sofa with a rather dirty cushion beneath her head. Alice was kneeling on the floor beside her. She got up and looked towards Monica.

'I've offered to call Social Services to help Mrs Paul, but she says they'll be able to manage OK.'

'Are you sure?' Monica looked down at Lyn, who nodded.

'We don't need no bloody Social Worker,' Jason confirmed from where he stood in the doorway. 'And we don't need no fucking cops either!'

He lunged towards Monica, who deftly dodged his fist

and, catching him off balance, brought him down. He fell face down across one of the armchairs. Alice leapt forwards and held his hands behind his back, while Monica reached into her pocket for her handcuffs.

'Jason Paul,' she said, as she clipped them on to his wrists, 'I am arresting you on suspicion of assaulting your mother, Mrs Lyn Paul. You do not have to say anything. But, it may harm your defence if you do not mention when questioned something which you later rely on in court. Anything you do say may be given in evidence. Do you understand?'

CHAPTER 16: FRIDAY MORNING

'Hmm!' Jonah murmured. 'We now have charges being brought against Robin Fry and Jason Paul, and we've cautioned Tanya Lumley and Craig Jones, but that still leaves Redfern and Boulton. They're both nasty pieces of work, but I'm not sure that we have enough evidence to charge them.'

Much to Bernie's disgust, Jonah had insisted on going in to work first thing that morning, despite having taken a day's leave. Ignoring her protestations that he should have stayed at home until it was time to set off for the *Design Ability* offices and the interviews for their customer-liaison officer post, he had called his team together to discuss progress and make plans for the day ahead.

'I'm a bit doubtful about Jason Paul too, to be honest,' Monica admitted. 'It seemed like the only thing to do at the time. To get him out of the house and give his mother a break, but …'

'If Lyn and Ryan both stick to their story that Jason was out of the house when Lyn fell down the stairs …,' Alice continued mournfully.

'And neither of them will admit in court that he ever knocked her about …,' Monica added.

'What about his threatening behaviour while you were there yesterday?' Jonah asked. 'Is that enough to justify charging him – even if Lyn and Ryan stick by him?'

'I suppose so.' Monica still sounded uncertain. 'The thing is: if we do charge him, the magistrate will probably let him out on bail and then …,' she trailed off.

'It could make things even worse for his mum,' Alice finished for her. They had been talking the situation over together the previous night without coming to any satisfactory conclusions.

'OK,' Jonah said decisively. 'We've still got a few more hours before we have to charge him or release him. If you don't think we've got enough evidence to make a charge stick, let's work on the basis of letting him go this afternoon. Meanwhile, get on to Social Services and report Ryan as a child at risk. If his mother won't let anyone help *her*, at least we ought to be able to get them to keep an eye on the family to protect *him*.'

'Right! I'll do that,' Monica brightened up a little at this suggestion.

'I've got to go out shortly,' Jonah added, 'but I should be back before our 24-hours is up; so I'll interview Jason myself before we let him go and see if I can persuade him to admit to hitting his mum. You never know, he may get all remorseful once he sobers up properly – these sorts often do.'

'Do you really think Social Services will be able to do anything?' Alice asked dubiously.

'That's what I was thinking,' Bernie agreed. 'If I was a Social Worker with an impossibly heavy caseload, protecting a strapping fifteen-year-old with a reputation for anti-social behaviour wouldn't be top of my priority list.'

'You're right,' Monica agreed, 'but I suppose it's the best we can do – given that neither Lyn nor Ryan will give evidence against Jason.'

Now, to get back to Redfern and Boulton,' Jonah

intervened briskly, conscious that he had limited time before Bernie would be insisting on whisking him away. 'Do we have enough evidence to arrest either of them?'

'I've got the coroner's report on Jack Redfern's death,' Andy volunteered. 'I'd pencilled in this morning for reading it to see if there's anything there.'

'And the lab has done a re-test on that hair from the headrest of Boulton's car,' Alice contributed. 'They say that it probably isn't Jason Paul's after all, which leaves us clear to assume that it must have been Boulton driving on Friday night.'

'Presumably they don't have any idea who the hair does belong to?' Jonah asked sharply.

'No,' Alice shook her head. 'They weren't very communicative,' she added with a smile, 'after they discovered they'd got it wrong. They just said that the DNA profile was incomplete and it had been wrongly matched.'

'A lot of time and effort could be saved, if only people would do their jobs properly in the first place,' Jonah muttered. 'But no point dwelling on that. I think you're probably right. Everything points to Ian Boulton being the driver of the car, and even if he's not, putting the frighteners on him may prompt him to confess to being involved in the homophobic attacks or to grass up Redfern or one of the others for them. He told us lies about where he was on Friday evening, which justifies us bringing him in for questioning.'

'And we still haven't managed to interview *Mrs* Boulton,' Alice piped up. 'I'm sure he's been deliberately preventing us from talking to her. If we arrest him, maybe she'll tell us what really happened that evening when he claimed he was at home with her.'

'Good!' Jonah glanced down at the time on his computer screen. 'I have to go now, but it looks as if we have a plan. Monica and Alice – you go and arrest Boulton, and see if you can speak to his wife. Andy – get on to Social Services about Ryan Paul and then check out that coroner's report. I should be back about three, I hope, in time to give Jason a good talking to about the way he treats his mum.'

***

Despite his reservations about allowing anything to interrupt his investigation, Jonah was enjoying himself interviewing the candidates to become *Design Ablity*'s new employee. He had agreed with Graham that each applicant would be asked to take part in a short role-play exercise before the formal interview. Now he and Bernie were waiting for the third candidate to demonstrate her abilities at dealing with a customer who had come to complain.

Jonah was sitting in his chair, apparently busy with something on the computer screen. Bernie was a few feet away holding a small briefcase on her lap and watching the door. It opened and a young woman entered, dressed in a smart business suit. She looked round the room and caught Bernie's eye.

'I'm Imogen Camberwell,' she told her with a nervous smile. 'I'm the customer liaison officer. I hear Mr Porter has a complaint about the installation of the voice-activated internal doors in his house?'

Bernie stared back blankly, so Imogen continued, sounding even more nervous now.

'First of all, please accept my deepest apologies. This absolutely shouldn't have happened. If you can just tell me what Mr Porter would like us to do to put things right ...'

'I'm sorry?' Bernie replied in a tone of bewilderment. 'Are you talking to me?'

'Well yes.' The candidate looked from Bernie to Jonah and back again. Jonah, who had looked up at the sound of his name was now eyeing her with an expression somewhere between amusement and hostility. 'I thought ...'

'I'm sorry,' Bernie repeated, 'but you seem to be under some sort of misapprehension. I don't know this man. I'm an accountant. I'm here to review the company's first quarter 2018/19 financial report.'

'Oh!' Imogen went bright red and looked towards Jonah again. He stared stonily back without speaking. 'I'm so sorry! I just assumed … I didn't think …'

'That much is evident' Jonah said coldly. 'Now, about my doors …'

***

'Come in!' Maureen Boulton greeted Monica and Alice cheerfully when she saw them standing on the doorstep holding up their warrant cards. 'You've come about the car, I suppose. Did you want to speak to Ian? Come in and sit down while I get him for you.'

She led the way to the spacious room that Alice had seen on her previous visit to the house. She could now recognise that the elegant woman on horseback in several of the photographs adorning the walls was Maureen Boulton. In other pictures, Maureen featured alongside two well-groomed afghan hounds and, dressed for skiing, standing in front of an Austrian chalet with her arm around what looked like a younger version of herself.

'If you don't mind waiting here,' Maureen went on, waving her hand towards the cream-coloured easy chairs, 'I'll fetch Ian for you. I must say, I've been pleasantly surprised at the amount of trouble you're taking over this. Other people have said that the police just ignore minor crimes like car theft – and after all, Ian was asking for it leaving the key in the ignition like that.'

'But this isn't just car theft, is it Mrs Boulton?' Monica said coldly. 'Driving at over seventy in a thirty-mile-an-hour speed limit, smashing a pedestrian against a bus shelter and then driving on without stopping is hardly a minor offence, is it?'

'What are you talking about?' Maureen Boulton paused on her way out of the room and stood there with her hand on the door looking round at Monica and Alice.'

'We're talking about dangerous driving,' Alice told her. 'In fact, whoever the driver was, they're very lucky that it isn't *causing death* by dangerous driving.'

'Also speeding, failing to stop and report a road accident,' Monica added, 'and, if it turns out that it was anything more than an accident, we could be talking assault or even attempted murder.'

'But ...,' Maureen gasped, struggling to work out what this was all about. 'Are you ... are you telling me that the car was involved in some sort of accident while it was stolen?'

'That's right. Surely your husband must have told you?' Monica said in a calm voice, but inwardly excited to discover this strange lack of communication between Ian Boulton and his wife. Was this confirmation that he was guilty?

'No. He just said that the car had been found in a ditch and the police had taken it away for forensic examination. I just thought you were being very thorough about finding out who the joy-riders were.' She stood for a moment or two looking uncomfortable and as though she was thinking hard. 'I suppose he was trying not to worry me,' she laughed nervously. 'Anyway, I'll go and get him for you. Sit down. I won't be long.'

'Before you do,' Monica said quickly, pushing the door closed and standing in front of it to prevent Mrs Boulton from leaving. 'I wonder if you could just answer a few questions about last Friday night.'

'Yes, of course.' Maureen looked puzzled. 'But I don't see that I can add anything to what my husband has already told you.'

'I'm afraid there were a few discrepancies,' Monica told her. 'Probably just a simple mix-up, but it makes a difference to the timing of when the car could have been taken, so we'd like to get things straight. Let's all sit down, shall we?'

Maureen nodded with a rather bemused expression on her face. Then she sat down on the edge of one of the armchairs. Alice sat next to her, while Monica chose the larger black leather chair, which Ian Boulton had occupied when Anna had interviewed him. She looked Maureen directly in the eye as she asked her first question.

'Can we go back to when your husband returned to the house in the car? That was between six and half past, I believe?'

'No. It was much later,' Maureen looked even more puzzled now. 'He got back about … Oh! I see what you mean. Yes, he got back from his golf afternoon round about six, I suppose – or, actually I would have said it was earlier than that – but I don't see what that has to do with the car being stolen.'

'Why do you say that?' asked Alice eagerly.

'Well, because it was when he left it on the drive that night, after coming back from the *Bullnose Morris* that it went missing. Surely you know that?'

'No. We didn't,' Monica told her. 'The statement that he gave to our officer was that he brought the car back before six thirty and then stayed at home with you all evening.'

'What time did he go out to the pub?' Alice asked, taking advantage of Maureen's shocked silence to press on with their questioning. 'And when did he get home again?'

'He – it must have been nearly nine, I think, when he went out,' Maureen began. 'No! It was earlier than that – just after we finished dinner. And he got back … I'm not sure exactly. I was upstairs having a bath. Ten thirty – maybe a few minutes after that – definitely no earlier than twenty-five past.'

'And he was in the car?' Monica asked. 'He hadn't left it at the pub and walked home or got a taxi?'

'Yes. He was in the car … or at least I *thought* he was.'

Maureen's brow creased in a frown as she tried to come to terms with the knowledge that her husband had lied to the police. 'I didn't actually see the car – I was in the bath, as I said. I think I heard it come up the drive, but I could have been mistaken. Or, I suppose, it could have been a taxi.'

She paused and seemed to be thinking. Monica and Alice waited patiently for her to go on.

'In fact … yes!' Maureen's face suddenly brightened and she smiled round with a look of relief. 'A taxi would explain the sounds I heard afterwards. I didn't think anything of it at the time, but I'm sure now that I did hear voices in the front garden and then a car driving away. That could've been Ian paying off the taxi man, couldn't it?'

'So now, let me get this clear,' Monica said slowly. 'You're suggesting that your husband returned from the pub in a taxi. What about his car – the one that was stolen – where was that then?'

'Why, still on the drive here, of course!' Maureen said triumphantly. 'Don't you see? He must've walked to the pub – knowing that he was going to be drinking and so wouldn't be able to drive back – and then got a taxi back. I'm sorry,' she added with a nervous laugh. 'I'm not a very good witness, am I? Fancy my not noticing that he hadn't taken the car! But we were all in the back sitting room, you see, so we couldn't tell the car was still there on the drive.'

Monica and Alice both opened their mouths to ask who "all" included. It seemed a strange way for Mrs Boulton to refer to herself and her husband. Had there been someone else present in the house on Friday night? Maureen, however, was too quick for them. She jumped to her feet and pulled open the door.

'Now, I'll just go and fetch Ian, so that we can get all this cleared up properly. I won't be a minute.'

It was more than ten minutes before her husband entered the room. His wife did not return with him. By way of excuse, he muttered something vague about her needing to "see to the lunch". He looked flustered and red in the face.

'Why did you tell my colleagues that you spent Friday evening here with your wife?' Monica asked coldly, the moment he stopped talking.

'I'm sorry,' Boulton gave a nervous snigger, as if he were a schoolboy caught smoking behind the bike sheds. 'I simply forgot I'd gone out. You see, I wasn't planning to. We knew we were going to have a busy day on Saturday, what with Bethany coming home from school and everything, so we intended to have an early night.'

'And what made you change your mind?' Alice asked, when Boulton stopped speaking, apparently thinking that he had said all that was necessary to explain his behaviour.

'A phone call. A friend of mine rang and asked me to go for a few drinks with him. His business folded when Carillion went under and he's been very low ever since his son committed suicide a few weeks ago, so I didn't like to say "no".'

'I see,' Monica did not sound entirely convinced. 'That would be Gordon Redfern, I take it?'

'Yes. That's right. Do you know him?'

'We do.' Monica hesitated, wondering how much to tell Boulton about their investigations into *Protect our Kids*. 'But to get back to last Friday, you were telling us about what you did that evening – what you *really* did,' she added with emphasis, 'rather than the fairy story that you concocted for DI Davenport. What time did you leave to go to the pub?'

'I'm not sure – eight thirty maybe.'

'And you had a few drinks with your friend Gordon Redfern, and then came home. About when would that have been?'

'Ten-ish, I think. I'm really not sure.'

'And it was just the two of you? Just two mates having a drink together?'

'Yes – well, no. Rob Fry was there too. I don't know

207

him that well. He's a friend of Gordon's. He used to work for him, before the business went under. He's unemployed now, I think.'

'OK.' Monica paused again, trying out in her mind alternative ways of approaching the question of who had actually been driving the car. 'You set off home from the *Bullnose Morris* at, say, ten pm, on foot, I take it?'

'Yes. That's right.'

'About how long would it have taken you to get home?'

'Five – maybe ten minutes. Not long.'

'And was the car still there on the drive when you got back?'

'I – I-,' Boulton stammered, looking round at Monica and Alice, clearly trying to work out which answer would satisfy them that he was telling the truth. 'I can't remember,' he finished at last.

'You walked up the drive, past where you'd parked the car, and let yourself in at the front door, and you didn't notice whether the car was there or not?'

'I had other things on my mind,' Boulton blustered. 'I was worried about Gordon; and I was thinking about picking Beth up from school; and I wanted to get back because I'd promised Maureen I wouldn't be late.'

'Ah yes!' Alice put in, a small note of triumph in her voice. 'Your wife. She told us just now that she heard a car drive up just before you got home – and then she heard it driving away again. She thought you must have come back in a taxi. If you were walking, can you explain the sounds she heard?'

'She must have been mistaken,' Boulton said quickly. 'It must've been cars out in the road. I walked home, like I said, and came straight in. I only remembered the car later on – when we were getting ready for bed. I took my keys out of my pocket and saw that the car key wasn't with them. And then I realised that I'd left it in the ignition when I got out to catch Sadie.'

'If the car was there on the drive when you got back

from the pub, I'm surprised that didn't jog your memory,' Monica observed calmly.

'Yes, I suppose so,' Boulton agreed, visibly relaxing at this suggestion. 'I suppose it must have already been stolen and that's why I didn't see it.'

'Which leaves us with the little puzzle of where whoever took it went to, between taking it from your drive and mowing down a pedestrian outside the *Blackbird* at quarter to eleven,' Alice commented.

'You know, Mr Boulton,' Monica said, leaning forward and looking him in the eye. 'I'm becoming increasingly sceptical about this car theft. It seems much more likely to me that you had a few too many at the *Bullnose Morris* before driving it away yourself. Isn't that what really happened, Mr Boulton?'

'No! I told you what really happened. I left the car on the drive and it was stolen.'

'While you were out at the pub?' Alice asked disdainfully. 'Or was it while you were spending a night in with your wife?'

'I explained all that.'

'Not very convincingly, I'm afraid,' Monica told him bluntly. 'We've spoken to Gordon Redfern, and he didn't say anything about telephoning you. Your wife put the time you got home at half past ten, which means that, if the thief took the car from your drive and went straight down Watlington Road and into Cuddesdon Way, you'd have seen them as you were walking home. *Did* you meet a speeding car on your way back?'

'I – I – I may have done. I don't remember.' Boulton was clearly rattled now.

'Come on, Mr Boulton,' Monica urged with exaggerated self-control. 'Why not save us all a lot of time and just tell us what really happened?'

They sat for several minutes without speaking. Monica, having thrown out her challenge, knew that silence was now her most effective weapon. Very few people felt comfortable under the scrutiny of a mute police officer. It was not long before her patience was rewarded.

'OK,' Boulton said. 'I'll come clean. You're right. I was driving the car when it hit that guy.'

CHAPTER 17: FRIDAY AFTERNOON

'I think it's between applicants two and five,' Jonah said to Graham and Dean as they pored over the notes they had made of the morning's interviews. 'One and three both failed the role-play exercise, as far as I'm concerned, by failing to engage properly with me and-'

'Yes,' Bernie interrupted. 'That Trevor Williams was so cocky and sure of himself and wanted to tell you what was good for you all the time. I felt like punching him in the face just to get him to stop talking and listen for a moment!'

'The woman – what was her name? – number three, was just as patronising,' Jonah insisted. 'She assumed that it wasn't possible for me to be anywhere without a minder.'

'And once we got that sorted out, I think perhaps she was so frightened of saying something that would offend you that she was hardly able to say anything at all,' Bernie agreed.

'And number four?' Graham asked. 'You're ruling her out as well? That was Belinda Shakespeare, the pretty little brunette in the black dress.'

'She wasn't so bad when she was treating me as a customer,' Jonah conceded, 'but I'm convinced she never took me seriously as a member of the interview panel. She addressed all her answers to you and Dean, even when I'd asked the question. I think she knew all the theory about customer-relations, but still didn't believe that I was on the panel as more than just a token disabled person to make the company look good.'

'So that leaves us with Daniel Barker and Natalie Forrest,' Dean said, looking down the list. 'I thought they were both OK. What do you think, Graham? You've done a lot more interviews than I have.'

'Barker has more experience of customer service but Natalie has more qualifications,' Graham replied, flicking through their CVs. 'I'm not sure how relevant a degree in philosophy and theology is though, so probably Barker would be the safer bet.'

'Natalie Forrest has a brother with cerebral palsy,' Bernie pointed out. 'And she knew a lot about disability benefits and some of the practical aspects of living with a disability.'

'I agree,' Jonah nodded. 'I reckon she'd have a better chance of understanding where your clients are coming from.'

'Well Dean, it's your decision,' Graham looked at his son-in-law. 'What do you think? Don't forget, you're going to have to work with whoever you take on.'

'Well, to be honest, I found Daniel Barker a bit intimidating,' Dean admitted. 'He seemed to know such a lot and to have so much more experience of customer-relations than I do. I'd be afraid of telling him what to do in case he thought I was being stupid.'

'In that case, it's Natalie or no-one,' Graham said decisively. 'It's no good taking on someone you know you won't be able to manage. Do you think she's what you want? Will she be able to do the job?'

'I – I'm not sure,' Dean hesitated. 'I don't like … Wayne and I have always decided everything together.'

There was a long silence. None of the others could think what to say to this. Eventually Jonah cleared his throat and spoke, tentatively at first and then with more conviction.

'Why not ask him? He understands what we say, doesn't he? His *thinking* isn't affected – just his speech. You can tell him about how the interviews went and what we thought and ask him if he thinks we ought to take Natalie Forrest or to re-advertise. We're agreed that none of the others will do, so it's a straightforward question for him to answer.' He paused and then continued, 'and speaking as someone who's been in his situation, I think it would give him a boost to know that he's still making a contribution to running the company, even if he is still going to be stuck in hospital for a while longer.'

***

Ignoring Bernie's protestations that he had taken a day's leave and ought to go home and relax, Jonah insisted on returning to the police station as soon as the interview process was over. He was greeted by Monica, who was eager to relate her success with Ian Boulton.

'Once he realised that we knew he'd been lying to us, he gave in and came out with the whole story,' she told him. 'What actually happened, was that he *drove* to the *Bullnose Morris* for his few pints with Redfern and Fry, after having dinner with his wife.

'When he came out, he found some boys hanging around the car park messing with the cars. One of them was standing on the bonnet of his BMW. Another seemed to be trying to get the door open. When they saw him, they ran off along Cuddesdon Way. He saw red and decided to chase them in the car, which explains why he came to be going so fast when he turned into Blackbird Leys Road.'

'Not really it doesn't,' Jonah interrupted. 'If they were on foot and he was in a fast car, how come he didn't overtake them way before they got to the junction with

Blackbird Leys Road?'

'I suppose they'd got a head start while he was getting in the car and turning the ignition on,' Monica suggested. 'Anyway, he admits he was probably over the limit and not thinking straight. He careered round the corner and lost control as he was coming up to the bus stop. He hit Wayne and then panicked and put his foot down hoping to get away without being recognised.'

'But, unluckily for him, one of the witnesses was on the ball enough to get part of his registration number,' Alice added, coming across the room to join them. 'So his only hope of avoiding prosecution was to claim the car had been stolen.'

'He headed for the by-pass, wanting to get away from where there were any people watching. He had to go west, because the Sandy Lane junction doesn't allow you on to the other carriageway,' Monica resumed. 'He went right round the Littlemore roundabout, as we'd worked out he must have, and headed back, intending to come off at Watlington Road to go home.'

'So why didn't he?' Jonah asked sharply.

'He was in the wrong lane when he got to the junction,' Monica shrugged. 'He was overtaking a lorry, which turned out to be going faster than he thought, and couldn't get back to the left in time. Anyway, he missed the junction and had to carry on to the traffic lights at Horspath Road.'

'OK. So he jumped the lights and hared off through Horspath,' Jonah cut in. 'We know what happened then. A couple of traffic cops chase him until he crashes out in a ditch and makes off across the fields, pursued by Mel Stanton and PD Q.'

'We should have listened to Q telling us that it was the car's owner who was driving,' Alice put in, pleased to have been vindicated in her belief.

'He got home and rang 999 right away to report the car as stolen,' Monica went on. 'He must've got a shock when it turned up so quickly.'

'Yes, agreed Alice, 'I bet he was hoping it'd stay in that ditch for days – until everyone had forgotten that it went missing the same day as Wayne was knocked down.'

'Do you think he told his wife what had happened?' Jonah asked. 'Or did she really think it had been stolen?'

'I'm not sure,' Monica said slowly. 'She seemed genuinely surprised to hear it'd been involved in the accident outside the *Blackbird*, so I think whatever he told her, it didn't include him having nearly killed someone.'

'My guess is that, by the time we went round this morning, he'd told her that he'd been driving under the influence and crashed the car in Cuddeson Road,' Alice surmised, 'but I don't think she knew about the hit-and-run.'

'And he may not have told her even that much right away,' Monica added. 'I think his first plan was to keep her in the dark and to try to avoid us talking to her – in case she blew his cover accidentally. But then, he realised that she was bound to work out that he'd made up the story about the car being stolen, so he persuaded her to cover for him so that he wouldn't lose his licence for drunk driving. He's sticking to the story that she knew nothing about it at all and I don't suppose we'll be able to get either of them to budge on that. The main thing is that we've got a signed statement from him admitting to being the driver who hit Wayne and then didn't stop.'

'Yes,' Jonah agreed. 'Good work, both of you. I don't think I'm too bothered about not being able to charge Mrs Boulton with perverting the course of justice. As you say, she probably didn't even know how serious it was until you confronted her with it this morning.'

'We'll go ahead and charge Boulton then,' Monica got up to go, nearly bumping into Andy Lepage, who had been hovering on the edge of the conversation hoping to speak to Jonah as soon as he had finished with Monica and Alice.

'You do that,' Jonah called after her, 'and, just to make assurance doubly sure, see what you can find in the way of

CCTV pictures of the car park at the *Bullnose Morris* on Friday night. It would be good to know who the boys were who were climbing on Boulton's car and where they went when they ran off.'

He turned to Andy Lepage, who took the seat vacated by Monica and placed a manila folder on the desk next to it.

'I've been reading the coroner's report on the death of Jack Redfern. I think you'll be interested in the contents of his suicide note.'

'Go on.'

'It was rather long and rambling and full of remorse and self-loathing, but the nub of it all was that he was convinced that he had AIDS. He seems to have been unaware of any of the recent medical advances in treating it and to be expecting to die a horrible death as a consequence.'

'You're right,' agreed Jonah. 'That *is* very interesting. And was he right? Presumably, in view of the note, the post mortem will have included testing for HIV.'

'Yes, it did – and no, he was completely mistaken. The PM didn't find any health issues at all. According to his mother, he'd been complaining of headaches and hadn't been eating very well in the weeks before he died. She'd urged him to go to the doctor, but he wouldn't. In the light of the note, she said that she thinks he was afraid to go because of what he thought they'd find. He's a student at Oxford Brookes. A couple of his mates from there told the inquest that he'd also been having muscle pain, but they put it down to too much working out in the gym.'

'It sounds to me as if he worked himself up into a state and made himself ill,' Bernie declared. 'But I wonder what put the idea of AIDS into his head.'

'Perhaps one of his sexual partners had been diagnosed,' Jonah suggested, 'but you'd think he'd have gone along to an STD clinic and got tested. The gay community are pretty clued-up about all that.'

'It sounds from the report as if he was too frightened,' Andy told him. 'Wherever he was getting his information from, all he seems to have taken in was that he was at risk and there was no cure.'

'Did anyone from the gay community give evidence at the inquest?' Jonah asked.

'Yes. As well as the note, he'd written to a few of them personally apologising if he'd given them AIDS and hoping that he hadn't.'

'Any names we know?' Jonah's eyes lit up at the prospect of establishing a definite link between Redfern and one or more of the gay men whose businesses had been targeted.

'Marcus Antonio was one of them. The others were all students, I think – youngsters of about Jack Redfern's age anyway. Antonio was the only one who spoke at the inquest. He admitted to having had sex with Jack, but claimed that they always took precautions and that he'd talked to him about being careful to avoid spreading infection. He seems to have seen himself as ... I was going to say a father figure, but ... I think he liked to think that he was looking after the younger ones – initiating them into the gay community and giving them the benefit of his experience.'

'Which is just the sort of thing that Gordon Redfern would object to,' Jonah commented grimly. 'Especially the initiation bit. My guess is that he blames Antonio for his son's death. The way he'd see it would be: Antonio ensnares Jack and turns him into a homosexual, which then leads on to him believing that he's got AIDS and killing himself because he can't face the consequences. I think it's time we paid another visit to Mr Redfern senior.'

***

Gordon Redfern was not at home when they called at the house in Horspath. The jaguar was also absent from the drive and Mrs Redfern confirmed that her husband had gone out in it shortly after lunch.

'He said he was meeting with some people in Evesham,' Sharon Redfern told them, looking anxiously at the warrant cards which Bernie and Andy were holding up for her to see. 'I'm afraid he didn't say what time he'd be back.'

'Then perhaps you could help us,' Jonah suggested, treating her to one of his endearing lop-sided smiles. 'May we come in?'

'Yes – yes, of course.' Sharon held the door open for them to enter and gestured towards the door into the lounge. 'Go on in there and make yourselves at home. Can I get you a drink or anything?'

'No thanks.' Jonah turned his chair to face her and indicated by a slight movement of his head that she should sit down. 'I'm sorry that this may be distressing for you, but we need to ask you about your son, Jack.'

'What about him?' Sharon looked from Jonah to Andy and then at Bernie, who had settled down on one of the leather-bound chairs and was setting up her laptop ready to take notes. 'I thought that was all finished. I mean the inquest and everything.'

'Yes.' Jonah thought for a moment, trying to see a way of finding out what he needed to know, without making any accusations against Sharon's husband. 'It's to do with an incident on Wednesday night. An arson attack on a club frequented by gay men. Our investigations threw up some uncorroborated allegations that some of the customers were under-age boys being preyed upon by older men – one man in particular.'

'Are you talking about that Marcus Antonio?' Sharon asked sharply. 'The fellow who gave evidence at the inquest?'

'What makes you say that?' asked Jonah, carefully refusing to confirm her suspicions.

'Gordon was always going on about him. He kept

telling Jack that he was nothing more than a dirty old man, filling him with all sorts of dirty ideas, and if he carried on like him he'd end up dying of AIDS.'

'So it was your husband who sowed the seeds in Jack's mind that he might get AIDS?' Andy asked eagerly. Then in a more subdued tone, trying to hide his excitement, 'I mean, he felt it was his duty to warn him about the dangers?'

'Oh yes!' Sharon's voice was bitter. 'Gordon was never much good at hiding his feelings and the prospect of his son having gay sex absolutely terrified him. He didn't realise that going on at Jack like that was only going to make him all the more determined to stick to his guns.'

'I'm not sure that I understand,' Andy ventured tentatively.

'Gordon and I were teenagers when the government launched its "Don't die of ignorance" campaign,' Sharon explained. 'We were bombarded with images of emaciated young men dying horribly. In Gordon's mind, being gay inevitably led to HIV infection and then to death. That's why he was so scared when Jack came out. He genuinely believed that it was a death sentence – and Jack believed him, underneath, even though he wouldn't take any notice of Gordon's demands for him to change his lifestyle.'

'And how did *you* feel about your son's sexuality?' Jonah asked quietly. 'I gather that you thought your husband's open hostility was counter-productive, but …?'

'I just wanted Jack to be happy,' Sharon replied with a sad smile. 'I won't claim to have been over the moon about it when he told us, but he was so clear that it wasn't something that he could do anything to change that I … well, I was worried he might be picked on if people knew, and I *was* concerned about AIDS, I will admit – but not the way Gordon was. I told him it was fine if he wanted to bring a boyfriend home to meet us – but Gordon blew up about that and started shouting at me that I was as bad as the rest of them and the whole world seemed to be intent

on corrupting his son and turning him into a pervert. So
... I just kept quiet and hoped Gordon would calm down
eventually, but he never got a chance!'

'You mean, because Jack died before your husband
came to terms with it?' Andy asked.

'Yes,' Sharon nodded, clenching her lips tight and
blinking away the tears that were threatening to fall.

'Take your time,' Jonah urged gently.

Sharon nodded again and wiped her eyes with the back
of her hand.

'I try not to blame Gordon,' she went on, 'because I
know it was only because he was so worried about Jack,
but I do keep thinking, if only he hadn't gone on and on
so much then maybe Jack wouldn't have got himself
worked up into a state about it – thinking he had AIDS
and was going to die. It's all so ... so stupid!'

'And do you think he blamed Marcus Antonio for
Jack's death?' Jonah asked, watching Sharon's face
carefully for any sign that she was starting to realise where
the conversation was going. Would she attempt to cover
for her husband once she was aware that he was being
investigated?

'Him and all the others,' she admitted. 'But yes,
probably him the most, because he was so much older
than Jack.'

'I don't suppose you know when Jack first met him?'
Jonah asked. 'You see, as I said, the thing we're trying to
find out is whether any of his sexual partners were under
the age of consent. How old was Jack do you think?'

'Oh! Definitely at least eighteen,' Sharon said with
certainty. 'I'm quite sure none of this began until after he
started at uni. I'm sorry,' she added apologetically. 'I can't
help you get evidence to prosecute him – even though
Gordon for one would be delighted if you did.'

***

220

When Jonah got back to the police station, intending to drop off Andy Lepage and then to go home, the sergeant at the reception desk called out to remind him that he had promised to speak to Jason Paul that afternoon. Wondering to himself – and muttering in an undertone to Bernie – why he had made this commitment, he made his way down to the custody suite, where Sergeant Pamela Gregson greeted him cheerfully.

'I don't think you'll have much trouble from young Jason,' she told him. 'He's feeling a mite sorry for himself, now he's finally sobered up. It's amazing what a night in the cells can do for a tearaway like him. A few more hours and he'll be crying for his mum.'

'It's his mum he's accused of assaulting,' Jonah said drily. 'Not that it sounds as if she'll be willing to press charges. Oh well! I said I'd talk to him, so I'd better get on with it.'

'Oh! And you ought to know,' Pamela said in a low voice as she unlocked the cell where Jason Paul was incarcerated, 'It's his birthday today. He's eighteen.'

'No longer a juvenile,' Jonah remarked. 'Perhaps he needs reminding that he's now eligible to join his dad in an adult jail if he doesn't mend his ways.'

Pamela opened the door and pushed it wide.

'Sit up Jason!' she commanded. 'DCI Porter wants to talk to you.'

She stood back for Jonah to enter. As the heavy door clanged shut behind them, he looked round the bare cell. The narrow bed attached to one wall was filled by the long, muscular body of a yellow-haired youth with a pale face and large, grimy hands. His blue eyes were slightly bloodshot. Had he been crying, as Pamela had hinted, or was it just the remnants of a severe hangover?

Those eyes opened wide at the sight of Jonah approaching in his wheelchair. He continued to stare as he raised himself slowly to a sitting position on the edge of the bed, planting his feet wide apart on the floor and folding his arms across his chest.

Jonah stared back for about half a minute without speaking.

'Happy birthday Jason,' he said at last. 'It's a pity you've had to spend it here, isn't it?'

Jason did not reply. For a few more seconds he continued to watch Jonah with a mixture of surprise and puzzlement. His eyes moved over the wheelchair, then upwards, taking in Jonah's useless right arm lying in his lap, and the straps holding his left arm in place so that he could manipulate the keypad that controlled his world. He noticed that there were more straps around his chest preventing him from falling out of the chair. Finally, he looked him in the face and caught his eye.

'Are you really a cop?' he asked suspiciously.

'Yes. Why wouldn't I be?'

'Have you always been like that?' Jason stared pointedly at the wheelchair again.

'No. It happened nine years ago. An angry young woman took a pot shot at me and hit me in the neck. She blamed me for putting her father in jail and causing her mother to kill herself. The bullet damaged my spinal cord. Luckily for me, a few of the nerves survived, so I can still move three fingers.' Jonah demonstrated by wiggling the first and second fingers and thumb of his left hand. 'And that means I can control this chair.'

'Aren't you scared of coming in here on your own?'

'Why should I be scared?'

'In case I did anything to you. You couldn't stop me, could you – stuck in that thing?'

'I'm relying on your intelligence not to try anything,' Jonah told him with a smile. 'Where would it get you? Assaulting a police officer's a serious offence, and you can't get away – we're locked in.'

'I could use you as a hostage – threaten to kill you if they don't let me out.'

'It wouldn't work.' Jonah shook his head and smiled

again. 'You'd have to take me with you, and I'm a terrible liability when it comes to travelling.'

Jason sat in silence, apparently thinking about this.

'I've never seen a cop in a wheelchair before,' he said at last. 'Why haven't you been pensioned off – put in a home or something?'

'Oh, they tried that! But I wasn't having any of it. I like the job, and I like to think I'm good at it. But I have to admit, *you*'ve got me a bit stumped.'

'How d'you mean?' Jason frowned in perplexity.

'I can't work out why you would knock your mum around the way you do, instead of taking care of her and helping her to hold things together while your dad's away.'

'Who says I've been knocking her around?' Jason demanded, some of his old belligerence returning. 'Who-?'

'Sergeant Philipson saw the bruises. Everything points to them being inflicted by you. Your mum's stories about her injuries all being accidental don't stack up.'

'Says who?'

'The doctors who treated her. Look Jason: for as long as your mum insists she's not going to press charges or testify against you, there's nothing I can do to bring you to book, but you must see that this can't go on. What if it'd been her neck your mum broke yesterday, instead of her collarbone? You wouldn't want to have put her in a chair like mine for the rest of her life, would you?'

'No, of course not,' Jason muttered quickly, suddenly on the defensive. 'I never meant her to fall down the stairs. I only gave her a bit of a smack round the face. I never thought … I never meant to hurt her – just stop her nagging at me. She's always on at me – do this – don't do that – get a job – wash the dishes – turn down the music … I never meant …'

His voice trailed off and he looked towards Jonah with something approaching pleading in his eyes.

'OK. I believe you didn't mean to seriously injure your mum,' Jonah acknowledged. 'And she seems to want to forgive you. But now you need to be thinking about the future. How are you going to make sure nothing like this happens again?'

Jason stared back in silence, seemingly completely flummoxed by this question.

'Well, let's go back a stage, shall we?' Jonah tried again. 'What makes you want to lash out at people?'

'I just told you, didn't I? She's always getting at me – going on at me to get a job and moaning about the house being in a mess.'

'Has it not occurred to you that she might have a point?' Jonah asked quietly. 'I mean, now you're eighteen isn't it time you were earning your own living?'

Jason stared back in sulky silence.

'And, with your dad away, you're the man of the house now, aren't you?' Jonah continued, hoping to divert Jason's vision of himself as a macho male towards that of protector and provider.

'Suppose so,' Jason muttered. Then louder and more forcefully, 'but it's all very well for you to talk. How d'you expect me to find a job? It must've been easy for you. I bet you've got GCSEs – gone to uni even.'

'Yes, I suppose it is really easy for me,' Jonah replied, speaking calmly and quietly, but with a slight edge to his voice. 'Employers are always queuing up to take on a cripple in a wheelchair. They're just looking for an excuse to install a few ramps and automatic doors. They love being criticised for the inadequacy of their disabled toilet facilities. They'd much rather have someone like me than a fit young man like you.'

'How *do* you manage?' Jason asked, his curiosity overtaking his resentment, 'if you can't move your arms or legs?'

'With a bit of help from my friends,' Jonah told him, flashing one of his lop-sided smiles at the bemused young man. 'I have a minder who drives me around to crime scenes and takes care of my bodily functions; and other people who look after me at home; and I've got a couple of good friends who keep thinking up new devices to make it easier for me to do things for myself. They designed this special chair, for example. It can do all sorts of things that a standard wheelchair can't.'

Jason stared in amazement as Jonah gave a short demonstration of the chair's capabilities. The seat rose so that Jonah towered above him; then it returned to its normal level before magically reclining to form something that looked rather like a hospital trolley; finally, and unexpectedly, it somehow managed to raise Jonah into an upright position so that he appeared to be standing over the bewildered youth.

'I owe a lot to them,' Jonah continued, returning to a sitting position and looking Jason in the eye, 'which is why I'm determined to find out who it was who was driving the car that knocked one of them down on Friday night and landed him in hospital.'

'It wasn't me!' Jason put in quickly, 'whatever them lady cops say. I never even-'

'I know,' Jonah said, cutting across Jason's protests. 'One of your mates told us where you were and we've got some CCTV pictures of you all round the back of the Evenlode Tower at the critical time. Don't worry,' he added, seeing the mixture of anxiety and truculence in Jason's eyes as he realised that the police were aware of the cannabis party with which they had celebrated Ethan's birthday. 'The shots aren't clear enough for us to see what it was you were smoking, and I don't have the time to be bothered with getting search warrants for all your homes to see if you've still got any illegal substances stashed away anywhere. However, we will be keeping a friendly eye on you all in future in that regard. I'm sure you understand what I mean.'

He paused, looking Jason up and down. Jason grunted and lowered his eyes.

'What I'm far more interested in,' Jonah continued, 'is

anything you can tell me about the car and the person who really was driving it. Its owner says he parked it outside the *Bullnose Morris* that evening. Did you happen to notice a silver BMW in the car park as you went in?'

'Ian Boulton's car, you mean?'

'That's right. Do you know him?'

Jason shrugged. 'Ethan's got something going with his daughter – Bethany, her name is. He saw the car and said maybe we'd go to the *Blackbird* instead, but we had to wait for Callum to come, 'cos we were meeting at the *Bullnose* and his job didn't finish until later.'

'I see. So did you go in right away or wait for Callum to arrive?'

'We went in and Ethan got us drinks from the bar. He pointed Ian out, but *he* didn't see *us* until later when he was on the way out.'

'And then?'

'He said something to Ethan about how he'd regret it if he didn't leave Bethany alone. Then he went out and got in the car and drove off home.'

'Home? Are you sure about that? Or are you just assuming …?'

'We watched him go, through the window. He turned left out of the car park and signalled right to turn on to the main road. Why?'

'I don't suppose you remember what time this was?' Jonah asked, carefully keeping out of his voice the excitement that he felt at this new information.

'Between ten and half-past,' Jason shrugged. 'Just before them fascists started harassing Callum and we got chucked out.'

'And you're sure he turned left out of the car park?' Jonah pressed him. 'He couldn't have gone right along Cuddesdon Way, towards the shops?'

'No. I told you. He went left and then he was signalling right at the lights.'

'Thank you. That's very useful.' Jonah smiled at Jason,

feeling suddenly very satisfied with the way the interview had gone. 'Now, we're going to have to let you go. I'm going to get one of our PCs to take you home, and I'm going to ask them to call in at a takeaway on the way to pick up a meal for you all so your mum doesn't have to cook this evening. And then, after that, I'm relying on you to look after her until her shoulder's better. Do you understand?'

Jason nodded, sulkily at first and then, to Jonah's surprise he looked up and flashed a brief smile. Jonah smiled back.

'Good. I'm glad we understand one another.'

**

Jonah finished giving Ben Timpson his instructions for the safe delivery home of Jason Paul, including a list of checks that he should make before leaving the house in order to safeguard Lyn and Ryan. He had just turned to go when he heard Monica calling after him.

'Sir! Can you spare a moment?'

He turned to see her hurrying down the corridor after him.

'I won't keep you a minute,' she added quickly, with a sidelong glance towards Bernie, who was tapping her watch anxiously to indicate that it was time they were leaving for home. 'I know you've got to go, but I thought I ought to tell you that we've just had a call from Maureen Boulton to say that their daughter Bethany has gone missing.'

'When? Where? What happened?' Jonah demanded.

'It looks like she's gone walkabout,' Monica answered. 'Her mum thought she was in her room. She's been a bit difficult apparently, since she got home from boarding school, so she didn't think anything of her staying up there and not answering when she knocked. But eventually, she started to think it was strange that there'd been no sound from there for hours – not since we arrested her dad, in fact. So she went in and found that she'd gone. That's all I know so far, the call only just came in. I just thought you'd want to know.'

'Quite right,' Jonah agreed briskly. 'We'd better get over there right away and-'

'Oh no you don't!' Bernie intervened firmly. 'You and I are going home – now. Monica can handle this, I'm sure.'

'But-'

'No buts,' Bernie insisted, reaching out her hand to indicate that, if necessary, she was prepared to override his decision by removing his hand from the controls of his wheelchair.

'OK. I'll come quietly,' Jonah conceded, 'but there is one thing that I do have to tell Monica before we go. Something Jason Paul told me just now. According to him, Bethany Boulton and Ethan Roberts were in some sort of relationship and Ian Boulton didn't approve. Oh! And the other thing is that Ian was lying when he told you he drove straight from the *Bullnose Morris* to the *Blackbird*. Jason claims to have seen him heading *home* from the *Bullnose* – in the car – between ten and half past last Friday night.'

'OK. Is that it?' Bernie asked, determined not to allow Jonah to delay them further. This was becoming the most action-packed day's leave that she could remember for a long time.

'Yes. I won't be a moment,' Jonah muttered, turning back to give Monica some final instructions. 'Obviously the priority is finding Bethany and making sure she's safe. Keep me informed on how the search is going. You can ring me any time up to ten tonight. After that, email me with any developments so I can get back up to speed in the morning. OK, *OK!* I'm coming!' he added, seeing Bernie's hand hovering over the arm of his chair again. 'And yes, I do know it's Saturday tomorrow, but this is an emergency.'

CHAPTER 18: SATURDAY MORNING

'What is it Q?' Melanie called, seeing the big dog stop in her tracks and stand staring towards a dense patch of gorse and bracken, which grew at the edge of the field beneath a rather overgrown hawthorn hedge.

They had been out all night, searching for the missing teenager, with little to show for their efforts. While other officers did the rounds of Bethany's friends and visited her favourite haunts, Melanie and Q had been attempting to track her route from the family home across the Oxfordshire countryside.

While Q sniffed the air to pick up invisible scent clues, Melanie darted her eyes around in all directions, hunting for discernible signs that Bethany had passed that way. A discarded plastic bottle, which had once contained spring water, might have been a sign that they were following her trail. Prints in the mud at the edge of a stream were the right size to have been made by the walking boots that her mother had identified as missing from her bedroom cupboard. But there was nothing definite to prove that they were on the right track.

Overhead, the helicopter made another sweep of the area, resuming its hunt, which had been called off when it grew dark the previous night. Melanie looked up at it briefly before turning her attention back to PD Q, who was now moving forward, her nose down, sniffing earnestly.

'Good girl!' Mel encouraged. 'Track on!'

***

'I've been thinking about what Pam Gregson said yesterday,' Jonah announced over breakfast. 'Being held in police custody probably *is* a bit of a wakeup call for youngsters who've committed offences. We ought to be doing more to take advantage of that shock-value to re-direct them before they slide further into criminality.'

'What did you have in mind?' Bernie asked. She was keen to encourage any topic of conversation that diverted Jonah away from his impatience to hear what progress had been made in the hunt for Bethany Boulton. As promised, Monica had emailed a brief note in the early hours, merely stating that their efforts so far had been fruitless. Jonah had been all for telephoning for an update the moment that he was dressed and settled in his wheelchair. It had been with the greatest of reluctance that he had accepted her argument that, if they waited until after breakfast, Anna would have been on duty for long enough to have got to grips with the latest developments and so to be in a position to give him the full story.

'Take Jason Paul, for example,' Jonah replied. 'He left school two years ago with no qualifications and no job to go to. His dad's in prison and his mum seems to fluctuate between bellyaching about his idleness and total indifference to him – when she's not scared out of her wits by his violence. It's not surprising if he's drifting into drink and drugs and other cheap thrills. He needs someone to show him how to make something of his life – to help him get a job and some life-skills.'

'But who's going to want to employ an unqualified

teenager with a police record?' Bernie asked sceptically. 'There aren't many jobs these days that only require brute strength. Even the bin men have to be able to sort out different types of re-cycling!'

'Just because he hasn't got any qualifications doesn't mean he's incapable of acquiring any skills,' Jonah insisted. 'By all accounts, he's quite nifty at rapid re-wiring of vehicle anti-theft devices! It's a matter of finding what he's good at and channelling it into something more worthwhile than house-breaking and car-theft.'

'I read about something along the lines of what you're suggesting,' Peter said suddenly. 'It's a project that's been going on in the Met[14]. It was the bright idea of an inspector in Brixton, I think.'

'You're right!' Jonah agreed. 'I remember reading about it too. It's called DIVERT[15]. That's the sort of thing we could do with in Oxford. We need someone to talk to these youngsters and find out what they *can* do, and show them how to put their skills to use lawfully. We should be pro-active instead of-'

He was interrupted by a call coming in on his mobile phone. It was Anna.

'Monica said you wanted to be kept up-to-date with the search for Bethany Boulton,' she said. 'The good news is that she's been found. She's being checked over at the hospital, because she was out all night and she was pretty cold by the time Mel and her dog reached her; but she seems basically OK. Her mum's with her and so is Sergeant Burton. I thought she's a safe pair of hands to see they're both OK.'

---

[14] The Metropolitan Police Service is responsible for policing Greater London, excluding the historic City.

[15] For an illustration of the work of the DIVERT project see this BBC report: https://www.bbc.co.uk/programmes/p03bpgpq

'Yes,' Jonah agreed. 'Tracy's a good officer and knows when to give people space. Presumably she'll bring them back for questioning once Bethany's been given the all-clear by the medics?'

'Yes. And we've still got her father here in custody as well. He's demanding to see her, but I'd rather like to get her side of the story *before* he has a chance to influence what she says.'

'Absolutely!' Jonah concurred. 'He's been lying through his teeth all along. The last thing we need is for him to get to her and persuade or intimidate her into telling us something other than the truth. OK. That'll do for now. I'm just having my breakfast and then I'll be with you. You can bring me up to speed with everything while we wait for Bethany to get back from the hospital.'

He ended the call and looked defiantly across the table at Bernie.

'Stop glowering at me like that. I've only got a couple of more weeks to go. At least let me make the most of them.'

***

'It's no wonder Ian Boulton wanted to stop us talking to Bethany,' Anna told Jonah as they sat together in his office going through the latest developments. 'The unidentified fingerprints on the wheel of the car are hers. It looks like she was driving, which would be bad enough even if she hadn't lost control and hit a pedestrian. She's only got a provisional driving licence and she only has insurance for driving her mother's car.'

'So, she can be charged with driving while unqualified and driving without insurance, just for starters,' Jonah observed. 'Then there's causing serious injury by dangerous driving and she's lucky to have avoided causing death by dangerous driving. It'll be interesting to hear what she says about *why* she did it.'

'And why her father lied to protect her,' Anna added. 'I mean, I can see why he would *want* to protect her, but he was taking a massive risk on himself.'

'Only after he'd tried and failed to shift the blame on to car thieves,' Jonah pointed out. 'I think he kept telling the first lie that came into his head until he found he'd painted himself into a corner and didn't have much option but to agree with the assertion that he was driving.'

There was a knock at the door and Andy Lepage's head appeared round it.

'Bethany Boulton's here,' he announced. 'They've put her in Interview Room 2. Her mother's there as well, and also the family solicitor.'

'Thanks Andy.' Jonah turned to Anna. 'Are you OK for us to do this together, or ...?' He left the sentence hanging, hoping that she would agree to his being involved, but not wanting her to feel that she was being sidelined.

'Sure. I'll be glad of your help.'

'You don't think I ought to step aside and let Monica ...? It is more her case than mine.'

'I think that Mrs Boulton will find the presence of someone as senior as a DCI reassuring.'

'OK then. Let's go for it.'

**

Bethany Boulton looked very small and very young, sitting between her mother and her solicitor. The lawyer was a portly middle-aged man with a very small quantity of grey hair and watery grey eyes behind half-moon glasses, which he removed in order to watch Jonah and Anna as they crossed the room and took their seats opposite him.

Jonah scrutinised both women carefully. Maureen was dressed in tweeds with pearl earrings and a silk scarf at her neck. She had dark brown hair and brown eyes, both of which were mirrored in her daughter. Bethany had a crisscross pattern of scratches on both face and hands and a yellowing bruise on her left cheek.

Anna made the introductions and went through the formal caution, speaking calmly and quietly in an effort not to appear intimidating.

'Do you understand all that?' she asked at the end. 'Or do you have any questions or anything you'd like me to go through again?'

'No. I'm OK,' Bethany answered in a whisper, nodding briefly and looking towards her mother.

'Good. Now Bethany – is it OK for us to call you Bethany?'

The teenager nodded again.

'Now Bethany,' Anna resumed, 'we realise that this has all been very upsetting and frightening for you, but it *is* important that you answer some questions for us. And it's very important that you tell us the truth – even if that means grassing on someone else. Do you understand?'

Another nod.

'OK. Now, do you think you could tell us, in your own words, exactly what you did on Friday of last week – that's not yesterday I'm talking about, but the week before?'

'Mum came and fetched me from school,' Bethany began. Her voice cracked and she took a sip from the beaker of water that stood on the table in front of her. 'That was in the morning, about ten.'

'You're sure that was Friday?' Jonah asked gently. 'I thought you didn't come home until the Saturday.'

'No, it was Friday, wasn't it Mum?'

'That's right,' Maureen Boulton confirmed. 'I picked Beth up at about ten, as she said, and we got home in time for lunch at twelve fifteen.'

'I see,' Anna resumed. 'And was your dad there when you got home?'

'No. He was having lunch at the golf club. He came back later, after I'd gone out.'

'Where did you go?' Anna asked.

'Do I have to say?' Bethany looked first towards her mother and then to her lawyer.

'You don't *have* to answer any of our questions,' Jonah told her, 'but it will help us a lot if you co-operate.'

'I'd really rather not say,' Bethany reiterated.

'Do you mind if I hazard a guess?' Jonah asked. 'I think that maybe you went to see Ethan Roberts.'

'How did you know?' Bethany gasped.

'A little bird told me that you and he were close. The same little bird said that your dad wasn't too happy about it. Is that right?'

'Yes!'

'Did he try to stop you seeing each other?' Jonah suggested quietly.

'He did more than that!' Bethany retorted, suddenly seized with indignation as she thought about her father's intervention. 'He – look, I'd better tell you all about it. Then maybe you'll understand.'

CHAPTER 19: FRIDAY

'Isn't that your dad's car?' Ethan asked, as a silver BMW glided silently past at twenty miles per hour. He and Bethany were walking hand-in-hand along Cuddesdon Way towards the junction with Watlington Road.

'Dunno.' Bethany gazed after the car as it came to a stop at the traffic lights. 'I've never seen it. Mum told me he'd got a new one, but he was out in it when we got back.'

'I reckon it is. I've seen him in it before.'

'We'd better wait here until he's gone then,' Bethany said, stopping suddenly and pulling Ethan with her under the shade of a large tree growing at the edge of the *Bullnose Morris* car park.

'Why?' Ethan put his arms around her and gently directed her back on to the footway. 'He's got to know sometime. And I bet he saw us just now anyway. What are you frightened of?'

'I just know he won't like you,' Bethany insisted.

'Well, we'll never know if I never get to meet him. Come on Beth! We can't be always jumping behind trees to hide from him, like we're in a spy movie or something. Come on! Just act natural. The lights will probably have changed by the time we get there anyway.'

They walked on together towards the junction. Two more cars pulled up behind the silver BMW, but the lights remained on red. As they approached the silver car, its passenger window opened and the driver leaned over towards them. Ethan had been right. Ian Boulton had recognised his daughter and was now intent on speaking to her. His expression made it clear that he was not pleased about what he had seen. He opened his mouth to speak, but he was interrupted by the sound of a horn from the car behind. The lights had changed and the driver of the next vehicle was impatient to move off. Swearing angrily under his breath, Boulton straightened himself in the driving seat again and released the handbrake. Bethany and Ethan watched as the car turned out smoothly into Watlington Road and then accelerated away.

***

When Bethany got home, she found her father waiting for her in the hall. She had left Ethan at the end of the drive and walked up to the front door alone. She was determined that they should not be allowed to meet – not yet – not for a very long time.

'Who was that boy you were with just now?' Ian demanded before she even had time to close the door behind her.

'That's none of your business,' Bethany retorted, attempting to push past him into the passage that led to the stairs.

'Oh yes it is! I'm your father. I need to know what sort of riff-raff you're getting yourself mixed up with. Where did you meet him?'

Bethany stood staring back at him stony-faced. Then she made another attempt to get past him. He grabbed her by the shoulders and held her firmly.

'Let me go! You're hurting.'

'Not until you tell me his name and where he lives. I'm your father. It's my duty to keep you safe from undesirables.'

'Bollocks!' Bethany shouted rudely, struggling hard to get away. 'It's my life. I can go round with who I like.'

'Not while you're living under this roof, you can't! Tell me his name or I'll-'

'What's going on?' the door behind him opened and Maureen stood on the threshold staring at them. Ian let go of his daughter and dropped his hands to his sides.

'Bethany's going out with some delinquent from the estate,' he told her. 'And she won't tell me his name.'

Released from her father's grip, Bethany seized the opportunity to slip past her mother and head for her room. Maureen stepped aside to allow her to pass. As she clattered up the stairs, Bethany could hear her parents' raised voices arguing over the best approach to dealing with adolescent love-affairs. She slammed her bedroom door closed behind her and hurled herself angrily on to the bed.

A few minutes later, there was a knock at the door. It was her mother.

'Beth love! Will you be a darling and take Sadie and Jo-Jo for their walk? I'm trying to get your trunk unpacked and they're into everything.'

'OK Mum.' Bethany got up and went in search of the leads for their two dogs – successors to the pair of Afghans from the photographs in the lounge. Airedale bitch Sadie cavorted excitedly around her legs at the prospect of a walk, while the more staid Labrador, Jo-Jo, stood waiting patiently for his leash to be clipped to his collar ready for their departure. Soon they were striding out along a footpath across the fields.

Bethany scowled to herself as she thought about her father's tirade against Ethan. It was so unfair! Why did he have to interfere? She had known he wouldn't understand. That was why she had been so careful not to let him know about their meeting during the Easter holidays or their ongoing relationship via text and social media. What excessively bad luck that he had driven past like that! Now it would be even more difficult for her to get away and snatch precious time with Ethan. And they had planned so many things that they were going to do together that summer! It was just so, so unfair!

***

Dinner, an hour or so later, was a tense affair. Bethany maintained a sulky silence, answering her mother's attempts at making conversation with grunted monosyllables. Her father was also taciturn, having been persuaded by his wife that it would be futile and counterproductive to continue to cross-examine their daughter about her boyfriend. As soon as the meal was over, Bethany returned to her room, while Ian declared his intention of going out.

Bethany watched from her window as the silver car disappeared round a bend in the long drive. Then she sat down on the bed and resumed the texted conversation that she had been having with Ethan before her mother had called her for dinner. Looking up briefly, her eye was caught by a small corner of paper sticking out from the top drawer of her desk, which stood against the opposite wall. She was sure that she had not left it like that.

She got up and went across to investigate. She opened the drawer. Yes! The contents had been disturbed. She took out the stack of revision notes, which she kept at the top of the drawer to deter prying eyes from digging deeper, and picked up the sturdy cardboard box, which held her personal private diary. It felt strangely light in her hands.

She fumbled to open it. Her haste made her clumsy and it was several seconds before she had the lid off. As she had feared, the box was empty. Someone had been in her room while she was out and had taken it!

She ran downstairs to confront her mother, carrying the two halves of the empty box, one in each hand.

Maureen was in the lounge reading a copy of *Oxford Life*. She looked up anxiously as Bethany stormed into the room.

'Have you taken my diary?' she demanded angrily. 'Where've you put it?'

'I'm sorry, love. I don't know what you're talking about.'

'Was it Dad then? Has he been in my room?'

'I shouldn't think so. I'm sure he wouldn't go in there without asking you.' Maureen attempted to placate her daughter with reassurances that she did not really believe herself. 'Don't you think you might just have mislaid it yourself?'

'No. Don't be stupid! It was in this box, at the bottom of my drawer. I never leave it out. He's been in and stolen it!'

'Don't talk like that, love. I'm sure he hasn't stolen anything of yours. If he has taken it – which I doubt – he'll only have borrowed it. I'm sure it's quite safe.'

'But it's my *private* diary!' Bethany screamed. '*Nobody's* allowed to read it.'

'I'm sure when he sees what it is he'll-,' Maureen began.

'No he won't!' Bethany interrupted, not waiting to hear what excuses or assurances her mother might be planning to offer. 'He's taken it deliberately, because he's spying on me. I hate him!'

With that, she slammed out of the door and stamped back upstairs. She threw her bedroom door open, allowing it to crash noisily against the small chest of drawers that stood behind it. Then she strode into the room and hurled the door closed behind her, before throwing herself face down on the bed and bursting into angry tears.

She reached for her phone. That was odd! It didn't seem to be working. She tried switching it off and back on again. Still no joy. She slid the back off and removed the battery and SIM card. Then she replaced them and put the phone back together again. No. It still refused to connect.

Dad! He must have done something to it. He didn't like her texting Ethan, so he'd blocked her phone somehow. The bastard! Why couldn't he leave her alone?

There was a gentle knock on the door. Then her mother's voice called from outside.

'Bethany love! Won't you come down and we can talk about this?'

'Go away! Leave me alone! I hate you both!'

Sobbing, Bethany got off the bed and dragged the chest of drawers across the door to prevent her mother opening it. Then she sat on it and put her ear to the crack between the door and its frame. She could hear her mother's breathing as she pondered on whether or not to call out again. Then there was a sigh and the sound of soft footsteps on the landing carpet followed by louder steps going downstairs.

Bethany slipped down to the floor, stomped across the room and flung herself down on the bed again. Why were they doing this to her? It was all so unfair!

***

Bethany woke from a fitful sleep at the sound of her father's car approaching up the drive. In a flash, she was up off the bed and dragging the chest away from the door. She raced downstairs, along the passage, through the hall and out of the front door. There he was! Just pulling up in front of the garage, all ready to put his precious car away safe from the attentions of vandals and thieves.

She strode across the cobbles and grasped the handle of the driver's side door, flinging it wide and standing, legs apart in the most aggressive pose she could muster.

'You stole my diary!' she screamed in his face. 'You hacked my phone!'

'Now Bethy, don't carry on like that,' he remonstrated.

'The whole neighbourhood can hear you.'

'Good! I want them all to know what a bastard you are. How dare you go in my room and steal my things!'

'That's enough of that,' her father said sharply, getting out of the car and trying to grab hold of her. 'That's no way to speak to your father. If we could trust you to behave yourself, I wouldn't *need* to go poking around in your room. We haven't spent thousands on your education just to have you taking up with some good-for-nothing from the council estate.'

Bethany slipped beneath his outstretched arm and slid into the driver's seat. The engine was still running. Her father reached towards her. She responded by pulling the door shut and pushing the catch down to lock it. Then she looked down at the controls. She had never driven this car before, but it looked simple enough. The automatic gearbox enabled her to move off more smoothly than she had ever achieved in her driving lessons or when practising in her mother's manual car.

She headed down the drive, slowly at first, then, as her confidence grew, more quickly. She would pay him out! Let him see how he liked it, having *his* things stolen!

She turned out on to Watlington Road, heading towards Oxford. Where should she go now? She would find Ethan. He would be impressed to see her driving the car, which he had openly admired during the short walk home after their encounter with her father that afternoon; and he was clever about electronic things. He might know how to make her phone work again.

She turned left into Cuddesdon Way, allowing the car to pick up speed again and enjoying the adrenalin rush as it bounced over the speed bumps. Where next? She had never been to Ethan's house, but she had an idea that it was on the left somewhere down Blackbird Leys Road. She took the corner a little too close, clipping the kerb as she skidded round. Then, all of a sudden, she found herself heading for a pair of bollards in the middle of the road. She wrenched the wheel round in a panic. The car veered to the left and mounted the pavement. There was a sickening thud as it collided with something soft.

In desperation, she pulled the wheel back round to bring the car back on to the road. As it bumped down off the pavement, she became aware of people running towards her shouting and gesticulating. She must get away from them. She put her foot down hard on the accelerator. The car gathered speed again and surged off up the road towards the by-pass.

What next? If she continued this way, she would soon be over the ring road and heading for the city centre. There was a mini-roundabout ahead. If she went left, she could get on to the by-pass and get away from all those angry people shouting at her and waving their arms.

***

A sign loomed up. It said "City Centre and Science Park" ahead. That was no good! She would have to turn round and go back. She needed to get home. Mum would know what to do. She signalled right and proceeded to go all the way round the roundabout and back on to the other carriageway of the by-pass. That was better. It wouldn't take long now.

Was that the junction for Watlington Road? It couldn't have been so soon, could it? Oh no! Yes, it was! Too late now! In hardly any time there was another junction coming up. It was traffic lights this time. If she turned right, she must surely be able to loop back home somehow.

Without remembering to signal, she moved out into the right-hand lane, causing the driver of a white van to slam on the brakes and sound his horn angrily. She hardly noticed that the lights were against her. Her only thought was to get off the by-pass and find a way back home to safety. She was vaguely aware of a screeching of brakes and more hooting as she skidded round the corner into

Horspath Road.

She knew where she was now. All she needed to do was to follow the road through Horspath and then on to the T-junction beyond. Then, not much further and she would hit Watlington Road, not far at all from her own house.

She slowed down a little as she approached the village. There were people standing around outside the Village Hall. It looked as if some event had just ended and they were getting ready to go home. She passed a filling station on the right and then a sharp bend brought her to the village pub. There were more people here, standing around chatting in the warm July night. Another bend and under a bridge and she was heading out into open country again. As she left the last houses behind, she accelerated again. Surely it couldn't be far to the junction now?

A glimpse of flashing blue lights in the rear-view mirror set her heart racing even faster than before. Oh no! Was she being pursued? She pushed her foot down on the accelerator. The powerful car leapt forward: 70, 80, 90 miles an hour. The road stretched straight ahead of her. This was easy! 100, 110 ... she would have no difficulty outrunning the police car.

There was something on the road ahead. What was it? The headlights cast strange long shadows making it difficult to work out its real shape or size. Instinctively, she pulled the wheel round to the right to avoid it and found herself skidding across the road and into a field entrance on the right. The soft ground gave way and the car came to an abrupt halt as one wheel subsided into a ditch and the engine stalled.

Frantic with fear of being arrested by the police, Bethany scrambled out of the car and set off across the field. Home could not be far off, as the crow flies. If she could only keep going roughly in a straight line, she should hit Oxford Road to the west of Garsington and then it was only a matter of a few hundred yards to Watlington Road and safety.

Keeping to a straight path was more difficult than she had imagined, but she pressed on doggedly. Looking back, there was no sign of pursuit. It looked as if she had thrown them off. She splashed through a stream and crawled beneath a barbed-wire fence. Surely, she must be nearly at Oxford Road by now? She pushed her way through a hedge, slid down into a ditch and blinked in the lights from a car, which passed in front of her.

Not much further now. She slithered down into the ditch on the other side of the road and forced her way through a dense hawthorn hedge into the field beyond. Her hands and face were bleeding from numerous scratches, but she pressed on regardless. Nothing mattered now except reaching home.

At last, her feet were back on tarmac again. This must be Watlington Road, but whereabouts had she come out? It was very dark. She was grateful when a car came past, its headlights blazing. As it headed to her right, towards Oxford, she saw, lit up for a few seconds, a familiar brick pillar. It was one of the gateposts at the end of her drive. She was almost home! She staggered forward, her relief making her feel suddenly weak, and, with a great effort, arrived at the front door.

Her father must have been looking out for her, because he was there even before she had time to press the bell.

'What's happened?' he demanded brusquely, looking her up and down. 'How did you get into that state?'

'I – I – I,' she panted. 'I'm sorry, Dad. I crashed the car!'

She lurched forward and collapsed into his arms.

***

The next thing that Bethany knew was her father's voice on the telephone.

'Yes. That's right. It must have been sometime this

afternoon or evening. ... Thank you. ... Certainly! I'll be here.'

She realised that she was lying on the couch in the lounge, with a tartan rug, which they used for picnics, thrown over her. Seeing her stirring, her father came over and bent down to speak to her.

'I've rung the police and reported the car as stolen,' he told her. 'They'll put it down to joy-riders from the estate. Mum's already in bed, so we won't disturb her. You'd better have a shower to clean all that mud off you and then get off too. I'll deal with everything.'

CHAPTER 20: SIX WEEKS LATER

So this man Boulton invented a story about his car being stolen to protect his daughter from being prosecuted?' Graham asked with a mixture of indignation and astonishment in his voice. He had been very busy recently; what with taking a lead role in managing *Design Ability* and doing everything he could to support his son's continued rehabilitation. Now, during a rare evening of leisure, he was listening to Jonah recounting the full story of Bethany's escapade. 'I hope he's going to pay for all the police time he wasted.'

They were in a large function room in Oxford Town Hall with more than a hundred other guests – mainly serving or retired police officers – celebrating Jonah's retirement from forty-one years in the police service. They were eating dinner, which was to be followed by speeches and presentations. At Jonah's insistence, the top table included Wayne (recently discharged home from a three-week spell as an in-patient at the Oxford Centre for Enablement[16]) and his parents, Dean, and all of Jonah's

---

[16] The *Oxford Centre for Enablement* is a regional rehabilitation unit providing rehabilitation services for people with persisting

"family" (Peter, Bernie and Lucy). As he intended, this left little room for the police establishment, which was represented by Chief Superintendent Alison Brown, accompanied by her husband David, and, at the other end of the spectrum, by Police Cadet Stella Gilbert.

It had been Peter's idea to invite Stella. He had argued that, as well as being symbolic of the inclusion of all ranks from Chief Constable down to Cadet, her presence would provide company for Lucy, who would otherwise be by far the youngest person there. Bernie resisted the temptation to comment that Lucy had never shown any sign yet of being unable to hold her own in adult company. She was well aware that Peter's true motivation was to bring his protégé to the attention of the senior ranks, with the hope of furthering her career.

To Jonah's great relief, neither the Chief Constable nor his deputy were available that evening. He was no lover of ceremony and would be relieved when the whole affair was over. It would have been made infinitely worse by the presence of top-ranking officers who would inevitably feel obliged to turn this into a solemn occasion with an uncomfortable degree of pomp and circumstance.

'I'm more interested in re-educating him about attitudes towards gay men,' Bernie replied to Graham from across the table. 'In a way there's something almost noble about the way he confessed in order to shield his daughter, but-'

'It would have been more noble if he'd done it right away, instead of trying to lay the blame on kids from the Blackbird Leys estate, who already had enough problems of their own,' Lucy cut in sharply. 'And it was the least he could do for the poor girl after the way he'd treated her! I bet he felt responsible for what she did – and he jolly well ought to!'

---

disability across the "Wessex region" of the National Health Service in England.

'I suppose he thought he was doing the right thing by her,' Peter began, always keen to see the best in anyone. 'After all, this Ethan Roberts doesn't sound like the ideal boyfriend for your only daughter, does he?'

'But reading her private diary! And switching her mobile account so he could send texts to all her friends, that looked as if they came from her!' Lucy exclaimed. 'You'd never do that to me, would you Peter? You know you wouldn't!'

'Of course not,' Peter agreed hastily. 'That was well below the belt.'

'What's that?' asked Wayne, picking up on Lucy's indignation. Thanks to the passage of time and some intensive therapy, his speech was now fluent, if occasionally a little stilted. Only those who had known him before his injury would be likely to be aware of the intense concentration that he still required in order to convert his thoughts into words. 'How did he …?'

'The account was in his name,' Jonah explained. 'Bethany's still a minor, remember, and she'd had her phone for several years. He simply told the service provider that the phone had been destroyed in some way and asked them to transfer the account to a new SIM, which he then used in his own phone to reply to any texts that came in from her friends, including Ethan, telling them that she was chucking him.'

'That's awful!' Dean endorsed Lucy's sentiments, remembering how carefully he had guarded his own communications with Wayne, during the early stages of their relationship before he had "come out" to his family.

'I'm sure we can all agree that Ian Boulton is a bastard of the first order,' Jonah said grimly, 'but at the end of the day, we couldn't justify the expense of taking him to court for wasting police time and attempting to pervert the course of justice. And we couldn't nail him for anything in relation to the homophobic attacks. So he's got off with just a formal police caution.'

'At least you managed to nick Fry for attempted arson,' Peter commented, 'and I don't suppose that other couple will be so free with the spray paint in future either. It's just a pity you haven't been able to prove that Redfern sent those death threats or to establish who attacked that poor taxi-driver.'

'Redfern? Fry?' Dean asked, not recognising the names.

'Redfern's son killed himself, thinking he'd got AIDS,' Jonah explained. 'Redfern blamed gay men in general and two or three individuals in particular, for "turning him gay" and driving him to suicide.'

'Actually, it's most likely the lad was influenced by his dad's paranoia about homosexuality automatically leading to AIDS,' Bernie added.

'Anyway, Redfern told his friends and we think that's what prompted the couple Peter was talking about to spray your van and property belonging to the other businesses featured with you in that Oxford Mail article,' Jonah continued. 'We think – but we can't prove – that he was the one who sent them some very nasty threatening letters. I put in my report to the CPS[17] that I thought he should be prosecuted for incitement to violence and stirring up hatred on the grounds of sexual orientation, but they decided it wasn't in the public interest to pursue it.'

'Not that Fry seems to have needed much in the way of incitement,' Bernie chipped in. 'Our Robin appears to enjoy violence for its own sake.'

'He's been charged with attempted arson, aggravated by homophobic motives,' Jonah told them.

'And Bethany?' asked Wayne, focussing on the aspect of the case that most affected him. 'What's going to happen to her? I mean, I know she pleaded guilty, but none of us made it to the court to hear the sentence.'

'The magistrate gave her a fine and Community Service

---

[17] Crown Prosecution Service: the body responsible for conducting criminal prosecutions in England and Wales.

and banned her from driving for two years,' Jonah told him. 'In view of your injuries, we could have pushed for a custodial sentence, but … , well she's still going to have a criminal record; and she'll see all her friends learning to drive – and getting their own cars from their rich daddies, no doubt – while she'll still be disqualified.'

'It seems quite harsh to me.' Wayne said, after a moment's thought. 'She didn't mean to hurt anyone. She was just angry with her dad. It was just bad luck that I was in her way.'

'That's no excuse!' Dean's sympathy for Bethany's treatment at the hands of her father suddenly evaporated as he remembered the enormity of what she had done. 'She must've known she wasn't safe to drive that car. And she didn't even stop after she'd hit you!'

'I think it's all just very sad,' Barbara intervened, concerned that anger at what had happened to Wayne would spoil what was supposed to be a celebration of Jonah's career. 'She didn't mean to hurt anyone; her dad thought he was protecting her from a boyfriend with a police record; I suppose the boy probably had his own problems …'

'You're right there,' Jonah agreed. 'Apart from his gran, who seems to be way out of her depth when it comes to dealing with teenage boys, Bethany is probably the first person who ever cared a toss for him. It's much the same with Jason Paul. They both need someone to come in and give them some sort of purpose in their lives. That's why Pamela Gregson and I are going to start our own project, working with youngsters in police custody, trying to get them off the streets and into a job.'

'When you're not busy in your advisory role with *Design Ability* and starring in promotional and training videos for them,' Bernie added. 'I can foresee your retirement being even busier than your working life!'

The conversation paused while waiters removed the empty main course plates and brought in the dessert.

'I hear you're going to be joining us full-time soon,' Alison said to Stella, taking pity on the youngster, who appeared rather overwhelmed by the occasion.

'Yes. I'm going to start after Christmas – to give me time to get my CKP.'

'It's nice when a cadet decides to join the force. I've heard lots of good reports about you,' Alison continued kindly.

'Thanks.' Stella felt rather tongue-tied at being addressed by such a senior officer. She racked her brains to think of something else to say.

'You're not tempted to do a degree then?' David Brown asked. He was a teacher at one of the local high schools and was keen to encourage students from ethnic minorities to go to university. 'Alison tells me that there are several good policing degrees out there now.'

'No. I'd rather have a job right away. And it's not as if I've got brilliant A' levels like Lucy.'

'There's nothing wrong with Bs and Cs,' Lucy cut in quickly. 'I only needed so many As because I want to do medicine.' She leaned across Stella to speak earnestly to Alison. 'Stella had offers from lots of uni's. You're dead lucky she'd rather come to you instead!'

'Yes. I know I am,' Alison smiled. 'Your dad keeps telling me so!'

'Peter's been awfully good,' Stella said gratefully. 'He's fixed up for me to be DI Davenport's nanny, while I'm doing my course, so I won't have to sponge off my gran.'

'It was a no-brainer,' Peter intervened from across the table. 'Anna has a place in nursery for Donna, but it doesn't start until January. And Stella here is an experienced childminder and needs some extra cash while she does the CKP. It all just slotted together perfectly.'

'Yes, but it took you to collect all the pieces and fit them together,' Bernie pointed out. 'Credit where credit's due.'

'So you're going to be a doctor are you, Lucy?' David

Brown asked, smiling across at her. 'Where are you going?'

'Liverpool. I wanted to go to Oxford, so I could stay at home, but they wouldn't have me.'

'I think she intimidated them,' Peter put in loyally. 'At the interview, she told them all about how she'd watched a post-mortem with Mike Carson, and all sorts of details about the long-term effects of spinal cord injury and what she does to help look after Jonah, and they were afraid she'd show them up with all her knowledge and experience!'

'Don't be silly, Peter!' Lucy blushed red. 'I expect they just had other people who did better in the test.'

'I heard on the grapevine that they were trying to save her from herself,' Bernie said to David. 'She told them about wanting to stay in Oxford so she could still help with Jonah's care, and they thought it would be better for her to get away from home. That's what a friend of mine who knows the tutors who interviewed her told me. But that's all water under the bridge now,' she added, smiling round at everyone. 'Lucy's off to Liverpool, which, as I keep telling her, is …'

'The best city in the world!' Lucy and Peter joined in.

The waiter cleared away the dessert bowls and placed steaming pots of tea and coffee on the table. Dean poured coffee into Wayne's cup, to prevent him from attempting to lift the jug with his partially paralysed right hand. Movement and sensation were coming back, but slowly, and Wayne was gradually learning to make more use of his left hand; however, Dean was still anxious about allowing him free rein with boiling liquids.

'I hear you had Carl and Harry over yesterday,' Bernie said to Wayne and Dean. 'How did it go? Did they like their room?'

'Yes,' Dean smiled happily. 'They loved it – and the garden! And we took them for a walk into Oxford and they thought it was much nicer than Redditch!'

'They are going to come to stay at half-term in

November,' Wayne added, 'and then, maybe they can move in with us at Christmas.'

'We've got places for them at the local primary school,' Dean continued. 'They can start in January or wait until after Easter, if they need more time before they move in with us permanently.'

'We're all really looking forward to it,' Barbara added, her eyes moist at the remembrance of her son's distress when he thought that his injury might prevent the adoption going ahead. 'Graham and I have found a house in Oxford, which means that we can be on hand to help out.'

'And it will be nice for the boys to have an adoptive grandmother, as well as new parents,' Alison suggested.

'Well, I'm not sure about that,' Barbara answered with a nervous laugh. 'The reason Carl and Harry are in Care is because of the bad experiences they had with their mother and grandmother. That's why the adoption agency thought Wayne and Dean would be ideal parents for them. They find it hard to relate to women and their psychologist thought that they would benefit from an all-male home environment, where they'll feel secure. So we're taking it very slowly and trying to build up their confidence gradually.'

The Chief Superintendent stood up and tapped her spoon against a glass to call for silence. Conversation gradually subsided across the room and heads turned expectantly. The lights dimmed and an image appeared on a large screen behind the top table. It showed Jonah in his wheelchair, dressed in police uniform and looking somehow smaller than usual, while another uniformed officer pinned a medal to his chest. The caption across the top read: 'DCI Jonah Porter QPM[18] 1977-2018'. The room erupted into spontaneous applause.

---

[18] Queen's Police Medal: an honour awarded to police officers for gallantry or distinguished service.

'As you all know,' Alison announced, walking over to the lectern that stood at the front of the room, next to the screen. 'We are here to celebrate the distinguished career of a very special officer; someone who refused to allow a bullet in the neck to force him into premature retirement; a detective with a string of successful cases to his name; but more importantly, a loyal colleague and friend.'

There was more applause. Alison waited for it to subside before continuing.

'As I look around the room, I can see officers from across the Thames Valley region and beyond, who have worked with Jonah during his forty-one years of service. I see officers long retired, who can remember him as a young, eager police constable. I see his contemporaries, many of whom have been drawing their pensions for a good few years now! I see young up-and-coming officers who owe their promotion to his support and mentorship.' She paused for dramatic effect and picked up the controller in readiness for moving on to the next slide. Then, looking directly at Jonah, she continued, 'as we all know, you're never one to blow your own trumpet-'

'If only!' Peter commented in a loud stage whisper that sent a ripple of laughter round the room.

'- so I asked some of your oldest friends to collect together some memories to remind us all of some of the most significant elements of an illustrious career. So … Detective Chief Inspector Jonah Porter … this is your life!'

She pressed a button and the picture on the screen changed to display a montage of photographs of Jonah from childhood (supplied, at Peter's request, by his sister, Sarah) through various stages in his career and family life up to a recent picture with his youngest grandchild, Rachel, on his lap.

Then followed a sequence of video-recordings in which family members and police colleagues related anecdotes and personal memories of incidents in Jonah's life. As the applause died down at the end, Alison got to her feet again and called for silence.

'We made a collection for a retirement present,' she announced to Jonah, 'but when we asked your friends what you might like, nobody could think of anything. In the end, we came up with this …'

She bent down behind the lectern and took out a large framed photograph of the police station with Anna Davenport, Andy Lepage and the rest of Jonah's team of CID officers standing on the steps in front of it. She held it up for everyone to see and then set it down on a stand at the front of the room.

'We've also made a DVD of all the videos that you've just seen, so that you can play them over again whenever you need reminding about what your fellow-officers thought of you.'

She held up a DVD in a presentation case decorated in the blue-and-white check pattern symbolic of the police.

'… and we're going to put the rest of the money into a fund to support your new initiative with young people in police custody,' she finished.

Jonah backed his wheelchair away from the table and started forward to join Alison at the front of the room. However, before he could begin his speech of thanks, she held up her hand for silence and beckoned to Wayne and Dean. Evidently expecting this summons, they got to their feet and walked slowly forward. Wayne steadied himself with a stick in his left hand, while Dean supported him with a hand under his right elbow.

From somewhere at the side of the room, they were joined by another young man, smartly dressed in a dark suit, with black hair and a neat black beard. The three of them stood at the front of the room while Alison made the introductions.

'As you all saw in the presentation, Wayne and Dean and their *Design Ability* company have been crucial in enabling Jonah to continue as a police officer when most people would have taken medical retirement. Now, I'm very pleased to be able to reveal a new venture, which they are working on in conjunction with another company based at the Oxford Science Park. Nick Dove is one of several engineers who have been working on computer algorithms for controlling driverless cars. They've linked up with *Design Ability* to develop driverless car technology aimed at making people with disabilities more independent. They've been keeping it secret, but they are here now to show you all – and Jonah in particular – the prototype, which they're hoping Jonah will test for them now that he'll have a little more free time.'

She sat down amid more applause and the three young men proceeded to take the audience through a short presentation, showing photographs, diagrams and video-footage of a small car, which drove itself around an obstacle course, following voice commands from Nick sitting behind the wheel, in what looked like a *Design Ability* wheelchair. Finally, he demonstrated how the occupant of the wheelchair could manoeuvre it in and out of the vehicle without any human assistance, giving them the ability to travel with total independence.

'My word!' Jonah exclaimed at the end. 'It's not often that I'm left speechless …'

'You can say that again,' Peter muttered in Bernie's ear.

'… but that really takes my breath away. When can I have my first test drive?'

THANK YOU

Thank you for taking the time to read Rainbow Warrior. If you enjoyed it, please consider telling your friends or posting a short review. Word of mouth is an author's best friend and much appreciated. Thank you,

Judy

LIST OF POLICE PERSONNEL

The following police officers recur in many of the Bernie Fazakerley Mysteries. This alphabetical list is provided to give some background to them and for reference.

- **Rupert Andrews** Detective Sergeant 2000, Detective Inspector 2012.

- **Malcolm Appleton** Police Constable 2007, Sergeant 2018.

- **Alison Brown** Detective Inspector 1989, DCI 2004, Chief Superintendent 2015.

- **Tracy Burton** Police Constable 1999, Sergeant 2005.

- **Anna Davenport** Detective Sergeant 2007, Inspector 2015. Married in 2001 to Philip Davenport. Separated in 2017. 3 children: Jessica (2001), Marcus (2002), Donna (2017). Archaeology and Anthropology graduate from Cambridge.

- **John Gamble** Police constable 2017

- **Pamela Gregson** Custody Sergeant.

- **Gavin Hughes** Police Constable 1988. Specialises in community policing and building bridges with rough-sleepers.

- **Peter Johns** Police Constable 1969, Detective Constable 1973, DS 1978, DI 1993, retired 2011. Married to Angie in 1978 and to Bernie in 2006. Father of Hannah (1980) and Eddie (1982). Stepfather to Lucy (2000).

- **Arshad Khan** Detective Sergeant 2002, Detective Inspector 2006, DCI 2014. Specialises in cases involving ethnic minority victims. Married to Anita.

- **Aaron King** Police Constable 2001, Sergeant 2009.

- **Andrew Lepage** Detective Constable 2007, Detective Sergeant 2015. Graduate in criminology (1st class) from Leicester University in 2005. Lives with his mother in Headington Quarry.

- **Monica Philipson** Detective Constable 2002, Detective Sergeant 2008. An ambitious police officer, who studied at Keble College, Oxford.

- **Richard Paige** Detective Constable 1960, Detective Sergeant 1967, DI 1973, DCI 1981, Detective Superintendent 1995, died 1999. Married to Bernie in 1997. Father of Lucy (2000).

- **Joshua Pitchfork** Detective Constable 2015

- **Jonah Porter** Police Constable 1977, Detective Constable 1979, Detective Sergeant 1983, DI 1987, DCI 1996. Married to Margaret in 1982. Widowed in 2014.

- **Louise Otterbourne** Police Constable 2017

- **PD Q** Police Dog 2014. General Purpose dog. German Shepherd Dog.

- **Alice Ray** Police Constable 2015, Detective Constable 2016

- **Melanie Stanton** Police Constable 2009 and Dog Handler 2014

- **Ben Timpson** Police constable 2018

- **PD Wesley** Police Dog 2015. Drug and firearms search dog. Spaniel.

MORE ABOUT BERNIE AND HER FRIENDS

There are now ten Bernie Fazakerley Mysteries. The other nine (in chronological order of the action) are:

1. **Two Little Dickie Birds**: a murder mystery for DI Peter Johns and his Sergeant, Paul Godwin.
2. **Murder of a Martian**: a double murder for Peter and Jonah to solve.
3. **Grave Offence**: an assault and a suspicious death that Peter investigates, while Jonah is in rehab in the spinal injuries centre.
4. **Awayday**: a traditional detective story set among the dons of an Oxford college.
5. **Death on the Algarve**: a mystery for Bernie and her friends to tackle while on holiday in Portugal.
6. **Mystery over the Mersey**: a murder mystery set in Liverpool.
7. **Sorrowful Mystery**: Jonah investigates a child abduction and Peter embarks on a new journey of faith.
8. **In my Liverpool Home**: Bernie and her friends return to Liverpool to investigate a suspicious death in Aunty Dot's Care Home.
9. **Organ Failure**: a body is discovered under the organ in St Cyprian's Church and Jonah is called in to investigate.

Bernie also appears in two other novels:

- **Changing Scenes of Life**: Jonah Porter's life story, told through the medium of his favourite hymns.
- **Despise not your Mother**: the story of Bernie's quest to learn about her dead husband's past.

Peter narrates his side of the story in this book of short stories:

- **My Life of Crime**: the collected memoirs of DI Peter Johns. This includes some episodes that appear in other books, but told from a new perspective, as well as some completely new stories.

You can find them all on Judy Ford's Amazon Author page:
https://www.amazon.co.uk/-/e/B0193I5B1M

Read more about Bernie Fazakerley and her friends at
https://sites.google.com/site/llanwrdafamily

Visit the Bernie Fazakerley Publications Facebook page:
www.facebook.com/Bernie.Fazakerley.Publications

Follow Bernie on Twitter:
https://twitter.com/BernieFaz

ABOUT THE AUTHOR

Like her main character, Bernie Fazakerley, Judy Ford is an Oxford graduate and a mathematician. Unlike Bernie, Judy grew up in a middle-class family in the South London stockbroker belt. After moving to the North West and working in Liverpool, Judy fell in love with the Scouse people and created Bernie to reflect their unique qualities.

As a Methodist Local Preacher, Judy often tells her congregation, "I see my role as asking the questions and leaving you to think out your own answers." She carries this philosophy forward into her writing and she hopes that readers will find themselves challenged to think as well as being entertained.

37454598R00153

Printed in Great Britain
by Amazon